pharo and the
murder at
smoke lake

pharo and the
murder at
smoke lake

Steve Skurka

To Kyra,
Best of success in your publishing career
Enjoy my Pharo book.

atmosphere press

Dedicated to my mother,
Rene Skurka

Introduction

The young man, pallid and slender as a shadow, entered the tavern and searched for a table. The room appeared full, and he took a seat on a flimsy, wooden barstool and ordered a pint of lager. Later that afternoon, every patron in the room, including the few who had noticed the sapling at the bar, denied sensing a lurking danger. He was a stranger, of course, but a fresh face was a common sight in a tavern located near the main street of Sarajevo.

The room erupted in gasps when the young man in the double-breasted jacket bolted from his chair, a pistol in his right hand pointing to the door.

But by then, it was too late to prevent the calamity that followed.

The tavern owner who served him the lager was probed by a policeman in a cold storage room at the back. "Did he say anything to you?"

"He kept repeating the words, 'We are the broken Black Hand.' I asked him what his name was."

"What answer did he give?"

"Gavrilo Princip."

"Did Princip explain who this broken Black Hand was?"

"No, but I inquired if he was visiting the city to see the archduke. I knew that the archduke and the duchess were visiting from Austria, and a parade was planned in their honor. Princip clenched his fist and banged the table. I wiped off the froth that spilled and asked him why he was angry."

"And did he tell you?"

"Not a word."

"Did Princip eventually speak about the archduke?"

"Only that he'd come to the tavern from downtown and had watched the parade."

"Did he inform you about a plot to murder the archduke?"

The tavern owner flinched as he studied the policeman's face. He detected a scornful expression and measured his words carefully. "I'd have tied his hands to his stool and waited for you to cart him away if he had," he declared.

The policeman left the room to confer with his superior officer. Part of the tavern owner's story was confirmed by Gavrilo Princip's blurted account immediately after his arrest. He'd spoken candidly about belonging to the Black Hand and described the group arriving in the Bosnian capital city on a killing mission.

Princip admitted to entering the tavern and carrying in the deep pockets of his black jacket, a grenade, a loaded pistol and a vial of cyanide. The archduke of the Habsburg empire, Franz Ferdinand, had arrived in Sarajevo in regal uniform with the duchess, Sophie, to be received by the mayor and local officials and to inspect the troops in a decorous procession along the city's main avenue. Seven members of the Black Hand, a group of Serbian revolutionaries, weary of the Austro-Hungarian domination of their annexed homeland and dedicated to unifying Bosnia and Serbia, had plotted to assassinate the archduke. They lined the bridges along the procession route and one of them hurled a bomb at the passing open-top car of the royals. The bomb bounded off the car and exploded, injuring many in the crowd of people gathered to watch. Princip claimed that he had watched in despair as Franz Ferdinand's car was left undamaged, the chauffeur steering the car forward with the archduke and his wife unscathed. He sought refuge in a tavern to grieve the group's failure.

Then, in the frame of the window, a car stopped beside the tavern he chose. For a moment, Princip thought he was dreaming as he opened his eyes wide. The royal car of the archduke was visible only a couple of feet from the door of the tavern. Seated next to the archduke, the duchess held a parasol in a white glove, shielding her from the sun. The driver cursed, and Princip realized that the car had stalled.

A stroke of good fortune! Gavrilo Princip reached into his pocket for his pistol and rushed to the door.

Chapter One

The wicket gate sprang open, and Mortimer Hanus walked through, averting his eyes from the watchtower and the barbed wire fence. Freedom gained after thirteen years and one month in prison. Many men had preceded Hanus through that gate, spirits broken, absent a gleam of hope. They lacked Hanus's demonic constitution, which had kindled a bevy of fury to spur him through his captivity.

Hanus was departing with two front teeth missing after a prison yard scuffle; an arm resting in a sling, a token of a push from his cellmate off the upper bunk; and a jagged gash scarring his left arm, the result of a kitchen ambush. A coterie of inmates loyal to Hanus, lured by prospects of work in his organization, had redressed each injury. Retribution was swift: bruised cheeks swelled into pumpkins, battered legs reduced to hanging ornaments, and a couple of fractured skulls from the pounding of wooden spoons.

A beefy, thick-lipped man with a great bull neck and the alabaster face of youth greeted him on a patch of grass outside the gate. He'd been waiting in the blazing sun, his scarlet nose a beacon, as beads of sweat dripped from the crest of the moon tattooed on his rolling arm.

"Hungry, Boss?" he asked.

"What's your name?"

"Tommie Hendry."

Hanus examined his greeter warily. "How many men's jaws have you broken, Tommie?"

"Five—two of 'em I knocked out with a single punch, and the third was on his knees while I stepped on his knuckles."

"What of the other two?"

"They got mouthy, and I waited to break their jaw. That shut them up."

"Ever kill a man?"

"I threw a stool pigeon into a fire pit once. We caught him sharing information with the police. He wished he was dead."

This chronicle of his enforcer's duties was spoken with calm assurance, like a lumberman reciting sizes of timber on a loading dock.

Hanus nodded approvingly. Bullwater, the second in command of Hanus's illicit business schemes, had mentioned Hendry's name at the Easter service in prison. Or was it an ordinary Sunday service? He couldn't be certain.

In the prison kitchen, Hanus had learned of a faltering church in Tonawanda that needed a sizable donation to be saved. He had invited the minister from the Revival Catholic Church to visit and made a tempting proposition: the required funds would be deposited forthwith to the church on the condition that Georgie Bullwater be appointed as a subordinate minister at the church.

"Does he have any training for clergy?" the earnest minister had asked.

"You'll teach him," Hanus replied. "And you'll have one hour to finish the job."

Thus, the suitably dog-collared Reverend Bullwater had attended the jail for prison church services, and thereby had met Hanus at regular intervals. Tucked into his Bible, the Reverend Bullwater carried a single sheet listing profits and expenses from Hanus's companies and the tally of uncollected debts, with the pertinent direction from Hanus conveyed behind a curtain during confession. The bloated success of the gambling houses always pleased Hanus.

Now he told the hired muscle, "Just drive me to my office, Tommie. Bullwater and a few of the fellows in my company will be waiting for me—I have business to take care of."

"Do you need my help?"

"I'll let you know," Hanus snarled. "I may give you a chance to prove yourself."

"Anything you ask, Boss. I'm at your service."

A few feet from the car, Hanus stopped and stomped the ground. "I want her to suffer. I want her to endure pain. I want her to perish."

"Who?" Tommie asked, bewildered.

But Hanus kept silent, his face frozen in a scowl.

Chapter Two

The sealed letter from the Hungarian Prime Minister, delivered by a Viennese page, was accorded priority and opened first. Count von Berchtold, the foreign minister for the Habsburg empire, had been pressured by the chief of the general staff to attack Serbia without warning.

A solemn memorial service for the archduke and duchess was to be held in a public square the next day, and the clamoring for vengeance would readily mount. But Berchtold, prudent by nature, chose not to act hastily with a military response: he welcomed any concurring opinion of the Hungarian leader.

The content of the letter dated the first of July did not disappoint. The Count sighed in relief as he read it. The Prime Minister urged that the assassination of the Austro-Hungarian heir not be used to justify a reckoning with Serbia. Rioting against Serbian businesses, schools and churches had abated with the enforcement of martial law, and Serbia had denounced the violent murder of the archduke and duchess. Proof of the complicity of the Serbian government in the plot of the Black Hand was a necessary pre-condition for a retaliatory attack—and that was not evident, the Hungarian Prime Minister concluded. The Serbian government, in turn, was urged to adopt a cautionary approach to avoid war.

Berchtold had been alerted to the French government's overture to the empire that it maintain a heightened position of calm and composure. Similar messages of restraint were delivered from London and St. Petersburg.

All well and good to seek a measured peace, the Count reflected. But could his government control a newspaper from extolling Princip and his band of confederates as martyrs or suppress the fervor of a few Serb patriots condemning the Habsburg empire?

Despite Count von Berchtold's reluctance to accede to military action, he understood that Serbia's entry into war could be provoked by a singular act of turbulent resistance. Peace nestled on a delicate branch that might snap at any moment.

Chapter Three

At the bottom of the cast iron stairway, three women were greeted by Rose, a slight, grey-haired usher, carrying a lit candle and flashing a luminous smile. Rose had been carefully screened for her allegiance to the suffrage cause. Informers hired by the police to infiltrate the Suffragettes were rampant.

The three strangers mounted a flight and huddled in a dank stairway at the back of Lambard Music Hall. Each held the brim of a velvet-bowed hat in one hand and a hand-painted sign with the words "GIVE WOMEN THE VOTE" in the other. A narrow candle encased in a glass jar burned on a table in a corner, lighting their faces with a faint glow.

"I'd have brought a lantern if I'd known it would be this chilly," whispered Molly, the tallest of the group. A cool summer mist swept down on them from an open skylight above. She added, "I almost forgot my manners. Molly Tancer from Rochester."

"I'm Lizzie from the Westchester Suffragettes." The

speaker paused, eyes blazing and fists clenched, and added, "That political blowhard will regret the day he came to Buffalo to speak."

"And I'm Pharo Simmons," said the third. "Good to meet both of you." Pharo curtsied. "Welcome to my city."

The three women, each representing a suffragette club in New York, had arrived separately through a fire escape at the back of the hall to avoid detection. The police had been warned of a planned disruption to the state senator's speech and were on the lookout for agitators milling around the theatre and music hall entrance. Any woman holding a sign or placard would be suspected as a suffragette provocateur and immediately detained and taken to the police station for questioning.

Pharo had been the last to arrive. A telephone conversation with Clarence Darrow had delayed her. The famed attorney had called to speak to Burford, and Pharo duly informed him that her husband was at the office with Neeru Sharma preparing diligently for his upcoming trial.

"How are you faring, my treasured friend?" she'd asked.

"The travail of this charade cuts to the marrow of my bone. It's like a sack of coal welded to my spine. It's wearying," he'd said. "But enough of my troubles. Burford tells me you're composing a new novel of romance and adventure."

"Yes, only a few chapters remain. Do you believe that people's romantic lives are bound together by coincidence or fate? It's a theme I'm currently struggling with in my writing."

Darrow's response was etched in her memory. "I'm a firm proponent of coincidence, Pharo. I had a client once, Busby Williams, who robbed three banks across the state, and in each instance, the cash drawer was found empty with the contents locked in a secure safe. On the fourth robbery attempt, Busby was apprehended by the police leaving the bank in Springfield carrying two bags filled with bills. When I visited him in the city jail, Busby was grinning from ear to ear. 'My luck's improving, Mr. Darrow. The cash drawers were filled to the brim this time. Fate was on my side.'" Darrow chuckled as he told the tale.

Pharo ruminated about Clarence's welfare in the cab to the music hall. She had discerned a hint of lethargy in the lawyer's voice, like a prize-winning horse revealing a notable limp on a gallop around the track.

"Daisies," she uttered upon arrival, the code word devised to gain entry.

"Come in, dear," the usher said. At a plodding pace, she led Pharo Simmons up the narrow stairs. At the top, she pointed to a door. "I've checked to make sure that it opens. You will have a clear path to the stage. I wish I could do more to help. In my younger days, the cause we fought for was abolition. My cousin Rachel and I took a trip to Charleston and watched the slaves being sold at the harbor like a herd of cattle. It broke my heart, seeing families ripped apart like that. Enough with my chatter. I must return to my post before I'm missed," she said, her hand flitting farewell.

Pharo checked her watch. The lecture of State Senator Baxter Willoughby was scheduled to start in seven minutes. She heard murmuring beyond, a sign that Lambard Hall was filling. The pending lecture, advertised in newspapers across the state, was devoted to the topic of the supremacy of man. For Willoughby, a targeted adversary of the Suffragette movement with his bombastic speeches and ungodly writings, disparaging the suffragettes had become a constant theme of his stump speeches.

Pharo could recite parts of Willoughby's most recently published pamphlet by memory. In a snickering tone, she repeated a central passage: "It is declared *man*kind for a reason. Women folk are subordinate to men. Righteous women recognize their role and flourish. Foolhardy radicals devote their day to upsetting God's natural order. They deserve our pity rather than our scorn. Let men spill their blood on the battlefield while women folk spill a few drops with their needle and thimble."

"He published that bafflegab?" Lizzie asked.

"Word for word."

"Then I shall bop him one hard to his shiny head and see where the blood spills."

"Now ladies, we shall teach our state senator a memorable lesson, but not with violence," Molly cautioned. "When Nellie Hopkins threw her black suede shoe at the judge in the Old Bailey, it earned her eight nights in a London jail."

"It won't be a suede shoe that I'll be hurling at the judge sentencing me," Lizzie declared.

"Apparently, Willoughby was once asked whether it was true that women were excluded from the golf clubhouse that he belonged to. 'Of course not,' he replied. 'Who do you think makes the tea?' I have a gift for you, Lizzie." Pharo reached into her bag and pulled out a set of handcuffs.

"Where is the key?" Lizzie asked, grabbing the handcuffs.

"Hidden in my shoe... Oh, such mischief!" Pharo exclaimed.

She opened the door a crack and peered into the Hall. "Oh look, there's Kat—in the center of the front row."

Lizzie rushed to the door for a peek. Katherine Chatham, known by the suffragettes as Kat, worked in the national office in Washington and had travelled through the state to speak at local chapters.

"Look!" Lizzie whispered excitedly. "I can see Baxter Willoughby at his lectern, hovering over his speech with his spectacles. The crowd is being hushed by a matron in a navy lace wrapper dress. Fifty cents to anyone who pilfers the rascal's notes," she said with a wry smile.

"We in the movement all admire you so, Pharo," Lizzie said, turning to her. "The daring way you rescued your husband in Canada from the clutches of his kidnapper."

"Ah yes, the wicked Mortimer Hanus. His cruelty is boundless. I expect he has a score to settle with me—I've been informed that he's been released from prison."

"Are you frightened?" Molly asked.

"I don't scare easily," Pharo said. "But I've thought of purchasing a Colt revolver to keep tucked under my pillow."

The shrill sound of a woman's voice inside the Lambard Music Hall echoed in the stairway:

"Ladies and gentlemen, it is my great honor to introduce to you the distinguished State Senator Willoughby."

A smattering of applause was followed by the discordant voice of the speaker rallying the audience.

"Are you ready?" Molly Tancer spoke as a general commanding the troops to climb the bunker. "Go!"

The wooden door creaked open as Molly and Lizzie burst through, carrying their signs above their hats.

"Votes for women!" Their roaring cry resounded through the hall.

As Willoughby turned sharply, his silver-wired spectacles sprung from his face.

Pharo ran down the curving stairs and reached for the crank of the fire alarm. She grinned like a Cheshire cat at the edge of a milk bowl, imagining the chaos about to unfold.

Chapter Four

The Merchant Street Police Station had been constructed on the banks of the Buffalo River. At the detectives' office on the third floor, it was known as the Merchant Street Water Station. On a breezy day, with the wind howling like a monster's cry, drifts of water hurled across the side of the building and splashed the front steps.

Burford Simmons did not react to the cold spray of water on his pants as he hurdled up the wooden steps. He was focused on his wife Pharo's bleak predicament. What trouble with the suffragettes, he wondered, could have led to his wife being locked up at a police station in the late hours of the night? Burford had been stitching his closing address for a burglary trial earlier in the evening when a ring of the telephone interrupted a rehearsal of the peroration. The call was brief, its pungent effect not measured by words. "Simmons, your wife's been arrested," the gruff desk sergeant had announced, refusing to provide a single detail beyond Pharo's location: the Merchant Street Police Station.

Detective Eli Jacob greeted Burford warmly as he entered.

"Ah, *Monsieur* Simmons. I was told that you were coming. So good to see you again, although regrettably under such unfortunate circumstances." The detective's tone turned doleful. "*C'est dommage*—I was surprised to see Mme. Burford's name on the list of arrests. Perhaps you did not realize, but I am now in charge of the detectives' office at this station."

"What's this about, Detective?" Burford spoke directly. He had little interest in exploring the pleasantries of the detective's life and career in the thirteen years since the investigation into his kidnapping. Pharo's release was his paramount interest. He recalled the advice he'd received as a budding lawyer from his chipper principal, Rondell Kipp. "Liberty is a precious commodity, Burford," he said, walking one day from the courthouse, "and the clock keeps ticking while your client languishes in despair behind the bars of a locked cell... tick, tick, tick."

Detective Jacob guided the lawyer into his office and closed the door. "Please sit, *Monsieur l'avocat*," he said.

"I prefer to stand, thank you."

"As you wish... Ah, *Madame* Burford, what trouble she has caused this evening. State Senator Willoughby was beginning to deliver his speech at Lambard Hall when *un groupe* of suffragettes interrupted him, Mme. Pharo among them, carrying signs and shouting. After a few minutes, Willoughby had to give up and was about to march off the stage spewing angrily—but one of the suffragettes had handcuffed his arm to a chair. The roomful of people who came to hear his speech were requested to leave. A fire alarm had been set off, and a fire truck soon arrived at the hall. A waste of time, *bien sur*."

"Not as much time squandered as the state senator's speech would have been. Willoughby rambles on with evangelical fervor about preserving the *sacred* vote for men. Now there, Detective Jacob, is a lost cause for the ages. I admit that I relish the image of Willoughby prancing around with a chair tied to his arm."

Jacob pursed his lips, hiding a glint of a smile. "The state senator is sulking in the parlor of his home with the handcuffs and chair. Mme. Pharo called me to her cell a few minutes ago to deliver the key."

"Where is my wife now, Detective?"

"A few documents to prepare, and she will be released, *tout de suite*. Under my command."

Puzzled, Burford looked at the detective.

"I apologize for my French. Mme. Pharo will be out very soon... I understand that you're the attorney chosen by Clarence Darrow to defend him. Bribing a juror, *mon Dieu*! Who can believe such a preposterous charge?"

"How did you know that I'm Darrow's lawyer? It isn't in the newspapers yet."

"Clarence and I have kept in contact since your kidnapping case was solved. A more honorable man I have never met. I wish you *bon chance*, great success with the trial. I have followed your career with great interest, *Monsieur* Simmons. Your defense of the headmistress charged with embezzling jewels to feed the poor was impressive. You christened her Saint Bernardine."

"Yes, Pharo is writing a novel about that case. The lawyer is dashing and handsome—total fiction, of course."

At that moment, Pharo burst through the doors, her arms flailing, her curly red locks matching her pink-flushed cheeks.

"Let me back in!" she shouted, turning back.

Burford went to her quickly. "Pharo, what's the problem?"

"I refuse to accept preferential treatment from the police."

"In more than twenty years of defending cases, I can assure you I've never had a client who wished to spend more time locked in jail."

"Well, there's always a first time, Burf." She turned to Detective Jacob without a hint of recognition of their shared past. "And what of Lizzie and Molly? Are they to remain confined to a cell for the duration of the night? The folly that man was spewing from the stage! '*We cannot trust women with the precious right to vote.*' And the rapturous applause he received, like a flock of sheep being herded to the edge of a canyon."

Detective Jacob spoke matter-of-factly, "Your colleagues will be processed and released in a matter of minutes. I give you my word."

"Come," Burford ordered. "We can trust the detective. Let's go home Pharo."

"I'm sorry, Burford, but I am not leaving until my suffragette colleagues are released. Among them, you'll find Kat Chatham from our national office. You will forgive me, Detective Jacob, but I don't trust *any* police officer after the horror we were subjected to this evening. Handcuffs tightly secured on our wrists, led across a hooting and hollering crowd, and pushed into a paddy wagon like we're common criminals! We've performed a great public service tonight."

An hour later, sipping tea at the kitchen table, Pharo still brimmed with anger about the evening's turn of events.

"I'm ready to go back to jail if that's what it takes," she said.

"You were fortunate that Detective Jacob was in charge. You may not be as lucky on the next round."

"Unfortunately, I'll be missing the excitement tomorrow at the boat club's July 4th regatta on Lake Erie. We're slipping in a couple of boats with all-women crews."

"Detective Jacob will be thrilled."

"I am disappointed in Jacob," she said. "A worldly man like that quoting Shakespeare and Greek philosophers, but supporting the forces of oppression."

"He's a policeman tasked with upholding the law, Pharo."

"Please don't lecture me about the law and justice, Burford Simmons. You've conceded that the Suffragette cause is righteous."

"True, you have my unwavering support." He was anxious to change the subject. "I'll be leaving for Chicago in a few days to prepare our client to testify. I'm waiting for Neeru to finish her thorny trial."

"Aren't all of your colleagues' cases filled with prickly problems? In your last trial, you complained of your client's desire to testify despite his incessant compulsion to agree to any proposition, farfetched or not."

"Yes, I'm afraid that Mr. Mockery would have accepted that the sun radiated a purple glow if the prosecutor had suggested it in his question. This trial of Neeru's, though, has a peculiar obstacle to overcome. But she's up to the task—I'm confident of that. Did you book your seat on the train to Toronto, Pharo?"

"Yes, the first-class carriage ticket is purchased. I leave tomorrow to interview Sir Arthur Conan Doyle. And I've read all the Sherlock Holmes detective stories over again—

The Hound of the Baskervilles still gives me the shivers. It mystifies me that a medical doctor could compose such intriguing tales of mystery."

"You'll have an opportunity to ask Sir Arthur when you meet him."

"I shall be careful not to call him Dr. Watson."

"Well, at least the good doctor displays some human emotion, even with all of his foibles. I find Sherlock Holmes to be a stuffy mechanical character."

"Burf, it's unbecoming of you to disparage the great consulting detective. He's a heroic figure to the members of my club, the way he thinks out his little puzzles and solves them."

"Heroic to me means something else entirely. A man swimming against a powerful current to save a drowning child."

"Yes, I've never known Sherlock Holmes to be a strong swimmer. But he's a brilliant detective who unravels crimes. An unsolved crime brings a swell of misery to the victim's circle and spurs the perpetrator to commit further harm. You must concede that."

"You carry the argument once again, dear Pharo. There is no concern about the supremacy of man in this house."

As the president of the Sherlock Holmes Club of Buffalo, Pharo had received an invitation to meet with Sir Arthur Conan Doyle in Toronto. He was a guest of the Grand Trunk Railway and set to travel by train across parts of Canada, in the company of his wife, Lady Doyle. The Doyles intended to stay in Toronto for a couple of days after arriving back from their last stop on the trip, a fishing trip to Smoke Lake in Algonquin Park, a provincial park north of the city.

"Kat wasn't pleased when I told her of my plans to meet

with the author of the Sherlock Holmes stories. Indeed, she threatened to seek my censure if I didn't desist from my participation in the Detective's Club."

"Whatever for?"

"Apparently, Sir Arthur is a vocal adversary of the Suffragette movement. Kat told me a disturbing tale of Sir Arthur Conan Doyle's speech at a public meeting in Tunbridge Wells, England. The local men's cricket pavilion had burned down, with all the bats and nets, and when the fire brigade arrived, copies of the suffragette newspaper *Votes for Women* were found near the gutted ruins. Sir Arthur posited in his speech that granting women votes would eventually deluge England with a new electorate in opposition to the constitution and the very laws of nature."

"Those were the exact words he uttered?" Burford asked in dismay.

"Yes, I had Kat repeat them at least seven times until I retained them to memory."

"Someone needs to rid the master of the detective tale of his moribund ideas."

"Prehistoric is a more apt description. Sir Arthur seconded a motion at the meeting's closure, holding that extending the vote to women would be against the best interests of women and of the British Empire as a whole."

"You must cancel your trip to Toronto, Pharo."

"But I simply cannot disappoint the members of my club. A new Sherlock Holmes book was published in the spring, and the members are anxiously waiting for its release in America. I've been asked to pry from Sir Arthur details of his new detective story."

"And to ask him whether you can be a character in his next book."

"I think that Mortimer Hanus is better suited for a role in his stories. Burf, could you inquire Detective Jacob about Hanus? He's a treacherous man and has likely been stewing in his prison cell all these years, plotting his revenge."

"After the passage of all these years?"

"I'm responsible for his apprehension and arrest. I'm an expert in pruning unsightly weeds from a garden."

"I will speak to the detective in the morning. Now you must get some rest. You've had a tiring day."

"Tiring? I'm exhilarated, bursting with energy. Our mission was a grand success tonight. We are one step closer to securing women the vote!"

*

"Counsel, I'm directing you to put the question to the witness more *carefully*."

Judge Cicero Maitland had ordered the jury excused amid Neeru Sharma's cross-examination of the main witness. The judge, who had adopted the name of the Roman philosopher after his appointment, fancied himself a ponderous thinker on the bench and sprinkled his rulings with philosophical maxims.

"Jurors must not be cast adrift by the current of lecherous thoughts," Judge Cicero added.

"Judge, I cannot avoid the fray of lechery," Neeru responded. "My client is accused of forcing this woman to commit an act of fellatio on him. He denies the charge completely. I must be permitted latitude to demonstrate the witnesses' mendacity."

"I agree, but surely it can be done..."—the judge hesitated before continuing--"without referring to the dimensions of his *manhood*."

Snickering abounded in the courtroom.

"But I must, Judge. The complaining witness testified that my client's anatomical feature is exceedingly small. The truth is quite the opposite."

The last statement was greeted by loud gasps in the gallery.

"Well, counsel. How do you propose to convince the jury of that? By your client's own inflated estimate?"

"By evidence far more probative than that. I shall call his former wife as a defense witness. She'll testify that she detests my client venomously, but that he is blessed with a masculine stick the size of a horse's."

"Here, here," the judge ordered as the courtroom erupted in chortling laughter. "If it is entertainment you're seeking, there is a Barnum and Bailey circus a few blocks away. This is a court of law and decorum will reign supreme!" A vein in the judge's forehead protruded as he banged his gavel. "There will be no evidence of the features of a horse in my courtroom, Miss Sharma. Am I clear?"

"Very clear, Judge."

He rested his head in his palms before continuing. "But you do have a point that I must address with fairness to your client. You can present the witness with a piece of paper and ask her to mark with a pencil the size of your client's anatomy. The paper will be shielded from the public. You may then take a second piece of paper and seek the dimensions from your client's former wife. The two pieces of paper will be sealed exhibits that will return to the jury during deliberations. The jurors will be entitled to draw their own comparisons."

Neeru sprang from her seat. "A resolution crafted with the wisdom of Solomon," she told the judge.

Chapter Five

"What did you think of the performance, Sir Arthur?"

"I thought it splendid. The actors were magnificent."

Sir Arthur Conan Doyle and Lady Doyle stood at the side of the Bonesteel Theater after watching a performance of the play "*Sherlock.*" Based on the Sherlock Holmes stories, the play had enjoyed a thriving success during its run in New York and had recently arrived in Toronto. The audience had given the author of the Sherlock Holmes stories a rousing ovation at his introduction before the performance.

"What are your plans during your stay in Toronto?" the *Star* reporter asked.

"Lady Doyle and I look forward to a tour of the city. We're most interested in taking a leisurely stroll along the lakeshore. I gather the kernels for my stories as I walk. We're off to a fishing trip in northern Ontario in a couple of days before we set out to return to England."

"Perhaps Canada will feature in your next Sherlock Holmes novel."

Sir Arthur paused contemplatively. "An inspiring thought," he said. "I've considered that Holmes and Watson are due for an overseas holiday."

The fishing trip to Algonquin Park had been Lady Doyle's idea. Her husband's success with his detective stories had elevated him to an international celebrity, and crowds jostled to gather around him everywhere he went. The restful outings they had once cherished were few now: indeed, pressure on the famous couple had mounted during their Canadian tour, and a respite paddling in a canoe and fishing in the serene setting of a log cabin camp on Smoke Lake sounded splendid. "It will quell our nerves," she'd said.

The recent assassination of the Austro-Hungarian heir to the throne by a disgruntled Serb patriot still dominated their thoughts—it had brought Europe to the edge of war.

Sir Arthur found it maddening that a catastrophic European conflict stacked up like a set of domino tiles. He'd gleaned from news reports that the Serbian government was accused by Austria-Hungary of complicity in the murder. Germany offered a "blank cheque"—unconditional support for any responsive action taken by the Austro-Hungarians; Russia took sides, protecting Serbia and France, who were bound by the Franco-Russian Military Convention to be aligned with Russia in any war with Austria-Hungary and Germany. Britain and Canada would be drawn into any military conflict in aid of France.

Sir Arthur used his influence as a renowned writer to secure a meeting at the University of Toronto with Canada's pre-eminent military historian and analyst, Professor Edwin Hildebrand. He hoped to probe the reasons for the brewing war, but garnered no satisfaction from the prolix explanation offered by the expert. The professor, in plaid tweed and smoking a well-lit pipe, merely recited a medley of reasons for Britain joining a war alliance.

Sir Arthur pressed him. "Surely a nation's safekeeping must be in jeopardy before enlisting in warfare."

The professor glanced at him scoffingly, his moustache twitching. "Covenants must be respected—it's all about treaties and the tethering bonds among nations."

Sir Arthur abandoned any pretense of formality. "You worry about tethers—I worry about scales of death and destruction hereby unknown to mankind. Wait for the casualties after the first passenger ship is sunk by a submarine." Fury caused him to shake, and he whisked around and departed without saying thanks.

While traveling across Canada, the Doyles learned that their son, Kingsley, had expressed a keen desire to abandon his plan to become a doctor at St. Mary's Hospital if war was declared, to join the British Air Force. The Doyles were scheduled to return home after the trip to Smoke Lake, and they harbored a genuine concern that they would return to their island in the throes of battle.

At first, Sir Arthur had resisted the idea of a fishing trip. His foremost thought was to cancel the trip and return to London immediately. But Lady Doyle's view prevailed in the end, and they were to sail for England on the steamship *Megantic* on July 11. She trusted the good sense of European leaders to accept that the folly of a war that would lead to senseless destruction and massive loss of life. "It might help if they were conscripted to the battlefield for a firsthand impression," her husband replied. "Conscription of our youth is a favored practice of the military. When the burst of a cannon splashes dirt in these fatuous leaders' faces, they'll pause to scurry into battle."

Doyle had spoken of the fishing trip to his host, Mason Caulfield, the head of the Grand Trunk Railway. Caulfield embraced the idea. "There are perfect fishing conditions in the lake," he told Doyle. "The bass and perch are plentiful, and your fishing nets will be full."

In the taxi back to the hotel, Sir Arthur reminded his wife that he was to lunch the next day at the hotel restaurant with the president of his fan club in Buffalo, who was traveling by train to interview him. "Pharo Simmons is her name. In her letters she showed an exquisite understanding of my novel's characters and deductive reasoning."

"Is that the only reason, Arthur? You've declined similar requests for interviews before."

"She wrote me a gracious note when I had that spirited debate with George Bernard Shaw about the sinking of the Titanic. One of Pharo's closest friends was a passenger on the doomed ship, and as she confided, describing tears dampening her cheeks, she saluted the officers crew and passengers as acting heroically."

"What a fool Shaw was to cite the British romantic demands for heroism in times of a shipwreck."

"Foolish and illusory."

"Meet this supporter of yours, Pharo, but don't be tardy. We have a visit to the Royal Ontario Museum set at two o'clock."

"I have something else to tell you, Jean."

"I thought you looked pensive. What secret are you holding back? Is war about to be declared in Europe?"

"No, not that, thank goodness. My mood is more remorseful than pensive. I met with Caulfield at the intermission this evening while you greeted the audience in the lobby.

He was congenial and lavished fulsome praise on my Sherlock Holmes novels."

"Like water to a wilting plant?"

"Hardly an apt comparison," he said, chuckling.

"But then Mason presented me with a strange request. He has a guest at his mansion visiting from America, a nephew of his wife's—Rudolph Mulino."

"The film actor from Hollywood?"

"Yes, that's the fellow. I'm told by Caulfield that he's a huge star."

"And a dashing man and heartthrob. He plays the romantic lead in his films. Can you arrange for me to meet him before we leave?"

"I'm afraid that won't be necessary. You see, our host mentioned that I was in Toronto and, I suppose, boasted that his company was sponsoring our trip. It turns out that Rudolph is a fan of the Sherlock Holmes stories. And when Caulfield told him about our plans for a fishing trip, young Rudolph insisted on tagging along."

"Surely you didn't agree," Jean said.

"Somewhat sheepishly, Caulfield explained that he'd been forced to let Rudolph join our fishing trip. Caulfield will be joining us as well—but we'll have three cabins and all the privacy we need, he assured me. My opinion wasn't sought on the matter. We'll handle our own canoe on Smoke Lake. I don't know if our film star knows how to put the bait on the hook, but he'll need to learn quickly."

"Arthur, I planned this as a peaceful trip for the two of us alone. A film star with a mad crush on your famous detective and a haughty business executive aren't the type of company I'm interested in keeping."

"I should have spoken up, I know, but Caulfield and his

railroad company have sprung for the cost of our trip. He's an amiable chap, not the disposition of a titan of industry you might expect. Do you want me to tell him that I've reconsidered?"

"No, it's fine. Just promise me that we'll carve out our own section of the campsite, and you'll zealously guard our privacy. I'm not in the habit of taking excursions in foreign countries with other men."

*

"Over here, Conan!" Mason Caulfield's stout hand was raised with a fork as he waved Sir Arthur to his table in the back of Jammer's Delicatessen.

"That can't be good for your constitution, Mason," Doyle said, plopping into the padded bench. "It's almost midnight, and you're feasting on corned beef streaming with gravy, peas and cabbage. You've spilled a few drops of gravy onto your shirt."

"Don't forget the loaf of rye bread that I've already feasted on," Mason said with a bellowing laugh. "Show me the edict that binds us to three meals a day?"

"You're quite right, but you'll excuse me if I order a glass of milk."

"Go right ahead!" Mason devoured a spoonful of peas in one hand and beckoned the waiter to the table with the other.

"Why did you press for this late-night meeting?"

"I wish my purpose was more congenial. I've been threatened." Mason reached into his jacket pocket and pulled out two pieces of paper neatly folded into squares. "Read these." His hands shook like a quivering leaf.

Sir Arthur studied the content of the typed notes. They were identical except that the word "Turner" appeared at the bottom of one and a couple of typing mistakes in the other. Addressed to Mason Caulfield, they referred to sticks of dynamite being placed at various listed locations along the Grand Trunk Railway unless he paid the sum of $5,000. A note would be delivered to him directly with instructions for the payment at a specified location; Mason was cautioned to appear with the money alone. Sir Arthur looked up and asked, "When did you receive these threatening notes?"

"They were delivered to my office by a courier last week. The first on Monday and the second three days later. The envelopes were inscribed with my name and nothing else."

"Handwritten?"

"Yes."

"And where are the envelopes now?"

"I ripped them up and discarded them. I realize now that was imprudent. Should I be concerned, Sir Arthur?"

"Have you notified the police?"

"Yes, but I first waited for the letter to arrive with the instructions for payment. Lilian told me that I was being foolish not to involve the police. I followed her advice, and a policeman showed up at my office yesterday—Detective Smart. He left his card."

"He didn't insist on keeping the typewritten letters?"

"He encouraged me not to be rattled by the letters—his nonchalant attitude surprised me. He jotted a few notes and warned me not to follow up with contact if I was approached further about the payment demand, saying it was strictly a police matter. I must notify the detective forthwith."

"That was the extent of his inquiry?"

"He asked if I'd received threats before, and I told him this was the first."

"Were you at your office when the courier delivered the letters?"

"Both times, they arrived when I'd left—once for a lunch with the mayor and the other for a meeting with a shipping contractor."

"Did the letter with the word 'Turner' arrive first?"

Mason nodded and added, "I don't know anyone by that name."

"We can safely assume that it's an alias. Any communication you receive from someone identifying themselves as Turner will link up to the typed notes."

"It's rather strange that two notes were delivered, don't you think?"

"I agree, but the second note was sent with a purpose." Doyle paused. "Do you have a legal will, Mason?"

"Yes, I changed it about a year ago."

"Who is aware of the change to your will?"

"Lilian, and my lawyer, of course. My wife argued with me not to make her my sole beneficiary, but I insisted. I trust her to distribute the content of my assets fairly. What does my will have to do with the second note?"

"I wanted to identify if anyone has a financial interest in your demise."

Mason scoffed. "The author of these notes underestimates me if he thinks I'll topple over in fright. But how can I be certain that if I pay the rogue's ransom that I'll be rid of him?"

"You'll never be certain—that is the extortionist's scheme. Extract payment with the lure of closure but always re-emerge from a dark shadow demanding more coin. The only sure way to end this is to apprehend the perpetrator. I have no faith in this Detective Smart. A team of detectives should have been dedicated to conducting a thorough investigation, starting with the employees of your railway company. The listing of the targeted locations along the railway is a curious fact. The courier company that delivered the letters must be traced and their records of each delivery checked. From the typeset, I detect that the typewriter used was a Remington 10 model. It was first manufactured in 1912, top of the line, and there may be only a few hundred of the models sold in the city of Toronto. The list of purchasers should be compared to all suspects and offenders known to the police. The person who sent you these notes is unlikely to be a novice in criminal enterprise."

"I feel like I'm being tutored by Sherlock Holmes," Mason said. "Although I can't fault the detective for being remiss in taking the matter seriously. I should have contacted the police when the first note arrived—Oh, Sir Arthur, I've bungled the investigation!"

"Don't be hard on yourself." Doyle paused before continuing. "You might reconsider joining Lady Doyle and me on the fishing trip to Smoke Lake. It's advisable for you to be immediately available when the next note is delivered."

"Now that the plans are finally set in place, you don't think that I'd abandon you on this trip. We're embarking on a train in Toronto that will take our group directly to the Highland Inn, a resort hotel built by my railway company. It's set on Cache Lake in Algonquin Park—one lake over from our log cabin camp on Smoke Lake. It's a magnificent lake abounding with perch and bass. I can't wait to dip my fishing rod in the water."

"You're looking forward to some outdoor recreation, I see," Sir Arthur said.

Mason appeared crestfallen. "I have a confession to make, dear chap," he said. "This fishing trip isn't a luxury for me."

"Why is that?"

"I recently remarried, and my two daughters are most unhappy with my new bride. They made their views known as soon as I announced my engagement to my Lilian. She had filled in for my personal secretary when she was beset with the flu. Twenty years my junior, with cheeks like the petal of a rose. I was smitten with Lilian from the start and sought her attention, but my daughters see her as a crusading interloper seeking my fortune."

"You mean *their* fortune more accurately."

"Correct—they have their palatial homes chosen for the day after I pass from this earth," Mason said, a strip of corned beef dangling on his fork.

"And what is Lilian's view of your daughters' antipathy toward her?"

"She's resigned to her designated fate of the wicked stepmother. Lilian has made valiant efforts to please the girls but to no avail. My daughters' resistance to their stepmother is as unabated as a cascading waterfall. They have chosen the cruel tactic of not speaking to me, causing me great distress. I need our fishing trip desperately—my health is deteriorating."

Sir Arthur sipped languidly from the glass of milk brought to the table. "All right. We'll be sure to announce with some fanfare that you're accompanying us on the fishing trip. That should keep our extortionist at arm's length until we return. And I'm sorry about your predicament, Mason. I'll keep your account to me confidential, of course. We'll have fun and adventure on this trip. I abhor dull routine and crave mental exultation."

Gravy slipped down Mason's smile. "Perched in a boat on a lake with a fishing rod doesn't strike me as exhilarating—restful and meditative, I hope. Tell me, did you enjoy your trip to New York?"

"Splendidly—Lady Doyle entertained a group of ladies at the Plaza Hotel while I met Colonel Roosevelt for lunch at his townhouse. We met in London years ago after the colonel returned from an African safari. I admire the old cowpuncher, climbing mountains and scouring choppy terrain. He's an avid reader of detective tales and had sought me out in London."

"When he was serving as president, Roosevelt spoke at a railway conference I attended in Washington. He had a pugnacious-looking face—it reminded me of a bull terrier. I recall his parting words of advice: 'Gentlemen, never draw your gun unless you intend to shoot.' I prefer the maxim of never drawing your fork unless you intend to eat."

Doyle playfully picked up his fork.

"He's an avid sportsman, a trait you share in common," Mason said.

"Yes, Colonel Roosevelt presented me with a pair of tickets to a baseball match. The New York Yankees played the Philadelphia Athletics—the Athletics' coach, Connie Mack, is quite famous in America. I must tell you, Mason, I fancy myself as an expert batsman with the cricket bat. I once made a century at Lord's and played for a celebrity cricket team, the Allah-Akaberries. But I cannot imagine hitting a baseball, considering the velocity of the pitch thrown at the batter."

"Fencing is Rudolph Mulino's choice of sport."

"Tell me more about this fellow."

"Oh, Rudolph—he keeps Lilian in giggles like a school child. She calls him her dashing Italian nephew. I admit that he's quite the handsome fellow and quite debonair. His smoking jacket has a crest with his initials sewn onto it. He's also quite the raconteur with his Italian accent—he was born in Italy. Rudolph's description of winning a fencing contest was so vivid that I felt his foil puncturing my vest. He regales us with stories of the exotic places he's visited around the globe. The latest is a scenic town, Ravello, on the west coast of Italy."

"He could easily learn the information from a travel atlas, Mason."

"You're suggesting he may be posing, a flimflam man? The thought crossed my mind when he appeared unannounced at my door and introduced himself. But I had Rudolph's credentials thoroughly checked by an investigator I trust at Pinkerton's, and he's certainly Lilian's Italian relative. My wife's sister married an Italian who owned a bakery on Spadina Avenue in Toronto. When they moved to Milan a couple of years later, Lilian lost contact with her sister... I'm becoming an expert on estranged relatives." Mason dropped his head in his palms and began to weep.

"I have a grand idea."

Mason pulled a hankie from his jacket pocket and dabbed his eyes. "What is it, Sir Arthur?"

"Let's depart for our trip to Smoke Lake a day earlier than planned. You can shuffle our travel arrangements in the morning. I'll make an announcement to the press from our hotel. I can't have you brooding about your domestic strife for one more day."

"I'll brood less in the fresh country air. It's a grand idea. I'm glad to be in the company of an esteemed author."

"I'll take my leave now. I left the hotel stealthily, and it's best that I return before Lady Doyle notices."

Mason Caulfield winked. "I'm your unshakable alibi if required."

*

Sir Arthur returned to his hotel room a few minutes later. Lady Doyle was in a deep sleep as he sat at the foot of the bed ruminating about Mason's threatening notes. He'd observed that they'd been typed on Crane stationery. What type of schemer employed the finest typewriter and paper to finagle money from Mason? And why the protracted delay in seeking the payout? Doyle concluded that it was more likely a cruel game rather than a criminal venture. But to what end, he pondered.

Chapter Six

"Burf, he's gone!" Pharo shouted into the receiver of the telephone. "I arrived at the Royal Tweesedale Hotel from the train station and the desk clerk informed me that Sir Arthur Conan Doyle had already checked out. He permitted me the use of the hotel telephone to call you."

"I'm aware of that, Pharo. A telegram came for you about an hour after you left. I rushed to the train station but missed you."

"What am I to do now?"

"In his telegram, Doyle invites you to meet him in three days for lunch. He'll be returning to the hotel in Toronto."

"Three days! I can't kick my heels in this dingy hotel waiting for him. The bed springs squeak with every toss and turn during the night. The carpet is stained with blotches of spilled ink and the walls are a sickly faded beige."

"Did you bring your writing pad and pen with you on the trip?"

"Yes, I managed to write a couple of pages on my train ride. I had a compartment to myself."

"Splendid," Burford said. "As you know, I'm off to Chicago with Neeru Sharma to meet Clarence to prepare him to testify at his trial. It's fortunate that Neeru can make the trip—her trial ended early, with the jury taking only an hour to return with a not guilty verdict."

"What will Neeru's role be? More than an adornment beside you at the trial, I hope." Pharo had great affection for Neeru as she had ably helped her in a recent quagmire.

"Clarence requested that she be part of his team of lawyers, and I readily agreed. Her cross-examination has the finesse of an Olympic fencer landing precise strikes. Clarence insists that she be merciless in our rounds of preparation. Neeru will assume the role of the prosecutor conducting a sample cross-examination. I've warned my esteemed colleague to bring several hankies to wipe the sweat from his brow."

"And your role?"

"Clarence has entrusted me with captaining his defense when the trial starts in Los Angeles."

"I'm delighted to know that one of us is occupied with affairs of importance."

"Why don't you stay in Toronto and continue to write? You will have the benefit of complete solitude. I suggest dropping a letter at the front desk for Doyle. He may return sooner than expected."

"I suppose that's a sensible solution. Did Sir Arthur provide an explanation in the telegram for his abrupt departure?"

"None, I'm afraid, but I'm certain that a profuse apology will be forthcoming." Her husband's voice turned solemn. "Be careful not to venture too far from your hotel. I spoke to Detective Jacob this morning. He informed me that Mortimer Hanus has returned to Canada after his release from prison."

"Well, he can't possibly know that I've traveled to Toronto."

"Unless he or one of his confederates is lurking about and sees you. Just be careful, that's all I'm asking of you."

"And you take care of Clarence. Your colleague and good friend is leaning on you now, Burf. He's in a heap of trouble."

"He will be sent to prison if a jury finds him guilty, and his career and reputation will be in tatters. The jury will need to hear a compelling account of Clarence Darrow's innocence."

Returning to her room, Pharo began to compose a letter to Sir Arthur. Burford had assuaged her, and she would follow his advice to patiently await her interview. She recalled the feverish excitement at the Sherlock Holmes Club when she had read out loud Sir Arthur's agreement to meet in Toronto. What disappointment if she returned with an empty trough! The letter was succinct, informing him of her extended stay at the hotel and her eagerness to meet at the earliest opportunity. Pharo deposited the letter with the hotel clerk with instructions to pass it on to Sir Arthur upon his return.

*

Willow Hooper entered the Bellevue Hospital in Lower Manhattan and went to the information desk in the lobby.

"Can you direct me to the room of Morris Levinter?"

The clerk opened a red binder and searched through the pages. "Room 5-C," she said. "You'll find the elevator at the end of the hallway."

Willow entered the room minutes later to find a bandaged man in a bed, his arms and legs raised in slings and his head wholly bandaged.

A muffled voice uttered under the bandage, "Is that you, Willow?"

"Yes, Morris. I'm terribly sorry to find you in this condition." She placed the flowerpot she carried on the windowsill.

"Don't fret. My doctors are confident that they will assemble me back into one piece again. I tumbled headfirst from my bicycle onto the road. Apparently, I lost sight of a jagged rock in my path. My big nose took the brunt of my fall, probably saved my life. Please, have a seat beside my bed."

Morris had mentored Willow Hooper when she began as a reporter at the vaunted New York Times. Morris's beat was the downtown courthouse on Foley Street, and he covered the major trials in the city.

"Alfred Ochs visited me yesterday, and I recommended that you take over a story I'm working on."

Willow had worked for the newspaper for two years but hadn't yet been invited to the top floor of the New York Times building to meet the paper's publisher. "Did Mr. Ochs recognize my name?"

"Oh, don't be silly, Hooper. He reads the newspaper thoroughly every morning, even the baseball box scores. He knows you're a crackerjack reporter. Let me tell you about the feature story. It's vitally important that you drop everything else you're working on and focus on this item." Morris's tone turned grave. "An innocent man, Leo Frank, is about to be hanged."

At the word 'hanged,' Morris coughed and began to wince in pain. "Call the nurse, Willow. I cracked a few ribs in my fall, and the pain is unbearable when I cough or sneeze. I keep a flask hidden under my pillow. Do you mind giving me a swig of whiskey before you leave? And please don't tell the nurse."

"Happy to oblige," Willow said.

Chapter Seven

Sir Arthur Conan Doyle stepped out of his cabin and breathed in country air to rival any poem by Woodsworth. He planted his Wellington boot on the first step of the porch. The horizon was framed by rolling hills across the lake and patches of royal blue sky with the golden greeting of an arching sunrise. A glorious day for fishing. He looked down to the shore of Smoke Lake, where their earnest guide, Terrence, was loading the canoes with paddles, fishing rods, landing nets and tin cans of bait. Terrence, a former missionary who had crossed the prairies of Manitoba and the Rockies of Alberta searching for converts, had organized a lively itinerary for the morning, including a stretching exercise on a patch of wild grass, a hike on a forest path and breakfast cooked over the campfire.

Doyle had arisen early to jot down a couple of pages of his next detective story. The seeds of the book had been planted—he'd await inspiration to add the trunk, sturdy branches and leaves. By the time he returned to England, he hoped to have an array of characters developed and a well-embroidered plot. The latest cable from London had reassured the Doyles that their children were in good spirits and fine health. Jean had asked that cables from London be forwarded to their Canadian camp, and Mason Caulfield had arranged for a policeman on horseback to deliver them daily. The cable with a few recent newspapers had been tucked into a thick folder.

The morning hike led the Doyles, together with Mason Caulfield and Rudolph Mulino, through a muddy path to a beaver dam constructed with strewn branches and foliage. Caulfield had mistakenly brought a suitcase packed for a planned business trip to Winnipeg. In his frock coat, pleated trousers and Oxford shoes, he struggled to climb a steep hill they encountered, so Rudolph kindly locked arms with him to guide him to the top.

On their return to the campsite, Terrence distributed lunch baskets with ham sandwiches and apples and canteens filled with water. He apologized that canned food would be served for the rest of the fishing trip as the heat had spoiled the meat and eggs he'd stored in the shed.

"We'll need to catch some fish for our dinner," Mason said. "I'm not accustomed to dining on canned food."

"Nor I," Rudolph said. "I was promised the finest cuisine when I agreed to take this trip."

Terrence pulled straw hats from a wagon and handed them out, cautioning everyone against sunstroke and burn: "The sun will turn your faces ruby red if you're not careful. I had a painter at the camp last week, Tom Thompson, and his face looked like he'd canoed through an inferno."

"Ah, rubies. My mother wore a ruby pendant on her necklace—her taste in jewelry was exquisite. She wore sparkling sapphire and emerald green charms on her bracelet," Rudolph replied cheekily.

"Mock me at your peril, sir," Terrence said, strumming his fingers through a grizzled beard that reached his belt. "I have seen men and women on a riverboat bedridden for days, their bodies and faces contorted in discomfort, all from the beating sun."

After breakfast, Terrence rolled himself a cigarette.

"Are there bears in these woods?" Rudolph asked.

"Bears, moose, wolves, rabbits, deer. We'll be safe from the bears if we're careful to burn our garbage." Terrence leaned toward the fire and lit his cigarette. "I'll get the life jackets," he said.

Lady Doyle had insisted that life jackets be brought on the trip after the tragic outcome on the Titanic, where an inadequate number of life jackets had been kept on board the ship.

Terrence led the group down a steep embankment to a rocky shore. The two canoes were tied to the dock.

Rudolph picked up a flat stone and skipped it across the calm water, sparkling like shimmering glass.

"Twelve skips!" he shouted.

"I skipped fourteen at the crack of morning," Doyle said, and watched in bemusement as Rudolph struggled to enter the canoe on a shoal without tipping it. Doyle had offered the American film actor a lesson on the artful skill of catching fish, but Rudolph waved him off with a haughty look. A supreme disposition for one so undeserving, Doyle commented to Jean.

"I find Rudolph perfectly charming. You must give him a chance, Arthur. He senses your dislike for him."

"Indifference is closer to the mark," he said. "I have no patience for the Rudolphs of this world, with their bloated sense of self-worth. And his boasting about his mother's extravagant jewelry—I doubt a word of it is the truth."

"I observed you speaking to Rudolph on the trail. I couldn't hear the conversation, but it appeared collegial and pleasant."

"We'll be in close quarters with the fellow for a couple of days, and it's pointless to be rude or belligerent. Rudolph was asking about Devon and Cornwall as he plans a holiday there in the fall. I cautioned him about settling a holiday itinerary in southern England with war brewing, and he gave me a lecture about rectitude and fate. Your movie actor's self-anointed destiny is to entertain and rouse the spirits of the common folk who watch his films. Rudolph's worldly view at his tender age is that the earth is populated by exceptional folk like him who serve their fellow man with their art and will be preserved by the gods. We, indeed, are fortunate to be graced by his presence. Bow to the boy wonder, Rudolph Mulino."

"Oh, please, he didn't say *that*, Arthur."

"He most certainly did. I answered that a bomb landing on a thatched roof doesn't take stock of the people residing below. He pursed his lips in a mocking grin. I will not be bothered with another moment of Rudolph Mulino's tomfoolery. Mason Caulfield can carry that burden."

"You're too harsh!"

"Really? He's inspired me to name a meek Scotland Yard detective Rudolph in my new novel. He will feebly attempt to outwit Sherlock Holmes, only to be chagrined when his ineptitude and folly are exposed."

"Don't you dare," she said.

Terrence stood at the shore, watching as the two canoes drifted to separate sections of the lake. Sir Arthur and Lady Doyle stopped close to shore, shaded by clumps of overhanging green foliage. Rudolph paddled in tandem with Mason until the canoe reached a mid-point in Smoke Lake, where he was directed to place the paddle on the ribbed floor of the canoe. Leaning over the bow, Rudolph swung his fishing rod awkwardly, barely missing Mason Caulfield's leg with the hook as he cast the line behind him.

"Just drop your line in the water and wait," Mason instructed.

*

By the end of the day, a tally of exactly one fish was reached, but it was magnificent: Jean Doyle had landed an eight-pound black salmon trout. She eagerly regaled the group at the late-night campfire with her perilous adventure while landing the giant fish.

"I thought at first my fishing line was stuck on a log," she said. "But then suddenly, a fish jumped out of the water and I knew I had my prize. The fish fought fiercely and there were moments when I felt I might be dragged into the water. But I did prevail!"

"A pair of combatants on a battlefield." Mason took a sip of gin from his canteen.

"How did you fare on Smoke Lake, Rudolph?" Doyle asked.

"I didn't believe there were fish in the water until I heard of Lady Doyle's spectacular catch. The fish must sense that a novice is holding my fishing line, unworthy of a catch."

"Oh, that's nonsense, Rudolph. You'll have a basket filled with fish tomorrow."

"Thank you, Mason. I'm grateful for your hardy spirit

and encouragement. But if I catch a single perch, I shall consider the fishing trip a grand success. And I'll have a tale of my catch to take back with me to Hollywood."

"When do you return? Tell us about your next motion picture."

"I've been told by the film studio to keep the project hush-hush, ma'am. I can tell you that I play a cowboy drifter. I am quite handy with a pistol. I devoted hours learning to twirl it in my hand. We move into production soon—I'll be returning to the west coast after our fishing trip. I have to guard against too much sun swelling my face into a giant tomato." Turning to Sir Arthur, he asked, "What about you, Doyle? A Sherlock Holmes novel in the works?"

"My latest novel was published in the spring in England. It will soon be released in America and the Commonwealth."

"Have you started your next project? I caught sight of you with a writing pad on the porch on my way to the shed to get a fishing net."

"A writer's capacious mind never stops pumping out new ideas for stories. I haven't decided yet, Rudolph, if it's a blessing or curse."

"A blessing for your legion of devoted readers," Mason said.

"Curious name for a renowned detective. *Sherlock* ..." Rudolph uttered the name with a hint of derision.

"Your uncle informed me that you are a fan of the Sherlock Holmes stories."

"Yes, but I'd much prefer a name like Sharpton or Cleverly for such a crafty detective. Sherlock seems more fitting for a bumbling policeman or an absconding soldier."

"Come now, there is no cause to disparage Sir Arthur. His books on Sherlock Holmes are eagerly awaited and read around the world."

"It's quite all right, Mason. Rudolph is entitled to the reason I chose my principal character's name. You see, I once roundly defeated a bowler named Sherlock by making thirty runs in cricket—it presents a pleasant memory to introduce the character. I'm an excellent billiards player too. Top amateur on the island."

"What island is that?"

"England," Doyle replied curtly.

Rudolph looked at him in bafflement. "Why did you decide to visit Canada?"

"With my book finished, the opportunity presented itself to accept Mason's railroad company's invitation to cross the ocean and visit this vast country. We spent a week in New York, and this is our last stop on our Canadian tour. We've been traveling for almost a month now. We traveled the Great Lakes in steamers and traversed Western Canada and the Rocky Mountains in a private car provided by the Grand Trunk Railway."

"The lakes are ice cold in the mountains and the fish plentiful," Jean said.

Doyle sipped whisky from his own flask and asked Rudolph, "I'm curious, what brought you to visit your aunt and uncle in Toronto? Mason tells me you've never met until this trip. That's an ambitious voyage to undertake to see a stranger."

"I had a yearning to travel to the Canadian frontier, and the visit with my relatives was a bonus. The Caulfields have treated me splendidly. I shall never forget the hospitality of Mason and Lilian and this trip."

"When did you arrive at their home?"

"One week ago, Sunday. Is there a reason that the date is important?"

"Tell me, Mason," Doyle said, turning to his host. "I thought I'd take the canoe out early in the morning. The park fishing guide says it's the ideal time to catch a batch of fish. The mosquitos and black flies are still asleep. Are you interested in joining me at sunrise?"

"Why yes, I'm an early riser. Count me in. Sunrise it is, Sir Arthur."

"I'll say goodnight then." Rudolph picked up an empty can of beans lying by the campfire, crickets chirping in the thickets behind him. "A bit of kicking a can around before I rest," he said. "Fencing is my first sport, but I've recently developed an affinity for the sport of soccer. I've become rather adept at kicking the ball into the corner of the net."

"Did you play on a team?" Jean Doyle asked.

"I latched onto a team while I lived in Rome filming a movie inside the Colosseum. I miss the splendor of Italy that I grew up with. The language, the rich history, the lovely *signore*. The Italian food is *magnifico*."

"Unlike the mash of canned food we're about to be served here," Jean said with a chortle.

*

Willow Hooper took the elevator to the eighth floor of the New York Times Building and was ushered into the office of Alfred Ochs, finding the publisher in an animated discussion with the features editor about an anti-war protest in front of the Woolworth Building. Officers mounted on horseback had circled the group of protestors, and the newspaper had a photograph of a blistering confrontation with a protestor. It was decided that the photograph would be placed on the front page of the paper's next edition.

"Willow Hooper, come in," the publisher said, motioning her to a chair. "Do you know Jim Barnweather?" he asked.

"We haven't been introduced."

"Barnweather, I'm sending Hooper to cover the Leo Frank travesty of justice. I want the two of you to work closely on this story. I've been sent the court records of the trial. There isn't a shred of credible evidence that Leo committed the murder. A jury in Georgia needed to avenge the brutal killing of a young girl, and a Brooklyn Jew made a convenient sacrificial lamb."

"May I ask you a question, Mr. Ochs?"

"Certainly."

"Why am I chosen? There are a lot more experienced reporters at the paper. I've never covered a criminal trial."

"Well, you were recommended, and I approved. You covered the McKinley assassination and the kidnapping of the anarchist assassin's lawyer, Burford Simmons. Simmons's law firm in Buffalo is leading Leo Frank's efforts to have his death sentence commuted by the governor. I expect Simmons will give you access that he'd deny to other reporters. I also believe that you'll do a stellar job on the story. Any other questions?"

"No, sir."

"Good, then get going. You'll send your original reports to my attention."

Chapter Eight

The treasurer of the Buffalo Sherlock Holmes Club, Godfrey Hines, a retired accountant and stamp collector, had been the first member to join after Pharo placed an announcement of the Sherlock Club's formation in the *Buffalo Morning Express*. In his interview, Godfrey expressed unbridled affection for the array of characters in the Sherlock Holmes stories and told Pharo of his peculiar habit of fixing on a character in a story of the great detective and assuming the role in his daily affairs. His latest venture was Mr. Frankland of Lafter Hall, an elderly good-natured man with a passion for costly litigation, equally ready to take up either side of a question and occupied by a plethora of lawsuits. He arrived at the first Sherlock Holmes Club meeting limping with a cane, a white wig adorning his head, complaining that his soup at lunch had come with a beetle on the spoon and promising a lawsuit against the offending diner. Frankland threatened litigation against any club member who openly mocked his dress.

So, when a letter arrived at the Queen's Hotel from Mr.

Godfrey Hines, Pharo opened it with trepidation. "I expect I'm being sued for overstaying my visit," she mused.

But the letter started warmly, wishing Pharo great success at her meeting with Sir Arthur Conan Doyle. The article in the *Morning Express* detailing her upcoming interview with the master of the detective novel had resulted in requests for Pharo to speak at the Sherlock Holmes fan clubs in Niagara Falls and Albany. Godfrey implored her to press for physical details of the character of Professor Moriarty, the scheming scientific criminal described in Doyle's latest story. "I shall relish playing the part of this organizer of devilry," Godfrey continued. "I imagine Moriarty with a bulbous shape to his nose, his eyebrows furrowed, a ruddy color to his cheeks, a sinister inflection in his voice, and a wispy frame."

But the letter continued with an ominous message for Pharo that caused rage to build up in her like an overheated kettle and made clear Godfrey's purpose in sending it:

"Beware, in your interview with Sir Arthur Conan Doyle, of requesting his views on female suffrage. He is no friend or ally to your cause, Pharo. The slightest hint of your predilection for the suffragettes will sour your interview. The papers report that Doyle was asked about an incident at the London National Gallery where a suffragette attempted to slash a nude masterpiece, and he lamented such 'outlandish behavior' and spoke of his fear that the disruptive tactics of the suffragette movement might eventually lead to lynching."

"Lynching!" Pharo exclaimed, her devotion to the author Doyle dissipating like melting wax. Pharo recalled Kat's stern admonition about meeting with Doyle—her banishment from the suffragettes was now assured unless she could convert Sir Arthur to the cause. "I shall enlighten the master of the detective story with the strides of progress made by the suffragettes. The vote for women is coming soon, Sherlock Holmes be damned!"

Pharo continued to read.

"Some good tidings to share. Three new members seek to join the club," Godfrey went on. "Daisy Francis, Macauley Simpson and Robert Planter. The membership committee will review their applications before our meeting tomorrow evening."

Pharo paused and studied one of the names. It had a familiar but alarming ring—it dawned on her at once that 'Robert Planter' was the alias used by Mortimer Hanus in his criminal misdeeds.

Hanus was on her trail! Burford had been right to warn her to be careful. Her arch enemy hadn't wasted any time tracking her down. She regretted granting the interview about her trip to the newspaper.

She must be on constant guard now. The bell had rung for Round Two.

*

"The next applicant to be considered for membership to the Sherlock Holmes Club is Mister Robert Planter." The speaker, Louise Champion, a retired schoolteacher and writer of children's stories, clasped her hands and smiled earnestly as she addressed the applicant with his coiffed side whiskers and his bespoke suit. "Mr. Planter, we are convened to consider your formal request to join our club. Before you can become our thirty-first member, we must test your proficiency in the Sherlock Holmes stories."

"I'm curious; how did you learn of the Sherlock Holmes club?" Godfrey Hines asked.

"Pharo Simmons recommended it. We attended the same Bible class at church. I'm not certain if she yet belongs to your club."

"Pharo is our president. She's in Toronto waiting to interview Sir Arthur Conan Doyle."

"Pharo is meeting with Doyle today?"

The question was ignored. "His correct title is Sir Arthur," Louise said, her cheeks flushing. "Let us begin with the first question. What were the circumstances that led to Dr. Watson's introduction to Sherlock Holmes?"

"They moved in together?"

"Correct. In *A Study in Scarlet*, Watson searches for lodgings and is introduced to Sherlock Holmes, who offers to share a suite in Baker Street."

"Am I now a member of the club?"

"Our committee is tasked to pose the questions," Godfrey said sharply.

"Not yet, Mr. Planter." Louise Champion's grey curls swayed as she turned to confer with her colleague. She checked her notes and began: "Why did Sir Henry Baskerville leave his farm in Canada to reside at Baskerville Hall?"

"He grew tired of milking the cows and feeding the chickens."

For Godfrey Hines, the answer was the equivalent of the dart missing the dartboard and landing in a different room. "You demonstrate a woeful lack of knowledge of a classic Sherlock Holmes novel! Sir Henry was the rightful heir to the manor after the sudden death of Sir Charles Baskerville." He peered at his colleague. "Is there any need to continue this charade?"

"I think not," Louise said.

Godfrey reached for his flat straw hat on the table. "Mr. Planter, your application is hereby dismissed."

"May I have one more chance?" Planter pleaded.

"Here is the simplest of questions," Louise said sternly. "What is the birthplace of Sir Arthur Conan Doyle?"

"Dublin?"

"The correct answer is Edinburgh, the capital city of Scotland. Please leave at once, Mr. Planter."

"That's not fair. I'm supposed to be tested about Sherlock Helms, not Sir Arthur Conan Doyle."

"You mean to say Sherlock *Holmes*, but you make a reasonable point. Godfrey, pose another question."

"Whose murder, Mr. Planter, did Sherlock Holmes travel to Birlstone Manor House to investigate?"

"Excuse the interruption, Godfrey, but I dare say that *I* have no idea of the answer."

Godfrey turned to his colleague and sheepishly apologized. "I traveled to England in the spring and purchased a copy of *The Valley of Fear*. The answer is Mr. Douglas. I was interested to see if Mr. Planter might venture a guess. A beguiling technique that Sherlock Holmes might employ to expose a charlatan."

"I'm not the charlatan here," replied Planter. "You are by attempting to deceive me with a counterfeit inquiry."

Louise spoke firmly. "Control your temper, Mr. Planter. *Ad hominem* challenges to our committee will not be tolerated. The next question represents your final chance and is most certainly not a trick. May I proceed?"

"Yes, and prepare to add my name to the list of club members."

"In the novel, *The Sign of the Four*, what external element does Sherlock Holmes take that is stimulating and clarifying to his mind?"

"A cup of coffee."

"Did you hear Mr. Planter's answer, Godfrey?"

"I did, Louise. He answered that he chose a cup of coffee as the stimulant." His voice simmered with rage as he stared ahead. "Mr. Planter, in a memorable episode, Holmes injected himself with cocaine. Your application to join the Sherlock Holmes Club is dismissed. Depart at once, sir!"

Chapter Nine

"Where is Mason Caulfield?"

Rudolph Mulino had knocked and entered the Doyles' cabin in one motion, his tee shirt untucked and his shoelaces not tied.

Sir Arthur swung his legs out from under a writing table and dropped his fountain pen.

"I was in Mason's company no more than an hour ago," he said. "I walked him back to his cabin."

"Is he missing?" Lady Doyle asked, sitting up in bed. "You appear distraught."

"Mason asked me to meet him in his cabin to discuss my train route home. His company has arranged my tickets. But when I arrived, the door to his cabin was open, and there was no sign of him inside. His fishing rod and boots weren't there, and I assumed he must be by the water. I went to the lake and found one of the canoes missing. I've searched the path and perimeter of the campsite. There is no sign of Caulfield anywhere."

"Did you speak with Terrence?" Sir Arthur asked.

"He was busy chopping firewood behind the shed."

"Did you check to see if a paddle and life jacket are missing?"

"I counted the paddles on the rack, and one is gone. The life jackets are all there."

"Then there's no cause to be concerned," Jean Doyle said, relieved. "Mason is gone for a solo canoe ride on the lake. He'll return soon."

"You don't understand." Rudolph appeared anguished. "He'd never take a canoe out on the lake alone without a life jacket, Lady Doyle. He told me before we left for the fishing trip that he didn't know how to swim. He asked me to save him from drowning if our boat ever tipped over. I assured him unreservedly that I would rescue him."

"A grand gesture on your part, Rudolph. You'd be prepared to sacrifice yourself, of course, to save Mason."

"I didn't consider the possibility that my own life would be in jeopardy."

"It might have been helpful if you'd shared the information that Mason couldn't swim."

"He made me promise not to tell. Mason worried that he'd be excluded from the fishing trip."

Lady Doyle clasped her husband's wrist. "We must alert Terrence to contact the police!"

"Mason Caulfield strikes me as a cautious man. He's likely paddling close to shore, where the water is shallow," Sir Arthur said. "Rudolph, come with me. We'll paddle along the banks of Smoke Lake and see if we can find our missing host. I'll first seek out Terrence and ask him to conduct a thorough search around the campgrounds. But I do agree with the prudent suggestion to enlist the assistance of the police."

The water was still, with a dewy mist hovering over the lake as the canoe set off. Vision was limited to a few feet, and Doyle asked Rudolph, in the prow, to use his paddle to check for jutting rocks as he steered the canoe to the shore's edge.

"Mason!" they began to shout, but only the wild cry of a loon echoed on the lake.

"Come on now, Doyle. Use your deductive powers. You're the creator of Sherlock Holmes. Where is our missing fellow?"

"Focus on keeping a proper lookout," Doyle replied, rankled.

As the minutes passed, the regular sound of the paddle curdling through the lake, accompanied by intermittent shouts of Mason's name, became an ominous chorus. Wind hummed across the lake and brought a strong current and waves that required forceful paddling to resist.

"It's my fault," Rudolph declared, slapping his paddle against the water. "I should have insisted that he take a life jacket into the canoe to cling to if he landed in the water. And I should have warned you, Sir Arthur."

"Heavens, yes, but if there was an accident, Mason must bear responsibility for his own feckless decisions. It's a curious fact, though, that when we were out on the lake earlier this morning, he never mentioned a desire to take a solo jaunt on the lake. Indeed, he seemed eager to return to shore. He picked up a sturdy branch from the water and told me that he planned to carve it into a walking stick. And yet, the canoe is gone without a trace, and so is he. We'll need to keep searching."

"There is one possibility that we haven't considered."

"What is that, Rudolph?"

"I recall that there is a connecting stream from Smoke Lake where it narrows to an adjoining lake. We'll never find it in this haze. Our guide's map will show us when we return to the campsite. Let's postpone our search and await the police."

"Mason struggled with his paddling—we needed to pause for a rest on a small island in the middle of the lake. He didn't venture very far."

A thumping sound could be heard under the canoe. "What was that?" Rudolph asked as the canoe swayed.

"Let's check it out," Doyle said, steering the canoe to retrace its course. "Watch for it with your paddle."

Moments later, an object floating in the water appeared in sight. Doyle guided the canoe to reach it.

"My God!" Rudolph exclaimed. "A paddle. It's Mason Caulfield's paddle!"

*

Two constables from the Huntsville Police Detachment arrived in a police auto at the campsite. Terrence updated the men on Mason Caulfield's disappearance, saying that Sir Arthur and Rudolph had searched the lake in a canoe, and he himself had hiked around the perimeter of the shore and searched the gorse bushes and dense grass around the campsite—all in vain. There wasn't the slightest hint of Caulfield's presence. The officers requested directions to Mason's cabin, where they found his clothing folded neatly on a shelf and a robe and jacket hung in his cupboard. A file thick with documents and a branch and pocketknife sat on his bed.

Sir Arthur entered the room with Lady Doyle. "Thank

goodness you've arrived—not a moment too soon. Look around this room," he said with authority. "Everything in perfect order. I stopped by during my search. An empty bottle of lager beer on the windowsill, and here's the branch Mason pulled from the water." Doyle picked it up from the bed and pointed to a few etchings on the wood. "He started the carving and stopped after a few minutes," he said. "Be sure to check out the business diary on the dresser beside the pillow. I briefly perused it—an agenda appears on the third page mapping out a schedule set to the minute for every date in the month of July after the fishing trip. Dinner with the Prime Minister in Ottawa on the 20th is circled with a sharp pencil. A corner of a page in the middle of the file is neatly folded. It refers to an invitation to the Royal Agricultural Fair next month. A punctilious man with no ability to swim wasn't foolhardy enough to wander off into the lake and risk his life to a gust and turbulent wave."

"You say he couldn't swim?" The larger of the pair of constables looked at Terrence.

"I wasn't informed that Mr. Caulfield couldn't swim."

Sir Arthur shot the policeman a stern look. "What does that matter? You have the information now."

"Are you the couple on the fishing trip? Doyle is the name?"

"I am Sir Arthur Conan Doyle, and my wife is Lady Doyle."

The police constable, startled by the mention of Sir Arthur's title, spoke carefully, not to betray his view that a fatal accident had unfolded. He pressed Sir Arthur for details of their early morning canoe trip.

Sir Arthur summarized it in one word: "Uneventful."

Mason had forgotten his sweater, and they returned after only a few minutes on the lake. "It's chilly out on the lake before the sun comes up."

He deliberately omitted one part of his conversation with his host on Smoke Lake. He had told Mason that he believed Rudolph might be the author of the two threatening notes. The timing of the trip to the Caulfield home coincided with the delivery of the notes: Sir Arthur made plain his distrust for Rudolph. Mason had scoffed at the theory, describing Rudolph as harmless, but Doyle's distrust had not been allayed.

As the first constable spoke, a second, youthful-looking officer, his rounded cheeks untouched by a blade, jotted notes.

"Do we know for certain that he couldn't tread water, Mr. Doyle?"

"Don't accept my word on it. His American cousin, Rudolph, reminded me of it today."

"And Mr. Caulfield never mentioned to any of you that he was heading out on the lake again?"

"That's what's so puzzling," Jean Doyle broke in. "Why the impulse to take a second trip so soon on his own? It defies common sense."

"Unless he was downcast and needed time to reflect on his own."

"What reason would Mason have to be upset? What are you keeping from me, Arthur?"

"We all have our stresses and demons. My mind feels encased in a vice over a brewing war in Europe. Mason had his own pressures and distractions."

"Distractions? You clearly have more knowledge than you're prepared to share. Are you suggesting that he suffered a malady of his heart?"

"It's a possible outcome, of course."

"We need to accept that he likely drowned," the second constable said. He looked admiringly at Sir Arthur as if at any moment he'd request an autograph in his police notebook. "We unfortunately, deal with a number of drowning accidents in Algonquin Park in the summer." At a glance from his senior, he added. "At least, so I've been told. It's my first week at the station."

Rudolph Mulino entered the cabin, announced his name to the policemen and sat on a corner of the bed. "It's all so tragic," he muttered.

"Well, let's not hurry to the conclusion that Mason has drowned," Jean said. "Surely, what's called for is a probing search of the lake and a rescue mission to be conducted. We're wasting precious time."

"Do you know who Mason Caulfield is?" Rudolph asked pointedly. "He's the chief executive and principal of the Grand Trunk Railway."

"Yes, we were briefed when the call came to the station about his disappearance. We'll get a police boat here and check out the lake. The lady makes a good point."

"Borrow our canoes. Please," Jean Doyle urged the two officers.

"We will tow the police boat to Smoke Lake and go motorboating to search for Mr. Caulfield."

Hours passed at the campsite as the Doyles and Rudolph waited for the return of the constables in their motorboat. Terrence, the guide, had been asked to join the search in his canoe.

"Let's consider that Mason Caulfield drowned," Doyle said to Jean. "Then where is the body, and where is the canoe? That's what puzzles me."

"Oh Arthur, perhaps at the bottom of the lake. If the boat tipped over with Mason underneath, it could have dragged him down as it sank. This is all too terrible to bear. We must pray to be pleasantly surprised."

"The canoe may have sunk or may be floating just below the waterline."

Rudolph spoke solemnly, "The discovery of a paddle leaves no doubt in my mind that Mason has perished."

"If you're right, who will share the grim news with his poor wife?" Jean asked.

"Poor Lilian," Rudolph said. "Both my aunt and Mason were exceedingly kind to me."

"The Toronto Police will notify her."

"We must stop by to pay our respects, Arthur, before we leave Toronto."

"Yes, and before the daily newspapers start hovering about in search of a story."

"I hadn't considered that, Arthur. No doubt a horde will rush to Algonquin Park after the first news is published. We must arrange to leave this campsite forthwith."

"I will join you at the Caulfield home," Rudolph put in. "Lilian will be devastated, I'm sure. She adored her husband. They were planning an autumn trip out west to visit me on the movie set. We can at least recount for her the moments of joy captured by Mason in his final days."

Conan took a hankie from his pocket and patted his forehead and brow. "There's something that you both seem to be missing..." he said.

"What is that, Arthur?"

"That Lilian Caulfield will blame the three of us for her husband's drowning."

Chapter Ten

Dear Sir Arthur,

I will deposit my letter with a clerk at the Royal Tweesedale Hotel and ask that it be turned over to you upon your return to the hotel. I missed your earlier message regarding your absence, and have kept my accommodations at the hotel as I await you.

I read in the newspaper of your fishing trip with Lady Doyle. I did enjoy a hearty laugh, imagining the consulting detective of your stories trapped in the confines of a boat waiting interminably for a fish to snap onto the bait. My husband, Burford and I embarked on a fishing trip in the Finger Lakes of my state, and dangled our string and hooks in the water for hours without attracting the attention of a single fish. I christened our boat, The Undesirables. I do wish you and Lady Doyle better success with the Canadian fish.

Before composing my letter, a disturbing telegram was delivered to my hotel. I was duly informed that my proposed meeting with you would have calamitous conse-

quences for my membership in the suffragette movement. I will be instantly banished.

Your harsh opinion of women's suffrage is widely known. It may not hinder the sales of your books, but it is not worthy of an author of your esteemed stature.

I have never padlocked myself to a railing or attacked a congressman, and I assure you that I will be a model of civility at our meeting. But I represent a legion of women who will never subscribe to your primitive view of women's rights. Women, not by decree or ordinance, but by the natural order of a just society, deserve the vote. The disenfranchisement of half of the world's population is a blight on progress and modernity. While my official status in the movement may be stifled, my protests will continue unabated, and my principles are ensconced as hardened clay.

I have reread your Sherlock Holmes stories and your propensity for featuring emboldened male characters is prominent. Sherlock; the army doctor, Watson; the Scotland Yarders, Gregson and Lestrade; and Dr. Mortimer, engaged in unraveling a mysterious death, are all men. You have chosen not to introduce women in your books with capacious minds to reason with the science of deduction. I assure you that the female of the species can think out little puzzles as ably as your consulting detective.

Your patronizing approach to women seeps into your writing. Sherlock Holmes tells Dr. Watson that he would not tell women too much. 'Women are never to be entirely trusted—not the best of them.' The doctor decides not to pause to argue over 'this atrocious sentiment.'

In one of your stories, the client, Miss Morstan, is described by Dr. Watson as entering the room 'with a firm step and an outward composure of manner.' He relates that in his experience with women extending over many nations and three separate continents, he had 'never looked upon a face which gave a clearer promise of a refined and sensitive nature.'

There, Sir Arthur, you illuminate for the reader the traits of women you treasure—decorous and delicate.

In The Hound of the Baskervilles, Miss Stapleton, the wife of the naturalist, Mr. Stapleton, posing as his sister, is described as having 'a proud, finely cut face, so regular that it might have seemed impassive were it not for the sensitive mouth and the beautiful dark, eager eyes.' Eyes eager for lasciviousness or love? The reader is left to speculate. What defines the woman's face as regular? Is there a standard of regularity for women and exceptionalism for men that you abide by?

I admit to not being cut from the silky cloth of your fawning audience of readers who will swoon in your midst. Burford has accused me of harboring a fiery spirit and independent mind. Guilty as charged! Yet, as a fellow author, I have the utmost admiration for your mastery of the detective novel. My devotion to your stories is amply proven by the Sherlock Holmes Club I established in Buffalo.

I look forward to our meeting.

With great admiration (but not unreservedly),

Pharo Simmons

PS I seek your guidance as to the use of 'Royal' for this hotel. There is a paucity of connection to the sovereign—apparently, the King spent a couple of nights here on his first tour of the Canadian Dominion in 1902. When my taps leaked onto the floor in the middle of the night, I had a royal view of a puddle forming beside my bed.

Chapter Eleven

Mitchell Harris sat by the paraffin lamp in his office at the law firm of Simmons and Harris. It was the end of a harrowing day.

He'd been summoned to Pastor Hutch's home as the attending physician had warned the elders of the church that the pastor's final moments on earth beckoned.

Pastor Hutch had been coughing but lucid as Mitchell greeted him in his bedroom.

"Come in, son," he'd said. "I have a message for you and Mr. Simmons."

Mitchell approached and forced a smile.

"I want you to watch over Booker." The pastor paused to cough into his blanket and was unable to continue.

Mitchell stopped at the doorway to say a prayer and took one final look at the priest who had served as a father to him his entire life.

As soon as he reached the office, he communicated Pastor Hutch's admonition to Burford.

Now Mitchell had dedicated the night to finishing his

review of the four weeks of court hearings of a trial in Atlanta, Georgia. After deliberating for four hours, the jury found the defendant, Leo Frank, guilty of murder, and Frank was sentenced to death.

A plea of commutation to imprisonment for life had been filed with the governor several weeks before Frank was to be hanged, and Governor John Slayton had called for a hearing before his fateful decision. Mitchell had been asked by Reuben Arnold, one of Frank's trial lawyers, to lead the argument at the hearing.

The murder victim was a thirteen-year-old girl. Her name was Mary Phagan; she had worked at the National Pencil Factory, a pencil factory in Atlanta, Georgia where Frank was the general superintendent. The young girl had been discovered by the night watchman, Newt Lee, in the basement of the factory in the middle of the night. Lee telephoned the police. She had been strangled to death by a cord tied around her throat and had a gaping head wound.

The police were summoned, and within an hour, a couple of police escorts brought Leo Frank to the pencil factory. He claimed to be uncertain if he recalled the name of Mary Phagan, but his cash book revealed that she had been in his office the previous day, a Saturday, to collect her pay of $1.20. His memory jogged, Frank told the police that he hadn't seen the young worker again before he left the factory at around 5:00 in the afternoon. Only the night watchman remained back at the factory.

The police officer who came to take Frank to bring him to the factory observed that he appeared very nervous and trembled. The next day the police located spots of blood and hair in a metal workroom about two hundred feet from Leo Frank's office. Six or seven strands of hair found on a lathe were identified by witnesses familiar with Mary Phagan as similar to her hair. When it was determined that Frank had been the last person to encounter Mary Phagan alive, the police arrested him on suspicion of murder.

Mitchell was familiar with the Frank case. Burford Simmons had been contacted by a close friend, Allbrighton Williams, shortly after the arrest of Leo Frank and asked to join the team of lawyers representing Leo. "He's innocent!" Allbrighton shouted into the telephone. "Leo is one of the gentlest people I've ever known. He didn't kill this girl any more than I did. It's an outrage!"

Instructed by Burford at the time of the arrest to collect more information about the case from the local attorney, Luther Z. Rosser, Mitchell had telephoned him at his home the next day.

"Let Burford know that the newspapers have turned this murder into a charade," Rosser said. "The *Georgian* has a front-page story calling it 'the greatest news story in the history of the state, if not the South.' The papers are demanding justice, and Leo Frank's arrest calmed them. A newspaper photographer barged into my office this morning and snapped my picture. I chased away the next photographer with my black cane."

"Where is the evidence to convict your client?" Mitchell asked. "There is a patchwork of suspicious evidence, but nothing more."

"What suspicious evidence are you referring to? That Leo was exceedingly nervous when the police came to get him and when he viewed Mary Phagan's body at Bloomfield's, the undertaker. Some of the biggest rascals on earth can sit stolidly and never tremor, while a man of undisputed honesty will quake and tremble on examination."

"Do you have a theory of who the real killer is?"

"We're working on the belief that it's the sweeper, Jim Conley. He had an equal opportunity as our client to commit the murder. Either Leo Frank or Jim Conley murdered Mary Phagan. And our client is innocent."

Burford had to reluctantly turn down a role in defending the sensational case because of his busy trial calendar. He was certain that the jury's guilty verdict was a miscarriage of justice, and he had encouraged Mitchell to be involved in the commutation hearing. Burford had learned from Frank's lawyers in Atlanta that the trial judge recommended to Governor Slayton that he commute the death sentence because he doubted Leo Frank's guilt.

Indeed, the seven volumes of notes taken by the court stenographer at the trial made clear that the verdict at the trial hinged entirely on the testimony of the factory sweeper, Jim Conley. Conley tied Frank to the murder and admitted assisting him in moving the dead girl's body to the basement. Conley had given the detectives a statement and three affidavits where he initially denied seeing the girl on the day of the murder, and changed it to a version that showed Frank planning the murder one day earlier. When the police pointed out to him that a premeditated killing would not fit and was not a reasonable story, Conley changed it again.

Mitchell read the stenographer's record of Conley's explanation for repeatedly lying to the police: "I do not want people to think that I was the one that done the murder." Precisely the motive, Mitchell thought, for Jim Conley to shift the blame to Leo Frank, to falsely implicate him in the sordid crime and prevent his own state execution.

Conley testified that Frank had given him a $200 bribe to move the dead girl's body on the elevator from the metal work room on the fourth floor to the basement and then to return to his private office, where Frank dictated two notes for Conley to write, one on brown paper and the other on a leaf of a scratch pad. The notes, labelled at trial as the murder notes, and scratch pad were found on the ground of the basement close to Mary Phagan's body.

Conley at first denied that he could write, but after the detectives on the case confronted him with proof, he admitted that he could. By the time of the trial, his physical authorship of the murder notes was not in dispute.

In his testimony, Leo Frank denied that he'd directed Conley to draft the notes in his office.

Indeed, since the trial, Frank's lawyers had uncovered evidence that the scratch pad used for one note had a dateline that read "190--," indicating that the form must have been at least four years old. The defense lawyers verified that these order pads had been used by a factory official who left the pencil company in 1912. His scratch pads had been taken to the basement, close to the location where Mary Phagan's body was discovered, thereby refuting Conley's claim that he wrote the murder note on a pad given to him by Frank in his office.

The pair of murder notes purported to be Mary Phagan's description of the perpetrator of her crime: "Mam that negro hire down here did this I went to make water and he push me down a hole a long tall negro black did it. I write while play with me."

"He said he would love me, lay down play like the night witch, did it, but that long, tall black negro did boy hisself."

The murder notes troubled Mitchell. The stenographers' notes from Conley's trial testimony indicated that Frank had requested the money back and received it. Mitchell's mind swirled with doubt. Conley was described in the lawyer's notes as a strong and powerful man and Frank as delicate as a wilting rose. Why would Conley willingly return the roll of greenbacks?

Mitchell studied the carbon copy produced by the police of Jim Conley's final affidavit. The affidavit was typewritten, and it stopped after the following sentence: "Here is $200, and Frank handed the money to him." At the bottom of Conley's affidavit in handwriting was written the following: "While I was looking at the money in my hands, Mr. Frank said, 'let me have that and I will make it right with you Monday if I live and nothing happens' and 'he took the money back and I asked him if that was the way he done, and he said he would give it back Monday."

The payment of $200 by Frank must be a fabrication. Conley had prepared his affidavit, and then when pressed by the police to account for the large sum of money, he had no explanation. He eliminated the problem by adding this ludicrous story that Frank had demanded it back.

Mitchell imagined the jury address he'd have delivered with flourish:

"Gentlemen, we've all enjoyed a hearty dinner with some mock mince pie served for dessert. But if you stick your knife in the middle to cut the first tasty bite only to discover that it's rotten and spoiled—would any of you take a chance with another slice of pie and swallow it? You'd throw the whole pie out just as you should discard every word uttered in this courtroom by 'con man Conley.' Jim Conley tells you that he returned a bribe on the solemn assurance—of a child murderer!—of the money being

restocked at a later date. A lie rotten in the middle!"

Conley had admitted to helping carry Mary Phagan's body to the cellar of the pencil factory. Yet the prosecution had been keen not to indict Jim Conley as an accessory after the fact to the murder. The reason was obvious to Mitchell: an indictment took the luster off their star witness, and the prosecution couldn't risk harming the state's case against Leo Frank.

Mitchell pored over the notes in the file relating to the physical evidence in the case. Blood stains and hair found in the metal workroom had been identified positively as the dead girl's at the trial. Conley had testified that he found Mary Phagan's dead body in the metal room and blood beside her. The gaping wound to the girl's head had reached her skull, and blood would flow freely. Yet the record was clear that there was no pool of blood found there.

Mitchell discovered a report in the file from Dr. Harris, who compared Mary Phagan's hair with the samples of hair found on the lathe. Mitchell was puzzled that the content of this report had not been introduced at the trial. Had the prosecutor held it back? And why hadn't the defense attorneys conducted their own scientific inquiry? Dr. Harris's report noted that he had examined the hair under a microscope and concluded that the hairs found on the lathe were not Mary Phagan's hair. A report in the file from the state biologist reached the same conclusion.

The only blood found in the workroom was untraceable. The splotches amounted to no more than scattered drops of dried blood and could have been present for months.

The physical evidence plainly showed that Mary Phagan

hadn't been killed in the metal work room, contradicting a key element of Conley's evidence.

Conley had also testified at the trial that he carried Mary Phagan over his shoulder to her resting spot in the basement. Yet the appearance of the girl indicated that she had been dragged through the cinder and debris of the basement.

Mary Phagan was strangled by a cord. Leo's knots could be different from those found around Mary's neck and Conley's knots could have matched the signature ligature linking him to the murder. Mitchell found nothing in the trial notes about knot samples.

Leo Frank had testified at trial that he knew nothing whatsoever of the cause of the death of Mary Phagan and that Jim Conley's accusation was a mountainous lie.

Leo Frank had introduced in his defense approximately one hundred witnesses as to his good character. A fifth of the witnesses attesting to Frank's good character were girls and women who were employed or formerly employed at the National Pencil Factory. The state, in rebuttal, had introduced ten witnesses attacking Frank's character, with some describing that he had been seen making advances to Mary Phagan. Mitchell wondered what promises and bargains had elicited such false testimony. The defense had called every girl who worked on the fourth floor of the factory to ask them if they had ever been inside Frank's office or seen other girls there. Frank's conduct had been exemplary.

Conley had testified that he was asked by Frank to attend the pencil factory on the Saturday of the murder. Frank told him that he was expecting a young lady to arrive at his office to chat for a while. Conley explained that he'd been the lookout for the superintendent in other instances when ladies arrived to chat and that a signal system had been devised for Conley to lock and then unlock the front door. The prosecutor failed to call a single witness to buttress Conley's account.

Mitchell's review of Leo Frank's file did not absolve Frank's own lawyers from blame. Problems abounded in their conduct of the defense. With bountiful evidence that John Conley killed Mary Phagan, the defense had instead raised the specter that the night watchman, Newt Lee, was the guilty party. Lee had telephoned the police after discovering the young girl's body. In his cross-examination of Lee, Rosser announced to the judge that "there are a good many suspicious circumstances against Lee."

Rosser and his co-counsel, Arnold, cross-examined Conley for sixteen hours. Three days of hectoring questioning—three hours should have been more than sufficient for the task, Mitchell considered. The risk to the defense was that a prolix and withering cross-examination might engender sympathy from the jury for even an unsavory witness.

Disconcertedly, Leo Frank's lawyers had probed at length the other occasions when Conley described watching for Frank while he entertained young women in his office, crediting Conley's story as worthy of challenge when it was manifestly a proven lie. Conley had been ready for the questions and added copious details to his stories of Frank's lecherous conduct in his office. The prosecutor had set a trap that the defense attorneys fell into. Rosser and Arnold had moved to have the damaging testimony they drew from Conley struck from the record, but the judge ruled that the damage had been done and it was impossible to remove it from the jury's mind.

Mitchell resolved to be unsparing about any deficiencies of the defense accorded to Leo Frank. He believed that no man deserved to be hanged by the state because of the grievous failings of his lawyer.

But then Mitchell was interrupted by the thumping sound of feet on the stairway outside his office. Mitchell checked the clock on the mantel. The time was 7:30—he'd worked through the night.

The door opened, and Mitchell saw a familiar face from the past.

He rose immediately. "Detective Jacob, it's good to see you again, although it isn't customary to greet detectives in my office."

"*Mais oui*, Mitchell. I checked your apartment first; when my knock went unanswered, I assumed that the esteemed lawyer must be at work. I'm surprised that you recall me after the years that have passed since Mr. Simmons's kidnapping."

"But why are you here?" Mitchell asked, perplexed.

"I am aware that you are working on the Leo Frank case. I recommended you to Rabbi David Marx. Leo is a member of his congregation in Atlanta, Beth El, and the rabbi has counseled and supported him during his ordeal. He attended every day of the trial, believing that the jury would cast aside the shackles of prejudice and decide the case fairly. We were all confident of a not guilty verdict."

"I've communicated with Rabbi Marx. He will be meeting me at the Terminal Station when I arrive."

"Leo Frank is a Jew, as am I, and I speak for many in my community when I tell you that his trial in Atlanta saddens me. I have spoken to Leo's uncle and the family is devastated by the verdict. His wife, Lucille, who visits him every day, is inconsolable. And rightly so—an innocent man has been convicted on the tissue of lies of a perjurer scrambling to save his life. The prosecutor's case was a tangled web of deceit from beginning to end. And why, *monsieur l'avocat*? Because Leo is a Jew, and it is convenient to sacrifice Jewish blood in a frenzy of bitter hatred of my people. Crowds gathered on the sidewalk outside the courtroom shouting through the open windows, 'Kill the Jew.' The verdict resting against Leo Frank is a familiar calumny. I am reminded of Alfred Dreyfus and his court martial in France, a soldier falsely accused as a Jewish traitor. As a *gendarme* in Paris, I witnessed the swelling tide of hatred against the Jew. Frank is the American version of Alfred Dreyfus."

"I must share with you, Detective, that I share your concern about the guilt of Leo Frank. I've reviewed the court hearing. An innocent man is facing the gallows."

"Mitchell, you are one of Buffalo's finest lawyers. I have followed the rise of your career with great pride. You must convince the governor of Georgia of your belief," the detective pleaded.

Observing tears rolling down his cheek, Mitchell rose again to shake Detective Jacob's hand.

"I give you my word," he said. "It will be my sacred mission to reverse this injustice. I won't rest until the mission is complete. I must return to my work."

"*Merci*, Mitchell!" Jacob embraced the lawyer in a tight hug, wiped his tears with a handkerchief and shuffled to the door without speaking another word.

Detective Jacob's visit altered Mitchell's view of the case. He had been wrong to attribute Leo Frank's charge of murder to sloppy police work or a flawed rush to judgment. Under enormous public pressure, the officials in charge of the murder investigation had to choose between a Jew and a Negro as the killer of Mary Phagan. Taking the Jew down made a bigger splash and harnessed greater rewards. Once the Jew had been selected as the prosecutor's prey, the forces of the state were all in to convict Frank of the murder.

"There, I've deciphered it!" Mitchell spread the sheet he'd prepared across his desk, illuminated by the glowing morning sun lighting the room through a paned window.

Booker, the student the law firm had hired for the summer, hovered beside him. His first two weeks had been devoted to assisting Mitchell with the file.

The murder notes were recast by Mitchell in sequence, with the punctuation removed. "Look at this," he said, using a ruler to guide him through each line like the baton of a conductor.

Mam
i wright while play with me
play like
i went to make water and he push me down that
hole
land down
he said he would love me
the night witch did it
that negro hire down here did this
a long tall black negro black that hoo it wase
long sleam tall negro
but that long tall black negro did but his self

"*The night witch did it!* Mary Phagan was supposed to be blaming the night watchman, not Leo Frank."

"Yes, Booker. The notes solved Jim Conley's dilemma as he sat on the ground of the basement with Mary Phagan's corpse a few feet away. He needed to find another culprit for the murder, and he knew that Newt Lee, the night watchman would arrive at the factory in a few hours, after he'd be gone. With a lantern beside him lighting the room, Conley prepared a note as if Mary Phagan had written it before she passed. The night watchman would surely discover the young girl's body on his rounds in the basement and contact the police. But the damning note would intimate that he'd committed the crime himself."

Mitchell sat back in his chair, suddenly tired.

"He is a conniving fellow, this sweeper. He added the description of a long, tall, slim Negro because it contrasted with his own short, stocky and broad-chested frame. He knew that no one had seen him in the factory other than the dead girl. Even Leo Frank testified that he wasn't aware that Conley was present on the day of the murder."

"But I don't understand, Mitchell. Why did the police suspect that Leo Frank was Mary's killer?"

"They didn't at first, Booker. When the police attended the pencil factory, Sergeant Dobbs read the murder notes to Newt Lee. The night watchman's response was that 'They's tryin' er lay it on me.' Lee was arrested and taken to the police station—he was kept in jail for three days of intense questioning by the police."

"Then why did the police turn to Jim Conley as a suspect? I'm confused, Mitchell."

"The Atlanta newspapers carried a banner story that the sweeper at the pencil factory admitted to writing one of the murder notes and identified Conley. But by that time, the police had decided to focus on Leo Frank as Mary Phagan's murderer."

"But why did Conley write two notes after he killed the girl?"

"I'm just as puzzled as you are, Booker."

The student picked up and read Mitchell's summary of the murder notes. "Was the last line in the second note?" he asked.

"Yes, it was."

Booker read the last line again: "but that long tall black negro did but his self." Then he shouted,

"I've figured it out! Jim Conley wrote that the tall black Negro, the night watchman, did it by himself. He'd realized that his first note didn't point the blame at a single killer. He prepared the second note to make it clear that Newt Lee killed Mary *all by himself.*"

"You're right!" Mitchell banged the table in fury. "Jim Conley murdered Mary Phagan and evaded capture. And another man now awaits execution, falsely blamed for the killing."

The lawyer stood resolutely and picked up a valise from beside his desk. "Have my files packed up and sent to the railway station. I'll wait for them there. I'm off to Atlanta to set the course of justice straight and save a man's life."

Chapter Twelve

Gordon, the fidgety clerk at the front desk of the Royal Tweesedale Hotel reluctantly accepted the business card of the man in front of him: a man with a trimmed red beard wearing a tailored Oxford grey suit and pearl-buttoned silk white shirt.

"Sir, I'm not sure why you're giving me your card."

The man's eyes locked on Gordon's in a contemptuous stare. "Read it!"

The clerk had twice rejected the extravagantly dressed man's request for the room number of a hotel guest. The decision was elementary as the hotel carried a strict policy of not disclosing guests' accommodation. Gordon read the card: Magnus Wilmot—Property Agent—and the address on the card listed the Temple Building in downtown Toronto.

"I'll keep the card on file," he said, slipping it into a drawer.

"Is your manager here? I wish to speak to him."

"I'm sorry, Sir. His child took ill, and he had to leave his shift early."

"You'll assume responsibility then for this charade.

I've told you that I forgot the sheet of paper with the room number in the desk drawer of my library."

"I'm bound to follow the hotel policy of not giving out a guest's room number," Gordon said.

"I hope you're aware that holding on to this ridiculous *policy* will not end well for you. Magnus Wilmot never forgives a slight!" He passed an envelope across the desk as he spoke.

"What's this?"

"Open it," the rancorous man said in a gravelly voice.

Gordon tore open the envelope and found two ten-dollar bills. He paused, looking up at the chandelier in the center of the lobby, its crystals shimmering like diamonds under the light. He'd been at the bank the day before checking his deposit tally in his savings account: thirty-four cents. Daily jaunts to the saloon after work had depleted his account.

Resistance waning, Gordon slipped the bills into his pocket. "What is the guest's name again?"

"Pharo Simmons. I'm here to discuss the purchase for a client of a building she and her husband own in Buffalo. Check your records, and you'll see she gave you a home address in Buffalo. Surely that will prove that my request is genuine."

Gordon's hand shook as he flipped the pages of the registry until he located the guest's listed address... *Buffalo, New York.*

"All right, sir, I'll make an exception in your case."

"Thank you," Wilmot said, his tone turning gracious. Smiling, he swung his body and extended his hand across the desk, flashing the shiny object tucked into the waist of his slacks.

The clerk's hand remained still. His eyelids began to flutter.

"What's wrong?" Wilmot asked.

No reply was forthcoming, just a trance-like stare.

Wilmot's voice rose, gentlemanly pretension abandoned. "What is Pharo's room number?"

The commotion had drawn the attention of another hotel clerk.

"Is anything wrong, Gordon?" she asked, propping her colleague's wobbly frame.

He muttered softly, "Pistol tucked into his waist."

"Pistol!" she shouted, halting three guests amiably chatting on the hotel sofa in mid-sentence.

Wilmot backed away and slunk quickly through the lobby.

*

Pharo Simmons was busy reading a newspaper story of hundreds of women suffragettes arrested in a failed effort to present a petition to the King at Buckingham Palace when she heard a sharp knock on her door.

"Who is it?" she shouted.

"Bellhop, Ma'am. I have a note to deliver to you from the desk."

Certain that it was a letter from Sir Arthur, Pharo rushed to the door and grabbed the envelope.

After reading the note, Pharo said, "Please let the desk clerk know that this note was delivered to me in error."

"I was told that the note was urgent. Are you sure?"

"I'm quite certain—and I'm perturbed that the clerk has frightened me so." Pharo pulled a lace handkerchief from a pocket and dabbed her eyes affectingly.

"Are you not well, Ma'am?"

"Clearly not!" Pharo shielded her eyes from the bell-boy's face and spoke sharply. "What is the desk clerk's name...Gordon? Inform Gordon that I need to see him at once about this dreadful note. My day is ruined."

The bellboy nodded and exited the room.

As she waited, Pharo reflected on the details contained in the note. The man described as carrying a gun must be a professional killer, and she his target. The killer had taken care to prepare a business card; the ruse was carefully plotted. Mortimer Hanus, the puppeteer holding these strings, was definitely on a mission to see her demise. She had underestimated his ruthless nature, to her peril.

Well, he had discovered her location in Toronto—perhaps Godfrey had let slip in correspondence with Hanus that she was visiting the city. The Royal Tweesedale was regarded as Toronto's finest hotel—not on merit, she might add. It was fruitless to surmise. She must arrange to leave the hotel as soon as possible.

The knock on her door came.

"Come in, Gordon," she said, opening the door and directing him to a padded chair.

"I'm terribly sorry to have frightened you, Mrs. Simmons."

"Can you recommend another hotel? Preferably one smaller than the Royal Tweesedale."

"My cousin Shirley works at the Davenport, on Jarvis Street."

"What is my bill for three nights' stay?"

"Ten dollars a night."

Gathering some bills from a table, she placed them in his hand. "Here is forty dollars. Telephone your cousin and book me a room for a couple of nights. The bellboy will pick up my suitcase outside my door in half an hour, and you will arrange to have an automobile waiting for me at the front door. Will you follow my instructions?"

"Yes."

"Are you an admirable desk clerk, Gordon?"

"I believe I am, Ma'am," he said with a gleaming smile.

"Can I rely on you? My life is in danger."

"You can trust me."

"Good. Let's put your aptitude to the test. I want three objects promptly delivered to my room. A cane, a piece of white chalk and a black veil. Can you manage that?"

Gordon looked at her, perplexed. "I suppose that I can."

"I have faith in you, Gordon. Use the extra ten dollars to purchase the items. I need them quickly. Save a dollar for the bellboy, and the rest is your reward."

"Reward, Ma'am?"

"You're a brave man. You've already saved me from grave peril. Now—are you able to send a cable on my behalf?"

"Certainly."

Pharo jotted a few words on a scrap of paper with an address in Chicago and handed it to Gordon. "Can you read it?" she asked.

Gordon unfolded the paper and read out loud: "*Burf, send Booker to the Davenport Hotel on the next train to Toronto.*"

"One further matter. Please keep me registered as a guest at your hotel."

"Why is that?"

"The jackal is likely to return. It's always prudent to be on guard and prepared."

Back at his front desk duties some time later, Gordon

glanced at the elevator as it opened and saw an elderly woman hobble out and cross the lobby floor stooped over, a silvery cane steadying her. A black veil covered her face, and her wrists and hands were ivory white. Gordon called the bellboy over to assist the woman, but she flagged him away with her bag.

As she passed the desk, Pharo lifted the veil and winked. "Bye, Gordon," she murmured.

"Mrs. Simmons!"

"Shush, Gordon, you'll disclose my disguise."

Gordon slipped his hand under the desk and pulled out a letter with Pharo's name inscribed on the envelope.

"Here, take this," he whispered, gazing around furtively. "Mr. Doyle left this for you."

Pharo waited until she registered at the Davenport Hotel and was secure in her room before reading the letter.

Dear Pharo,

I apologize for the delay in my correspondence, but it could not be avoided. I received your letter on my brief stop at the hotel in Toronto. Lady Doyle and I are engaged in pressing matters this afternoon, followed by a farewell dinner party hosted by the mayor of the city. We will forego the tango dance program and get an early rest.

We continue our journey to England tomorrow. There is the danger of an impending war. I have been reassured by the British ambassador to Canada that no civilized nation will torpedo unarmed and defenceless merchant and passenger ships. For the sake of everyone on our ship, I pray that he is right.

Our train departs for Montreal at 6:00 pm, and I recommend we meet inside the front doors of the train station one hour earlier. I promised to send you an interview in a Marconi message from the liner, Olympic, and you shall receive it.

There is a sharp division of opinion between us regarding universal female suffrage. My immutable view on the subject is that when a man comes home from his day's work, he does not want a politician sitting opposite him at the fireside.

The newspapers are filled with stories about the drowning tragedy that unfolded on our fishing trip to Smoke Lake. The papers insist on describing me as the most famous man in England, a distinction unappreciated by the electorate in England—I lost every election I ever entered. I assure you that fame is not foremost on my mind. I have a numbing pain in my shoulder from a cricket ball hit at full toss at a school field in Scarborough, my latest detective tale is as dull as a rusty screw, and of paramount concern, the host of my tour of Canada has vanished into a misty lake.

Our genial host, Mason Caulfield, is presumed dead after venturing onto the lake alone in a canoe. We devoted many anxious moments scanning the lake for him but returned with the scant discovery of a paddle. The police have fared no better.

I am unsettled and distraught about Mason's death, more so because my hunch is that he did not drown. A short time before he went missing, we ventured out on the lake together. I can conceive of no fathomable reason for a second trip by my convivial host. I mourn for Mason's family. He had a tight bond with his wife, Lilian, and enchanted me in our canoe with stories about his close bond with his stepson, Brian. Brian is autistic and, according to Mason, a gentle giant with a kind disposition who leaned on his stepfather for guidance. Alas, that guidance will now be wanting.

I owe it to Mason to unravel the mysterious circumstances of his death and to hold his murderer accountable for his dastardly crime. I have a proposal for you at the train station, which you are free to summarily reject. Until we meet then.

Sincerely,

A.C. Doyle

*

Sir Arthur and Lady Doyle arrived at the palatial home of Lilian Caulfield, entering through a cast-iron gate and a grazed path. Rudolph greeted them at the door and escorted them to a sparsely furnished living room adorned with tall glass windows looking over a castle.

"The Caulfields only moved into their new home three weeks ago," Rudolph explained. Lilian emerged from the kitchen and greeted the Doyles warmly.

"I understand you were the last person with my husband," she said to Sir Arthur.

"Yes, I was—he was in hardy spirits, and we enjoyed our time on the lake. His last moments were gay and happy ones."

"I must tell you, Sir Arthur, that I thought it a waste for my husband to join you on your fishing trip. Mason was not well-suited to outdoor life. But he insisted on taking the trip to Smoke Lake. The prospect of spending time with the author of the Sherlock Holmes stories enticed him."

"He spoke so fondly of you, Lilian," said Lady Doyle. "You have many memories together to treasure."

"You're very kind," she said, her voice breaking.

"We are sorry to have to miss the funeral. Our ship sails in two days."

"Rudolph suggests that I proceed with the funeral, but my mind is tumbling with farfetched ideas that my husband is alive. My nephew reminds me that the police have abandoned the search for Mason's body. I'll be compelled to proceed with a funeral without a casket—yet I can't abandon hope that he'll show up one day, apologizing for some frolic or misadventure. But of course, Mason would admonish me for not being sensible. Rudolph is spot on. We all know he's gone. You'll have to excuse me. I need some rest. The doctor's orders."

"We are so sorry," Lady Doyle said, clasping Lilian's hand tightly. She helped the grieving widow up the stairs to her bedroom.

"What are your plans, Rudolph?" Sir Arthur asked.

"I've delayed my return for a few days to stay with Lilian until after the funeral. The producer of my film wasn't pleased. The director, Bullhorn, will have to wait a few more days to scream at me on the set. Bullhorn—his real name is Bullard—carries a megaphone during the filming and shouts his instructions. I long for the day when actors can speak on film."

"Has Lilian received many guests at the house?"

"Mason Caulfield was a titan of industry, with a legion of colleagues and dedicated friends. The house is packed with visitors most of the day. Lilian's pastor and family doctor left minutes before you arrived. The doctor is carefully monitoring her."

"She doesn't seem to be—"

"Blaming us, Sir Arthur? You're correct. We had a chat on the first day of my arrival, and she told me that she understood that it was Mason's decision to take a solo trip on the lake. He knew the risks. That was her husband's character, fearless and unwavering. I shall miss my uncle."

Sir Arthur listened to Rudolph's effusive praise of Mason Caulfield and his thoughts turned immediately to a stage actor reciting scripted lines.

Chapter Thirteen

Booker exited the cast iron door of Toronto's Union Station with a sack slung over his shoulders, ready to count his paces. He took the sheet of instructions dictated by Pharo Simmons from his pocket and read, "Twenty paces forward followed by a sharp right turn, then a hundred paces to reach the street corner of Bay and Front." He steadied his straw hat and touched each step, counting out loud.

A woman and her child approached.

"Why is that man counting?" the boy asked.

A friendly grin rounded Booker's dimpled cheek. "I'm practicing my arithmetic," he said.

He soon reached the closed souvenir stand noted with an X on the sheet, but Pharo was nowhere to be seen. Peering across the street, he observed a clown holding a balloon waving in his direction. Booker looked around—he was alone on the street.

The clown waved him over, and as he reached within a few feet, he heard a familiar voice.

"Hello, Booker."

"Pharo?" he asked, bewildered.

"Yes, it's me." She let the balloon fly off and removed her clown nose and her baggy overshirt. "I found a costume store on a walk downtown," she said. "It's been great fun dressing up as a nun and a Quaker."

"Burford explained that you needed me here—I took the first train available."

"I'm so grateful, Booker. Mortimer Hanus's men are prowling the streets, stalking me."

"I have a revolver in my satchel. The bullets are in my pocket—I'll load the gun when we get to the hotel. Burford insisted that I not carry a loaded gun."

"I'd expect that from my prudent husband. He had a prosecutor discharge a loaded gun in the courtroom by accident one time. Come, Booker, we'll take a cab from the train station after I conclude a brief interview I've arranged. Have you eaten dinner?"

"They served biscuits and drinks on the train. Who are you interviewing?"

"Sir Arthur Conan Doyle. Come, there's a coffee shop inside Union Station. Let's stop there," she said, starting to walk. "It's been a few years since I saw you last. How are you managing your law school studies?"

"The first year was challenging," he said. "But I have an engaging criminal law professor and enjoy the course."

"Remember Mr. Simmons's promise that there is a position waiting for you at the law firm when you graduate."

"Simmons, Harris and Glover. I'm counting on it," he said.

Joining the criminal law firm as an associate was Booker's career plan. He'd waited for his first day in court from the moment he left school in Buffalo to start his university studies. He'd enrolled at the School of Law at Duke

University and was working as a summer student under Mitchell's mentorship at the law firm.

They mounted the steps and entered the grand rotunda with a patterned tile floor, and stopped at the coffee shop next to a board with a list of arriving and departing trains. Moments later, as Pharo sipped on her tea, she was startled to see Doyle briskly moving across the rotunda in the company of a woman—Lady Doyle, she presumed. The interview was scheduled to start in a quarter of an hour.

She ran to greet Sir Arthur, panting as she stopped to block his path.

"What do you think you're doing?" he asked angrily.

"My name is Pharo Simmons. I've been waiting for days to meet with you for my Sherlock Holmes Club."

"Ah, Pharo, you've tracked me down. Forgive me for being abrupt with you, and my sincere apologies for delaying our meeting."

"You've had a couple of harrowing days, Sir Arthur."

Lady Doyle interrupted. "I'll let you finish your chat, Arthur. Please be brief. I'll proceed to the gate and check that our suitcases have been placed on the train."

"I'll join you in a few minutes," he said, turning to face Pharo. "The memorial service for Mason Caulfield is tomorrow. I regret that we must miss it."

"The Toronto newspapers are filled with tributes to Mr. Caulfield. He's described as launching off in a canoe on a solo trip without the ability to swim. That spells danger."

"A tragedy, yes, but I'm not as certain as the police to conclude that it's an accident. What I'm about to tell you must not be repeated."

"You have my solemn word."

Doyle detailed Mason's account of the two disturbing notes.

"Do you think they're connected to his untimely death, Sir Arthur?"

"On the surface, they appear not to be. If the extortionist's purpose is to extract his ransom money, Mason's murder vitiates his plan."

"Might the author of the notes have any other nefarious purpose?"

"That will be for you to uncover, Pharo—if you're prepared to carry forward with the investigation."

"But what of the police?"

"Rank amateurs as far as I'm concerned. They started with the conclusion that Mason drowned in Smoke Lake and forced the evidence to fit to confirm their theory. I was with Mason earlier that morning on the lake. He made a comment that I dismissed at the time. I'm not certain that it's insignificant now, although the detectives are treating it lightly."

"What did he say?" Pharo asked, deeply interested.

"We had been paddling for a few minutes when Mason blurted out that he'd been startled by a sound in the middle of the night. He thought he saw the shadow of someone in the room but didn't hear any further sound and went back to sleep."

"Did he keep his door unlocked?"

"Yes, but he claimed there was no evidence of an intruder when he awoke."

"He must have suffered a nightmare. Perhaps the Hound of the Baskervilles!"

"Sherlock Holmes would deduce that the possible sighting of a mysterious intruder and Mason's disappearance within hours is a link worthy of investigating. I wish I could take on the task. I receive many appeals for help in the detection of crime. Mason was a generous host for our journey across Canada, and I owe him that much."

"Tell me more about your stay at Smoke Lake."

"It was uneventful until Mason vanished. We awoke in the morning to our chores and a hearty breakfast. Our guide, Terrence, led us on a nature hike. He'd prepared our canoes for a day of fishing on the lake—life jackets, two paddles in the bow, nets, pails, fishing rods and bait. We returned for a couple of hours of leisure and rest and capped the day with a delectable dinner and campfire."

"Were you and your wife and Mason alone except for Terrence?"

"Lilian Caulfield, Mason's wife, has a visiting Italian relative, Rudolph, who accompanied us on the fishing trip. He'll be staying at the Caulfield home until he returns to his movie business in California. An unlikeable chap and a possible suspect—keep your eye on him."

"Did Mason have any enemies?"

"You don't reach his stature in the business world without ruffling a few feathers on the journey up. I imagine he'd collected a few."

"Don't fret, Sir Arthur. I shall carry on with the investigation in the company of Booker, a student at my husband's law firm," Pharo said, turning to point out her companion.

Sir Arthur was already rising to leave.

"I never gave you the promised interview! Here is my address in London, and you may send me your questions in writing." He handed her a card from his suit pocket. "I'll be grateful if you can report your findings on Mason Caulfield. My hunch is that Mason is the victim of a devilish crime."

"I will sign my letters to you as Doctor Watson."

"Pharo suits you better," Doyle said with a warm smile. "I must be off to make my train. Good luck with your adventure."

As he descended into Union Station, Pharo trotted alongside the great man. "Where do you recommend I start my investigation, Sir Arthur?"

"A trip to our fishing lodge on Smoke Lake. A train will take you directly to a hotel close to the exquisite lake. Sherlock Holmes always familiarizes himself with the scene of a possible crime. In one of my stories, he traveled to the address a suspect had offered as an alibi to a crime at 2:57 in the morning, the precise time of the murder. Holmes was overcome with the pleasant scent of bread baking at a factory. When he interviewed the suspect, he recalled no unusual features at the location of the declared alibi—and Sherlock knew he had his murderer."

After waving farewell to Sir Arthur, Pharo returned to the table, stopping at the newsstand to buy a copy of the *Toronto Star*. Sitting across from Booker, she flipped through the paper.

"What are you looking for, Pharo?" he asked.

"Here it is! I've found it," she said, and read aloud,

"*A private memorial service for Mason Caulfield will be held tomorrow at 2:00 pm by the east entrance of Mount Pleasant Park. Lilian Caulfield, the widow of the deceased, will be hosting a gathering of family and friends at her home after the service.*"

Pharo read the tributes to the head of the Grand Trunk Railway that followed the announcement of his memorial service. She put the paper down and turned to Booker.

"I just finished chatting with Sir Arthur Conan Doyle—

he's entrusted us to solve a great mystery on his behalf, Booker! Come, let's eat our dinner and be on our way. Your room is booked at the hotel. We'll need to complete the arrangements for our trip to Smoke Lake. Prepare yourself for a grand adventure, Booker."

*

The judge, Montross McKean, charged with administrative duties in the Federal Courthouse, called Mitchell Harris's case first on the docket.

"You have a continuance motion, Counsel."

"Judge, my client in the state of Georgia is facing certain death if the governor declines to commute his capital sentence. I'm asking..."

But Mitchell was interrupted mid-sentence. "And what is the government's position?" the judge asked.

"We're in agreement. I'm familiar with the record of Leo Frank's trial, and I'm appalled. I wish Mr. Harris success at the hearing."

"Government's sentiment of support noted on the record. Continuance allowed. New trial date is to be set. God-speed, Mr. Harris. Next case."

Mitchell shuffled his documents into his briefcase and left the courtroom. Hearing his name called, he looked to his side.

"My name is Willow Hooper." The woman flashed her press badge as she spoke.

"Burford cautioned me to be on the lookout for you," he said. "You're aware that I can't say anything on the record until the governor announces his decision."

"Our conversation is strictly for background. I asked

Burford to inform you that I can be trusted. When are you traveling to the south?"

"My train to New York City leaves this afternoon—I'll take the Seaboard Airline to Atlanta."

"We'll be traveling companions on your first ride. You're garnering a lot of public support for your client. A petition for commutation for Leo Frank was presented to Governor Slayton today with 800,000 signatures."

"An impressive number," Mitchell replied. "But how many of those signatures are from the state of Georgia? Can I speak to you off the record?" Willow nodded in agreement. "Slayton will be burned in effigy if he offers clemency to Frank."

"But surely he must act to prevent the execution of an innocent man."

"I wish I shared your hearty optimism. Did you attend Leo's trial?"

"My colleague at the *New York Times* attended the trial for a couple of days. It took him three hours to be allowed entry. They didn't believe that he was a newspaperman. There are a lot of impostors clamoring for seats in the courtroom. It was steaming hot inside, even with the windows open. The people watching in the ranged benches had the luxury of using fans to cool themselves."

"I've tried cases under harsher conditions. One time in Binghamton, a crew was building a road just outside the courtroom. I struggled to hear the witnesses' answers."

"Do you believe you and Burford Simmons could have won Leo Frank's trial? I've seen a lot of criticism of his lawyers at the trial. They should have sought to move the venue from Atlanta."

"To where in the state? Mariota or Macon? Avenging

Mary Phagan's death percolated through every county in Georgia like a lightning rod."

"You make a valid argument. I have one request: I want you to grant me an exclusive interview with your client after the governor's decision."

"*If* Leo chooses to be interviewed by the press. The reporters have been most uncharitable to him in their coverage of his case."

"Not the *New York Times*. Our newspaper has published a number of articles favorable to your client. Our publisher, Adolph Ochs, is a member of the American Jewish Committee and is passionate about correcting the injustice of his death sentence."

"The slathering of virtue on your paper is undeserved. You speak of remedying a horrible injustice, but Leo Frank committed no crime. Saving him from the hangman's noose is a worthy goal—attaining his freedom is the ultimate pursuit. I am burdened by the melancholy of a lawyer seeking a slice of justice."

"But surely saving Leo Frank's life will be a glorious result."

"Undoubtedly, Willow. I'll use my best efforts to get you my client's interview—that is my solemn promise."

Chapter Fourteen

Shielded by a shady tree at the top of a rolling hill in Mount Pleasant Park, Pharo and Booker watched the grave-side service for Mason Caulfield. A pastor spoke for several minutes with a group of seven mourners huddled around him.

Pharo studied their downcast faces. She recognized the silent film actor, Rudolph Mulino, standing directly beside Mason's wife. He was that nephew deserving of scrutiny who had accompanied Mason and the Doyles on their fishing trip. The two couples in their twenties must be the Caulfield daughters with their spouses. A burly man in his sixties with a grey moustache closely cropped stood next to Lilian, nodding his head in agreement as the pastor eulogized Mason. In a magazine article about the Grand Trunk Railway, Pharo had read that Mason had a business partner, Samuel Solway, whom he grew up with; she pegged the older man as the partner.

The service ended, and the mourners wandered off in different directions. Pharo and Booker followed at a distance.

At the side of the street, Pharo observed the mourners: Rudolph standing idly by the curb, cutting slices of apple with a pocketknife; the two couples getting into a parked automobile, and Mason's wife, who walked to a waiting cab. The former business partner lingered to chat with the pastor.

"Anything stand out, Booker?"

"The fellow with the apple seems out of place."

"That's a perceptive observation. Rudolph Mulino was on the fishing trip with Mason and the Doyles. For a visiting relative from California, he's managed to be right at the center of the Caulfield family affairs."

"What observations did you make at the service, Pharo?"

"This isn't a close family. No-one bothered to say good-bye. The stepdaughters' auto drove off in the opposite direction to the Caulfield home—there won't be a family gathering after the service. Indeed, one of the stepdaughters didn't appear to be speaking to Lilian Caulfield. One of the children was missing at the service."

"How do you know that?"

"Sir Arthur described to me that Mason had a stepson named Brian. Did you see a youth pull up on a bicycle and watch the entire service from a railing on the street? That must be Brian."

Booker smiled. "You don't miss a thing!"

"Look across the street. I think that's Brian hiding partly behind a tree. I recognize the bicycle. Let's introduce ourselves."

Pharo walked first, and Booker followed.

"Hello, Brian," she said, reaching him.

"How do you know my name?"

"We came for the memorial service, but we arrived too

late and watched it from a hill. I saw you with your bicycle and figured you were Brian Caulfield."

"I wanted to see the service. My stepfather was kind to me."

"Why couldn't you be at the service with your family?" Booker asked.

"I can't tell you." Brian looked around restlessly as he spoke.

"Who are you afraid of, Brian? You can trust us." Pharo said.

"I have to go now." Within a moment, Brian had disappeared.

"That was a most unusual conversation. We'll drop by the Caulfield home tonight, to pay our respects. Perhaps we'll have a chance to continue our chat with Brian. He is holding vital information from us."

"How are we going to get inside the house?"

"I haven't got a clue. I'm relying on you to devise a workable plan, Booker."

*

Rabbi Marx had prepared his sermon for the Sabbath services and was leaving his office when he heard a faint knock on the door.

"Is someone there?" he asked.

The door opened, and a young boy appeared. "Are you Rabbi Marx?"

"Yes—and who are you?"

"My name is Alonzo Mann."

"How old are you, Alonzo?"

"Fourteen, sir."

"Why are you here?"

"I read in the papers that you are friends with Leo Frank. He doesn't have many friends."

"I remember you now, Alonzo. You were the timid office boy at the pencil factory. I was in the courtroom when you answered Rube Arnold's questions. The stenographer could barely hear you in court."

"It was my first time."

"I recall your evidence that you'd never seen any girls in Leo's office on Saturdays. And that you left the factory at about noon on the day of the murder."

"You have a good memory, sir."

"Alonzo, I remember every witness at Leo's trial. You were on the witness stand for less than five minutes."

"I was very nervous. All those people in the courtroom were staring at me."

"Please sit down and tell me what I can do for you."

"I'll stand, sir. Just wondered how Mr. Frank is doing."

"It's kind of you to ask. He's not doing very well. The judge sentenced him to death—and he's innocent."

"My father said Mr. Frank will be hanged. He always treated me nice, and I hope it works out for him."

"You took the trip to my office to tell me that?"

"Can you let Mr. Frank know I dropped by?"

"I sure will, but is there something else you want to tell me?"

"No, sir."

The rabbi escorted Alonzo to the front door of the synagogue and watched him walk in the direction of a trolley stop.

Alonzo's mother stood waiting for him on the porch after he returned from the trolley.

"Where've you been? You got off work over an hour ago."

"I went to see Leo Frank's rabbi."

"Why? Didn't your father and I order you not to say anything? There's nothing you can do now. The jury did their job."

"I didn't tell the rabbi about seeing Jim Conley carrying Mary when I went back to the factory. I promise I haven't told anyone except you and Pa. Conley threatened to kill me if I did."

"Then what business did you have with this rabbi?"

"I was just hoping he'd tell me that Mr. Frank isn't going to be executed."

"Did he tell you that?"

"No."

"No more chatter about that convict. It's no business of our family. Let them judges and lawyers sort it out."

*

Lilian Caulfield answered the doorbell of her home to be greeted by a couple of strangers carrying a basket of fruit and flowers.

"We're the Brickers," Booker said. "This is my stepsister, Betsy. We were staying at a cottage on Smoke Lake when the tragedy happened, and we wanted to leave the flowers and fruit with you to show our respect. We're sorry for your loss."

"Do come in for a few minutes," Lilian said, taking the flowers. "You have a long trip back."

Pharo assumed her role in the scripted plan. "We can't impose on you, Mrs. Caulfield."

"You're not imposing at all. Your company will be a great comfort to me. I'm alone in this house. My nephew has been staying with me, but he's leaving tomorrow. Let me brew some tea. Come in, please."

Pharo and Booker were led to the dining room, where they sat until Lilian returned with a tray, teapot and three cups.

"My husband and I enjoyed a cup of tea together in the evening. He always prepared my tea. My son, Brian, has resumed his duties of serving the tea."

"Where is your son? We'd like to express our condolences directly to him."

"Brian has gone to a friend's house for the afternoon. I do have a question for you. Did you see Mason canoeing on the lake during his fishing trip? He should never have been out alone. It was completely out of character. He was such a cautious and careful man."

"The water on the lake is very calm," Pharo said. "There isn't much danger that a canoe will tip. Do the police have a theory as to what caused the accident?"

"They're not sure. Apparently, a well-known painter, Tom Courtney, drowned last month in one of those lakes in Algonquin Park. Canoe Lake, the policeman said. They never found the painter's body either."

Rudolph sauntered into the dining room and demanded, "Who are these people?"

"They're the Brickers. They have a cottage on Smoke Lake and came to pay their respects."

Rudolph surveyed Pharo and Booker suspiciously. He told Lilian, "I'm packed—I've arranged to be picked up in the morning. Strange," he said, turning to Pharo. "I paddled around the lake and didn't notice any cottages.

I'll leave the three of you to enjoy your tea. I'll see you at breakfast in the morning, Lilian—oh, I nearly forgot to tell you. The policeman called while you were napping this afternoon. He's coming back in the morning. He'd like a list of what's missing."

He left the room.

"That is the nephew you mentioned?" Booker asked.

"Yes, Rudolph. He's been in an ornery mood since he returned from the fishing trip. I can't say that I'm disappointed he's leaving my home. My nerves are already frayed."

"Is there any reason for Rudolph to be angry?" Pharo asked.

"I think he blames himself for Mason's drowning."

Pharo didn't feel that the young man was suffering from guilt at all. "What further business do the police have with you?" she asked Lilian.

"We had a break-in here at my house. When I returned from the memorial service, the rear window was shattered. Some jewelry was taken from my bedroom. Come, let me show you." She escorted them to the living room, where a board covered the frame of a back window.

"Rudolph put the board up for me. He's been a wonderful guest, and I'll miss him."

"I think we'll say goodbye now," Pharo said. "You've had a difficult day. We'll let ourselves out, Mrs. Caulfield."

"Lilian, please, dear. And you're both welcome to visit any time."

After they left, Pharo turned to Booker. "Mason Caulfield is awoken by an intruder whose shadow he sees in his cabin; he drowns the next day under mysterious circumstances—then Lilian Caulfield's jewelry is plundered during her husband's memorial service. Are the three events connected?"

"There is one common link."

"What's that, Booker?"

"Rudolph Mulino had the opportunity to be involved in all of them."

"Correct. But first, we need to establish if this was a murder or accident. Get some rest tonight. We'll set off in the morning for Smoke Lake."

Chapter Fifteen

Dear Sir Arthur,

I pray that your trip across the Atlantic with Lady Doyle has been a safe one. You will receive my cable upon your return. Upon your instructions, I have begun my investigation into the mysterious disappearance of Mason Caulfield. I share your view that Mason met a nefarious end to his life. Nothing about his character or habits suggests a feckless misadventure in a canoe on a misty lake. I am ably assisted in my investigation by Booker, a student of law, who helped rescue my husband, Burford, from a diabolical kidnapper. Alas, that fantastic story for another cable!

We leave for Smoke Lake this morning and I shall duly report to you my findings. This actor, Rudolph Mulino, highlighted by you as a possible suspect in the crime, has piqued my interest. I felt a wary sense of one of the villains in your novels. He glared at me like an intruder upon our introduction at the Caulfield home. I learned that he was a surly and unappreciative guest of Lilian and Mason and lacked a morsel of compassion for his aunt's grieving state.

More study of Rudolph is required, as I am not quite sure what evil traits of character are lurking under the mask of his sullen face. He speaks little, but every word cuts like a buzzsaw. (I caution myself that being thoroughly unpleasant doesn't qualify the fellow as a killer.)

Accompanying your group on the fishing trip provided Rudolph the opportunity to snuff out Mason Caulfield's life. We have a narrow list of suspects to investigate for the dastardly crime. I immediately exclude you and Lady Doyle—any other thought is preposterous. That leaves only Terrence, the guide or an intruder. Heaven knows what motive Terrence might have to be the killer. A notorious murder at his fishing camp can't be good for future business.

Assuming that Mason was the victim of deliberate foul play, it is hardly serendipitous that the author of the great consulting detective was in his midst.

The theory I've developed is that the rascal was daring you to solve the crime, Sir Arthur. And under your tutelage, we shall ensnare the killer and cut the deadhead rose from its stem.

We have collected our first clue. Booker and I watched Mason's memorial service. We determined that Mason's stepson, Brian, was distressed that one of the guests had attended— we will follow up our investigation, but it is important to note that Rudolph was in the select group gathered there.

But I must mute my enthusiasm for the task ahead and be guided solely by the science of deduction. In this regard, any expert guidance and any tidbits of information about Rudolph, the manly siren, or your camp guide will be greatly appreciated.

Adieu!

Pharo

Chapter Sixteen

Arriving in Atlanta and going directly to the court square, Mitchell Harris stopped outside the Fulton County Tower. He gazed at the panoramic view of the Old City Hall and the Tower like a tourist peering over a cliff in wonderment, seeing the patterned squares of ploughed fields far below.

Here the patterned squares were replaced by edifices that harbored a manifest wrong: the adjudication of guilt of a wholly innocent man and his temporary confinement in a jail cell. Only a reprieve from the governor could now stop the life being snuffed from the prisoner's body.

Mitchell had pined for the moment he could dissect these surroundings for a clue, some remnant of insight into the grotesque injustice that pervaded this southern city. But it was Sunday, the Lord's Day, and except for a passing truck on a milk run, the peaceful square was empty.

He gingerly stepped around tobacco spit smeared across the sidewalk like blotches on a drawing and approached the steps of the Tower.

From across the square, a bellowing voice hailed him.

"Mitchell Harris!"

Mitchell peered at the speaker, a wafer-thin man with a cone-shaped beard wearing a long dark frockcoat and a top hat.

The man came briskly toward him, his hand outstretched for a greeting.

"I'm Rabbi Marx," he said, clasping Mitchell's right hand tightly. "I'm delighted that you agreed to make the trip to Atlanta to represent Leo."

"Rabbi Marx! You attended the trial, I understand."

"I didn't miss a day. My congregation, Beth El, granted me a sabbatical—I'd planned a restful trip with my wife, Allie, in Europe, but when Leo was arrested, of course, I cancelled my trip. I recall the first day of trial, waiting in the anteroom with Leo and his lawyers, everyone beaming with such confidence that a jury would find Leo not guilty. He asked if I liked his new fitted grey suit with stripes. The trial took place in that building." The rabbi pointed to Old City Hall. "Judge Roan decided to move the trial from the courthouse. I've arranged for the front door to be left unlocked to show you the courtroom."

Mitchell followed the rabbi through the entrance and into the courtroom. Rabbi Marx walked to an area the size of a boxing ring with seats prepared inside a railing.

"The lawyers and the prosecutors were seated here," the rabbi said. "Leo, his wife Lucille, and his mother, Mrs. Ray Frank, who came from Brooklyn, had seats allotted as well. I sat behind Leo at his request. The judge's stand was in the front."

"The benches were filled as Leo entered the courtroom

on the first day. 'This is all for me, Rabbi,' he remarked to me as many of his friends who came to support him approached past the railing and shook his hand." The rabbi paused, stricken, but regained control.

"And then the first witness testified, Mary Phagan's mother."

"I felt so sorry for that poor woman. The unimaginable loss of a child."

"The same sentiment shared by the jurors, of course. Pity that Luther Rosser didn't use the mother's testimony to bolster his defense."

"What do you mean, Mr. Harris?"

"Rosser showed her Mary's hat, and she agreed that it was worn by her on the Saturday she left for the pencil factory. She identified the hat by the pale blue ribbon on top. The young girl suffered a severe blow to the head. If the injury occurred inside Leo's office and the girl was found in the metal work room by Conley as he testified, the hat would be soaked in blood. Instead, the hat was found by a detective untarnished in the basement."

"I missed that crucial point."

"You weren't alone, Rabbi Marx, and you weren't tasked to defend Leo Frank. The police didn't locate Mary Phagan's hat when they were called by Newt Lee to the factory. It was discovered at a later time on the side of the basement, mixed with some trash away from the body. The killer had deliberately placed it there."

"But why, Mr. Harris?"

"Mary Phagan was strangled with a cord by Conley to rob her of her wages. The $1.20 she collected from Leo in his fourth-floor office was never found. But Newt Lee was a night watchman who had only worked at the pencil factory for three weeks—he wouldn't know that the girls were dropping by the factory on Saturday to collect their wages. So Conley schemed to make it appear like a savage killing, disguising the robbery. Mary was dead when he struck her head with his lantern or some other hard object. The hat was an obstruction and was discarded."

"How can you be certain that she was already dead?"

"Because there would be a pool of blood from a head wound, and the police found no trace of blood in the basement. A dead person doesn't bleed; without the heart beating, the blood in the body stops circulating."

"More proof that the trial was a farce, Mr. Harris. When Allie rushed to the court after the jury's verdict, she cried and urged me to leave this city. But my faith doesn't permit me to run away. Come, come and meet Leo. He's been returned to the County Tower for his hearing tomorrow, and he'll remain there until the governor's decision. Leo was confined there during his trial. I was with him when the shattering news of the jury's verdict came. And yet he's resilient. He never abandons hope."

"An innocent man awaiting his fate: death or a lifetime in prison. That would break most men."

"You'll find Leo lucid and composed—I've just come from the dining room outside his cell. He occupies himself reading books and newspapers. He's a scholarly man, a Cornell graduate like yourself." The rabbi observed Mitchell's perplexed reaction. "Detective Jacob told me," he said.

Moments later, they rode an elevator in the Tower that opened to the dining room.

Mitchell entered. Leo looked up, wiped his thick, slightly darkened glasses with a cloth, folded the cloth and spoke calmly.

"It's wonderful to see a friendly face," he said, motioning Mitchell to a chair at the table. "My dear wife and mother visit as often as they can. Rabbi's enduring support sustains me." Leo stared into Leo's face as he continued. "I am helpless and in desperate straits, Mitchell. My wife, father and mother are in the depths of despair. The mob spirit was abroad at my trial."

"I absolutely believe in your innocence, Leo," Mitchell said. "You are the victim of a great injustice."

"Many of the wisest and best men of the country feel that my trial is not a fair one. My lawyers and friends tell me the governor of Georgia is a good man. But they warn me that the outcome of my commutation hearing is uncertain. The jury was influenced by mob law—the governor may be similarly affected. I am a reviled and despised man, Mitchell. Yet I assure you, I am as innocent as I was one year ago."

"You must keep your faith," the rabbi said.

"I try, Rabbi Marx. My God, I have suffered much; some good men have condemned me, but they have done so in sorrow, while others have kicked me on toward the gallows. What do you say, Mitchell?"

"You show commendable grace and restraint, Leo; I am less forgiving. Your innocence should be patently obvious to any fair-minded person. Your conviction rested on the lips of a devious killer who was richly rewarded by a crooked prosecutor for securing your guilty verdict. I read on the train that Jim Conley pleaded guilty as an accessory and was sentenced to a year on a chain gang. A mere pittance for the true murderer of Mary Phagan."

"I am heartened by your belief in my innocence, Mitchell." Leo Frank dropped his head into his hands and began to weep.

117

"I will not rest with the commutation of your death sentence. Our struggle must continue to free you."

"My lawyers' efforts to secure a new trial were in vain. Rube compared the trial of a Yankee Jew to the trial of Mendel Bialis, a Russian Jew falsely accused of the murder of a thirteen-year-old boy as part of a religious ritual."

Mitchell glanced at the delicate frame and boyish face of the client. He had the sad eyes of a man beset by great adversity. "Impassioned speeches are hollow exercises. We need hard evidence to prove your innocence, Leo, and I intend to find it."

Leo spoke with a feeble smile. "You see, Rabbi Marx—I was right to insist that you bring this fiery lawyer from Buffalo." He turned to Mitchell with a probing look. "Tell me how I can help you."

Mitchell pulled a pencil and notepad from his valise, placing them on the table. "Let's start with the testimony of the police that you were trembling and nervous at the undertaker's."

"It is true that I was nervous. Coming into a darkened room, and then suddenly an electric light flashed on—oh! to see that sight—that poor little child. That was a sight that would have made a stone melt."

"I'm interested in knowing everyone you saw at the National Pencil Factory on the Saturday of the girl's murder," Mitchell said. "Everybody admits that Mary Phagan didn't come to your office to collect her pay before five minutes after noon."

"I didn't see Conley on that Saturday. Emma Clark and Carinthia Hall came to my office in the morning."

"The unchallenged evidence of those two witnesses was that they arrived at the factory at 11:35 in the morning and left ten minutes later. Conley claimed that after the girl was dead and he was in your office, you suddenly said, 'Here come Emma Clark and Carinthia,' and then hid Conley in a wardrobe."

"A habitual fabricator," the rabbi said.

"Did you see anyone else at the factory?"

"I do remember leaving my office once in the morning and seeing the office boy."

Mitchell checked a note he'd jotted. "When the police sent an automobile to pick you up and bring you to the factory, you described Mary Phagan's arrival at your office one day earlier: 'My stenographer and the office boy then left, and Mary Phagan came in right after that.' The stenographer, Hattie Hall, testified that she worked from about 11 o'clock until noon, left at 12:02 and didn't see Mary Phagan. Who is the office boy who left?"

"Alonzo Mann," Leo replied.

"Excuse me," Rabbi Marx said diffidently. "I hesitate to interrupt, but I saw Alonzo Mann yesterday."

Mitchell rose from his chair. "Yesterday! Where?"

"He visited my office at the synagogue. He asked how Leo was doing. It was a brief visit, but I felt that the boy's concern was genuine."

"Still, it's odd that the boy showed up at your synagogue. It wasn't a random visit. I wonder if he had more to tell you but was frightened. What can you tell us about Alonzo, Leo?"

"He was always polite and called me 'Mr. Frank.' I recall checking with him that Saturday morning about some mail that he was sorting. I don't recall any other conversation."

"Do you think he'll agree to speak?"

"I can't say. He is still working as an office boy at the pencil factory. You can try there. There will be a record of his home address in the payroll office."

Mitchell began to recount Alonzo's evidence from memory. "He testified that he started work on April 1st and that he was at the factory on the Saturday the girl got killed—he stayed until 11:30 in the morning. Was 11:30 his usual departure time?"

"He usually stayed till the afternoon on Saturdays. He may have asked to leave early that day —I can't remember."

"Your recollection the next day is that Mary Phagan came right after he left, not half an hour later. Why did Alonzo hide the truth? Perhaps he encountered Mary leaving the factory? We need to interview Alonzo."

"I can meet you at the pencil factory tomorrow morning," Rabbi Marx said. "We can talk to him there."

"Splendid. Now Leo, how long was Mary Phagan in your office that Saturday?"

"I paid her $1.20 in wages and she asked if more metal was delivered to the factory. It meant more work for her."

"So, not more than a minute or two?" Mitchell asked.

"Yes."

"Suppose that on her way out, Conley was lying in wait for her to commit a robbery on the young girl. But Mary was feisty and fought. He then killed her."

"And I became his scapegoat," Leo said, "when the police rejected his story. Aided by the police, he concocted a story that pinned the girl's murder on me—he knew he'd hang if he failed."

Chapter Seventeen

"It is plain to me why Mason Caulfield chose this site for the fishing trip."

"It is quite wondrous," Booker replied. He stood on a stony ridge glancing across the murky blue water of Smoke Lake.

Note paper, magnifying glass and pencil in hand, Pharo surveyed the curving shore of the lake. The law student from her husband's firm stood at her side, vigilant as always.

"Whatever I may jot down will not capture the surroundings of this splendid place. Look around you at the plentiful display of nature's wonders: the still blue-hued water, the rolling hills, the burly trunks of ancient trees dressed in foliage, the powder blue horizon."

"And the crisp flavor of the morning air," Booker said, inhaling.

Pharo and her protégé began their investigation in earnest with a tour of the cabins and campsite, examining every nook and cranny of the grounds. There was a shed with a bolt on the door, with firewood stacked in a pile at the side. The cabin doors were unlocked, and the rooms barren other than wooden bedframes, mattresses and the odd piece of furniture. A newspaper was found by Pharo strewn on one of the beds. The date marked at the top matched the date of Sir Arthur's fishing trip.

"What are we searching for?" Booker asked.

"Evidence of foul play. It is Sir Arthur's hunch that Mason Caulfield didn't wander into the lake and sink accidentally into its depths. We have Mason's account of a prowler in his room to consider as well. To accomplish the deed in time—between Mason's sojourn on the lake with Sir Arthur and breakfast—required a careful plan hatched by his killer. No one at the camp site was alerted to any danger by Mason's cries for help. That was essential to the killer's plan."

"Have you discovered any useful clues?"

"Not a clue leading to our culprit, Booker, but we must assume that every step on this camp is in the vicinity of a crime scene."

"But why, Pharo? What reason was there to go to such lengths to murder Mason Caulfield? And why in here of all places?"

"The motive remains a mystery that we shall uncloak. It may be greed and avarice or brewing anger and vengeance. Or perhaps a reason stranger than anything we can conjure. And as for the location, the killer chose it carefully to disguise his crime. 'Murder is a stranger to paradise.' This placid scene is unadorned with the obvious trappings of a dastardly crime. But somewhere captured here is the proof, Booker, and we shall be the wily sleuths and find it. Sir Arthur was reasonably certain—he'd still be here collecting the clues if he could."

"Have you seen anything of interest? I've watched you scribble a few notes."

"There are a few sets of boot prints leading to and from the shed. There is only one set that has a partial print, consistent with someone running to the shed."

"Do you know what's inside the shed?"

"I peeked through a window," Pharo said. "Its long, narrow shape is fitted to store canoes, paddles, bait, fishing rods, life jackets, canned food, bedsheets and blankets and lanterns."

"The camping guide would have held the key to the shed. The footprints you found are likely his. But why did he need to run?"

"We'll need to interview Terrence next to get his explanation. He was a guide and expert canoeist. And yet, Mason, a non-swimmer, chose to jaunt off alone in his canoe?"

"It doesn't seem logical," Booker said. "Did you make any other discoveries?"

"In one of the cabins, did you observe the small table in front of a bed? With my magnifying glass, I detected tiny strips of wax. A candle burned there. The table provided a useful station for a writer like Sir Arthur. He follows a strict regimen of writing on a camphor-wood desk in his study in the wake of night. A member of the Sherlock Holmes Club shared that tidbit with me."

"It seems that no-one has been in his cabin after he left. The table would have been moved as its use ended."

"Precisely, Booker." Pharo produced a scrap of blackened paper. "In the campfire, I found a charred wrapper for a Tootsie Roll candy, a chewy candy sold in the United States—but as I learned to my chagrin in a grocery store in

Toronto, not yet in Canada. Rudolph Mulino's stock, I surmise. Our prime suspect was likely present the last time the campfire was lit."

"This is exciting. What is the next step?"

"We're off to the shore, where the canoes set off." Pharo's curly red locks bounced off her back as she stumbled down the steep hill to reach the rocky shore.

Booker was waiting for her at the bottom.

"Did you fly?" she asked in jest.

There were three protruding stumps in the shallow water; a stray seagull perched on the middle one. Pharo picked up a dangling piece of tied rope lying on the shore.

Booker suggested, "The stumps and the rope are used to keep the boats from floating away?"

"So, if Sir Arthur and Mason paddled out in the morning, the canoe rested here when they returned. The group planned to go fishing again during the day."

"That explains why Sir Arthur and Lady Doyle assumed that Mason went on a solo canoe trip. They noticed the canoe missing. Their suspicions wouldn't be aroused at first."

"Something here is troubling me, though, Booker."

"What is it?"

"Mason's poor health. His photograph displays a portly middle-aged man. How did he expect to climb this hill on his own, after a tiring solo paddle in a canoe?"

"You're right. He'd find it a struggle to clamber up the hill alone."

"Totally unnecessary, however, if he was dead—and was rolled *down* the hill! The killer could have rolled him along the rocks to the water and flipped him into the canoe."

"It's the perfect crime, if you're correct, Pharo. A police

investigation would find it to be a drowning accident."

"But we still have no evidence of Mason Caulfield being murdered. We did our best, Booker, but it's time to return to Buffalo. Come, clasp my arm as we climb the hill."

"Mrs. Caulfield must be distressed not to be able to bury her husband. I remember when my older brother was killed with the others in Wilmington, my daddy and I took a carriage to bring back his body. Pastor Hutch gave him a proper burial. Every member of our church came. Even the little ones. I still go to the cemetery to talk with Gravesly. He's proud of me for becoming a lawyer."

"He should be mighty proud. Burford thinks you'll be a fine lawyer one day."

Booker beamed at the mention of Burford's praise.

"I'm ready for my push now," Pharo said.

At the top of the hill, the pair stopped to catch their breath; then Pharo crouched down, staring at the ground.

"Look at this," she said, pointing ahead at bunches of budding willows leading into the plush forest. "They've snapped. Someone walked through here."

As she brushed aside the willows, a narrow dirt path appeared.

"Let's follow it." Pharo was ablaze with curiosity.

A woodpecker chopped at a tree above like a carpenter's hammer and the call of a loon carried across the lake.

Booker forged ahead along the path as Pharo surveyed the brush and ground with her magnifying glass. The sun was shielded by an abundance of leaves that almost hid the sky.

"I've found something!" Booker shouted in delight.

Pharo raced to his side and found him on his knees, examining a bed of rocks.

"Look at the concave hole in the middle. There was a large rock here."

"Yes," Pharo said. "And a smooth patch of earth in its place. It hasn't rained since the rock was removed. A first-rate discovery, Booker. The missing rock was removed by hand: a possible murder weapon. We are amassing our proof that Mason Caulfield was killed on the fishing trip."

"His assailant may have followed him on this path and snuck up behind him and hit his head with a rock."

"If the trauma was to the side of Mason's head, it could rupture the middle cerebral artery, and death would be instant."

"How do you know that?"

"I've been reading a medical journal, researching my next novel. I have a spy fatally wounded after being shoved off a balcony and landing on his head. Our family physician, Doctor Ricketts, was very helpful."

"We must go to the police with our findings."

"But we're missing pieces of the puzzle. If Sherlock Holmes was here, he'd ask: 'Where is the blood?' There would be *pools* of blood spilled with this type of injury. And a second, perhaps over-arching question."

"What is it?"

"How was the body moved by the killer?"

"Perhaps Mason was dragged along the path and then kicked down the hill to the shore? It would require a man of great strength, of course."

Pharo pressed her open palm on her forehead and paused in deep thought. Beads of sweat poured down her brow. "That explains the snapped pussy willows. But where are the traces of blood? We shall start here and follow the path. You look to the right, Booker, and I'll cover the dense shrubbery to the left. Let's be careful as we walk not to smudge an imprint of blood on the path."

Back and forth along hundreds of meters of path, Pharo and Booker looked in vain for drops of dried blood. After an hour, Pharo called a halt to the search.

She leaned against a birch to rest and said,

"Our killer was cautious. He assumed that the police might check this path. He smudged the blood into the ground with his boots and covered it with mounds of dirt. An arduous exercise, but necessary to eliminate any traces of blood. We'll never find it."

"But if the surprise attack came from behind," Booker asked, "wouldn't the blood also have splashed onto the killer?"

"And on his hands. He'd need to wipe the blood from his hands, or it would smear on anything he touched. He'd need a harder surface than leaves."

"Like birch bark. Look behind at that tree you're leaning against."

Pharo turned around. There was a darkened brown smudge at her shoulder, and the shape of fingers and a palm were apparent. "Dried blood!" she exclaimed. "Take your pen knife and cut and peel a piece from the trunk with the dried blood. We must report our findings to the Huntsville police at once."

"Do we have enough to get them to investigate a crime?" Booker asked.

"Of course."

Any lingering belief that the police would take their findings seriously dissipated within moments of meeting the two Huntsville constables who had investigated Mason Caulfield's disappearance. The file was closed permanently—that was their official position.

As for Pharo's and Booker's discoveries:

The missing rock—"might have been taken to fill a rose garden or build a rock barrier in a yard." The sample of darkened birchbark—"even if we concede it was blood, likely from a scraped and bloodied hand after a tumble on sharp branches on the path."

Pharo's suggestion that a homicide investigation be commenced was scoffed at by the officers, who admitted they had not even conducted a cursory search of the campsite. Mason Caulfield's death was an unfortunate accident. There were more pressing investigations for the police to follow.

"What is the address of the guide to the fishing camp at Smoke Lake?" Pharo asked, undeterred by the constables' dismissal of her theory.

"Terrence Davis, but I'm afraid that it will be impossible to speak to him."

Pharo turned to the burly constable. "For you perhaps, but Booker and I will give it a whirl."

"I don't think you understand. Terrence is dead. He fell off a ladder climbing up to his roof a couple of days ago. The campsite is shut down until they find a guide to replace him."

"Then our task is completed here," Pharo said.

Upon exiting the room, she overheard the younger officer remark with a mocking laugh:

"First they want the vote, and now they think they're crime investigators."

Rankled, Pharo snapped to attention and strode back into the room. "What's your name?" she asked, pointing at the offending officer.

"Stewart...Stewart Costain," he said meekly.

"Splendid—you see, I write romantic novels, and I've been stuck on naming a character in my story. He's a foul-mouthed ruffian who steals from the trays of pennies of the blind beggars collecting on the sidewalk. You've helped me overcome my impediment, Constable, and I express to you my sincere gratitude. I shall name him Stewart Costain."

Outside the station, Booker turned to Pharo. "You've done your best. It's time to surrender and go home."

"Not quite yet. We must return to the campsite."

"For what purpose?"

"Two people on the same camping trip perish within a couple of days of each other. What are the odds of that occurring, Booker?"

"Quite low, just guessing."

"One can't swim and saunters off to perish in a canoe, and the other, an expert guide, stumbles off a ladder. Do you think that Sherlock Holmes would abandon reason and swallow the folly of those police officers' conclusions?" Pharo opened her notebook and flipped to a page. "There it is," she said, pointing. "The rope beside the stump was tied."

"Yes, I recall that."

"But in order to get the canoe free of the stump, the rope has to be untied before pushing the vessel out from shore. The tied rope we found wasn't used to hold a canoe."

"But for what reason, then?"

"I don't have the answer yet, but let's examine that rope again."

Chapter Eighteen

Burford sat in the office of Clarence Darrow, staring at the circles of smoke from his client's cigar.

"Eli Jacob sent me a telegram last night, Burf."

"What did it say?"

"Oh, I had been complaining to the detective in a telephone call about the plodding pace of my case. The caption was a quote from *Romeo and Juliet*, 'Wisely and slow; they stumble that run fast.'"

"Imagine the scandal if it became known that a detective was sending you notes of encouragement."

"We keep our unusual friendship a secret—I don't want to tarnish Eli's name with my tawdry association. For your benefit, the detective informed me that Mortimer Hanus had an appointment with his parole officer in Buffalo. Eli is concerned for Pharo's safety, and the police are watchful of his movements. He asked me to convey that to you."

"Fortunately, Pharo will be gone from the city. Hanus would never sully his hands with dirty deeds. He relies on his band of thugs and hooligans for that."

"Enough conversation about Hanus. Tell me about Mitchell's hearing before the governor."

"The governor asked probing questions and appeared to be a man of conscience. I told Mitchell before he left for Atlanta that in order to win the hearing, he needed to reach Slayton's soul and his mind."

"It will be a state-sponsored lynching if he hangs," Clarence said. "I read a description of Leo Frank: he's a smooth, swift and convincing speaker. If that's enough to condemn him, count me and a hundred other Chicago lawyers as guilty parties."

"Add a couple of attorneys from Buffalo."

Darrow flashed a perfunctory smile and plopped the ashes of his cigar in an ashtray. Leaning forward, he said, "I'm overwrought with despair, Burf."

"But why, Clarence? The evidence is heavily in your favor—and the pressing question for the jury is why you'd risk everything: your career, your good name and your liberty, to bribe a couple of jurors. And you'll have the opportunity to convince the jury of your truthful account. Judging from your answers to Neeru's probing exercise, you'll testify admirably."

"It isn't the fight against fearful odds that leads me to despair. It's the misfortune of no longer being a lawyer pleading another's cause. I've sat beside my clients for many, many years, giving them all my comfort and aid in their dire misfortunes. I have made their cause my own. I've worked with them and suffered with them, rejoiced in their triumphs, and despaired with them in their defeats."

"No one can question your dedication to your clients. Your skill in the courtroom is unrivaled. I shall harness your wistful mood in my jury address. To risk extinguishing the bright flame of your career for a measly bribe of two possible jurors is confounding logic. Now permit me to return to assist my esteemed co-counsel in preparing for her another withering round of cross-examination. Gather yourself, my friend. Neeru's like a thoroughbred at the Kentucky Derby, restless for the gate to open."

*

Detective Eli Jacob waited by the telephone in his office with a steaming cup of tea. He'd left instructions with the detectives at the station that he was not to be interrupted. He had attempted to read a James Joyce short story, ironically titled "The Dead," but it was a fruitless exercise. He'd done everything he could to gather signatures and letters to support the commutation of the death sentence of Leo Frank. *Quelle tragedie*. He had galvanized the rabbis and priests in Buffalo to rally their congregations in protest.

In normal circumstances he would have been reproached for acting beyond the ken of his duties as a Chief of Detectives. Instead, he'd received boundless support from his police colleagues. The superintendent had told him privately that Frank's trial in Atlanta was a travesty. "An innocent man sentenced to die," he'd said forlornly.

Eli glanced at his pocket watch. Thirty minutes—an interminable delay to wait for the governor's pronouncement. An uncle of Leo Frank had tipped the detective off that the Georgian governor's ruling was forthcoming. A reporter from the *Atlanta Constitution* had telephoned Leo's uncle seeking an immediate comment after Leo Frank's fate was known. The uncle had assured Eli that he'd contact him with the result.

Eli reproached himself for not aiding Frank during

the trial. From the regular accounts he'd received, Leo's lawyers were outshone by a bombastic prosecutor—who delivered a six-hour jury address over two days. One could read *King Lear* aloud in less time.

The Chief of Detectives' sterling recommendation had introduced Mitchell Harris to the case. But Eli worried that it might be too late.

The telephone rang, and Eli rushed to take the call.

He heard a man sobbing, struggling to speak. "I'm sorry, Eli. There will be no decision by the governor today." The receiver went dead before the detective could respond.

"*Mon Dieu!*" Eli declared, shaking his head in despair. "*Un autre jour à attendre.*"

Chapter Nineteen

Booker held up the piece of rope to inspect it closely. "Look, Pharo," he said. "Tying a canoe to shore requires one long rope end—this rope is tied with two short ends. The size of the loop created by this knot is very large."

"I missed that the first time. Come, let me show you why your discovery is important. Please bring the rope."

Climbing the embankment again, Pharo led Booker to the path beyond the willows, and to the concave hole in the ground.

"Take the loop in the rope and measure it against the ground where a rock was removed."

Booker kneeled on the ground and laid out the rope carefully. "It's almost a perfect fit!" he exclaimed.

"Just as I suspected. The rock wasn't the murder weapon, Booker. That's why we didn't find pools of dried blood. The rope around the rock was meant to be placed around Caulfield's ankle inside the canoe, to weigh it down and force it to sink. But when the rope was tied in a knot and secured around the rock, it must have come loose and dropped into the bed of rocks below—the rope was left on the shore."

"So, how was Mason's body weighed down with the canoe?"

"I'm not sure what the correct answer is. The killer succeeded in sinking a wooden canoe and corpse to the bottom of the lake."

"Or the body and canoe were dragged into the woods along the shoreline."

"Good thinking Booker! This murder wasn't carefully planned. We can be certain of that. The coverup was designed on the fly. Something occurred after Sir Arthur and Mason returned from fishing that led to him being killed. But what, I wonder?"

"How do you account for the dried blood on the birch bark?"

"I've reflected on that," Pharo said. "The killer got Mason to the path somehow. No one heard gunshots or a man's voice screaming for help."

"The killer had a revolver pointed at Mason's back."

"I believe so. But Mason Caulfield wasn't the type of man to surrender easily. He'd irritate the killer by mouthing off and earn a sharp strike to his head."

"I'm impressed, Pharo."

"Please don't be. I usually follow the deductive reasoning of Sir Arthur's master crime solver, Sherlock Holmes. But it isn't Sherlock who guides me now—it's Mrs. Vicker."

"Who is Mrs. Vicker?"

"Rosalie Vicker taught me English at Smith College. There were ten students at the start, but only seven survived the term. It was a rigorous class! Every day, we were given an assignment: ten words to use in sentences. "*The* abject poverty of the disparaged peasants..." We'd recite poetry by heart in front of the class—and woe to the student who mucked up a line:

"'I dwell in a lonely house I know
That vanished many a summer ago,
And left no trace but the cellar walls,
And a cellar in which the daylight falls,
And the purple-stemmed wild raspberries grow.'"

"You still recall the words."

"Well, no—that is from a new poem by Robert Frost that I read recently... But one morning, Mrs. Vicker assigned the class a short story to compose. I worked on it through the night and presented it proudly. This will show my mark as a serious writer, I thought. A couple of days later Mrs. Vicker asked me to remain behind after class.

"'I've read your short story, Pharo,'" she told me. "'And it's excellent in parts.'"

"The question blurted out of my mouth: 'In *parts*?' That was a harsh lesson about the discipline of writing that I carry with me. My short story concerned a young woman of privilege from New York who decided to spend her summer slumming—working on a steamship on the Mississippi River. She befriended an artist who sat on a stool at the back of the steamship, painting. Each day she watched in wonder as the canvas filled with rich color. On the last day of the journey, the artist gave her the painting as a gift, on the condition that it would hang on a wall in her home for the rest of her life. She readily agreed, but upon returning home, to her dismay, her mother loathed the painting and refused to hang it in their home. The consequences of that broken promise devastated the young woman—and, to make a long story short, led to her taking an apartment in the Bowery and staking a life on her own."

"The painting came to haunt her."

"Yes, but that was the problem. Mrs. Vicker pointed out gently that I had left a loose strand crucial to my story. *What happened to the painting?* And we have missed an important loose strand at Smoke Lake, Mitchell."

"What is the loose strand?" Mitchell listened raptly.

"Proof that Mason Caulfield didn't set off in the canoe on his own. There was only one paddle found. Terrence was careful to slip two paddles in the bow of both canoes. Sir Arthur told me that."

"And only one wooden paddle was recovered!"

"Sir Arthur and the guide scoured the entire lake and perimeter of the shoreline. The Huntsville police also searched, although I'm not convinced that they could distinguish between a foghorn and a moose call. When the floating paddle was retrieved from the lake, the assumption was that it was Mason's paddle. But where is the second paddle?"

"Assuming the killer is Rudolph, possibly he returned to the campgrounds with it," Booker said.

"We've conducted a thorough search—it's not here."

"What is your theory of what Rudolph did with his paddle?"

"He tucked it in with Mason when he sank the canoe."

"And then swam back. He'd need to be an accomplished swimmer."

"Excellent point. We must check that, Booker. Perhaps Terrence can assist—oh, I've forgotten already! Let's put our thinking caps on and imagine we're Terrence. A camping guide in charge of the equipment might notice a canoe missing in the morning and be alarmed. Terrence ran to the shed to check if the canoe was still stored there. He'd then be on the lookout on the shore waiting for its return. Most likely, he watched Rudolph swim to shore. And after Mason Caulfield went missing, Terrence confronted Rudolph."

"And threatened him?"

"Rudolph either threatened Terrence or inveigled him to keep silent with a bribe. Part of the bribe given on the spot, the remainder to be paid after Terrence's silence was assured."

"But instead of making the second payment, Rudolph showed up at his house and pulled the ladder from Terrence as he climbed to the roof. The execution of the murder was made simple for Rudolph."

"Of course, Rudolph could have returned from the lake and told Terrence that he went for a long swim; Terrence could have slipped off the ladder by accident—and Mason might simply have drowned and vanished in Smoke Lake."

"Oh, don't be a wet blanket," Pharo said with a wide grin. "It's only a working hypothesis.... But if all can be attributed to mere coincidence, account for the missing paddle."

Booker ruminated before answering. "I'm stumped."

"But there's a missing piece of the puzzle, if my hypothesis is correct: what reason did Rudolph have to kill the man in charge of the Grand Trunk Railway and his gracious host?"

"And his wife's close relative," Booker added.

Pharo's palm rested on her forehead. "I'm going to make a second check of the cabins," she said. "Perhaps we've missed an important clue. Can you secure another piece of that birch bark with the dried blood? We have a double murder here, my friend."

Minutes later, Pharo returned, one of her fists clenched.

"Did you find anything?" Booker asked.

"Just a small clue. It's pointless to mention until I check it out."

"Now you have me wondering." Booker stared at her hands. "Can I have a hint?"

"I will tell you, before I change the subject, that my discovery is either entirely worthless or is capable of solving the deep mystery of Mason Caulfield's disappearance. Come, let us leave this campsite," Pharo said, forging a path ahead of her piqued companion.

Chapter Twenty

Pharo and Booker found the hardware store in Huntsville, nestled between a butcher shop and a drug store. The sign read "Jim's Hardware." The obliging teller at the Commercial Bank had told Pharo they sold cans of paint there.

Pharo passed a horse and buggy perched in front and entered the store first, followed by her younger colleague lagging a couple of strides behind.

A fortyish-looking man with a scraggly beard, smoking a pipe, stood behind a counter—a blue ribbon hung from the lapel of his striped waistcoat. Pharo had noticed an older clerk at the hotel wearing a blue ribbon on his vest, and her curiosity was aroused. "It's a sign of support for Temperance," he'd explained.

Pharo had responded huffily. "What will be next?" she asked. "Ribbons in support of chastity and abstinence? I'll gladly adorn a ribbon to my dress in support of bohemian pleasures."

Now the man in the paint store approached. "Can I help you?"

"Are you Jim, the owner of this store?" Pharo asked.

"Sure am—you folks must be passing through Huntsville. I know everyone in these parts. What's your business here?"

"We're house painters from Bracebridge," Booker said. "We've been hired for a job in Huntsville and we're short a can of paint."

"What color of paint are you looking for?"

"Cream white will do." Pharo looked around at the stacked cans of paint on a shelf. "I do have a favor to ask," she said. "Do you have an extra painter's smock? I neglected to bring mine."

"I don't have any for sale. But you're welcome to borrow one I used to paint my shelves and porch in the back. It's full of paint spots, but you'll be accustomed to that."

"That will be ideal. We'll return it to you later today. Did you know Terrence Davis?"

Jim pulled the pipe from his mouth and shrugged. "Poor Terry! God bless his soul. He came by my shop a couple of weeks ago and I sold him some life vests for his fishing camp at Smoke Lake. He told me that the Sherlock Holmes writer and his wife were coming to his camp. How were you acquainted with Terrence?"

"We weren't," Booker said. "His brother has inherited his house and hired us to paint the front gate."

"I didn't know Terry had a brother. We talked mostly about his fishing camp in the store. He bought his supplies here."

"Did he mention anything else about the Sherlock Holmes writer?" Pharo inquired.

"Only that Cyrus would do anything to meet him—he claimed that he'd read every story and book ever written about Sherlock Holmes. Cyrus Delaney was Terry's financial partner, the one who invested the money to build the fishing camp."

"Did Terrence set up a meeting with Cyrus and the writer?" Booker asked.

"You'll need to ask Cyrus."

"I'm a keen fan of the famous consulting detective. Perhaps we can meet to discuss our mutual interest in Sherlock Holmes."

"His office happens to be in the grey stone building across the road from my shop. You can mention that I referred you. Let me get the can of paint and smock for you to take. You're in luck —paint is half-price this week."

"Can we reach Terrence's house from here on foot?" Booker asked.

"Just a couple blocks across the bridge over the river, and it's the first street on your right. The house with the door painted yellow. My paint, of course!"

*

Minutes later, her plan hatched, Pharo stood outside the office of Cyrus Delaney, pressing a chiming bell.

The door opened, and a man in a housecoat and red toque appeared, wiping his eyes as if awoken from a deep slumber, studying her curiously.

"You've interrupted my afternoon nap on my couch," he said, with a glint of a scowl. "What is your purpose here?"

"My sincere apologies. I happened to be shopping in Jim's hardware store, and I inquired about locating a book shop carrying the latest Sherlock Holmes story. He referred to you as the local expert."

At the mention of the fictional English detective, Cyrus beamed. He pointed to a chair in his office. "Please do enter and tell me your name."

"Pharo Simmons—I'm a literary agent from Toronto. My agency represents Sir Arthur Conan Doyle in Canada."

"Mulberrys on Main Street holds a first copy of every Sherlock Holmes story for me."

"On my travels, I make it a habit of checking the stock of my clients' books in the local book shop."

"This fellow Doyle was a guest recently at my fishing camp. I begged Terrence to introduce me—he ran the camp. But Terrence resolved that his distinguished guest couldn't be disturbed by a fan, not even for me."

"I've met Sir Arthur, and I'm also aware that Sir Arthur and Lady Doyle stayed at your camp on Smoke Lake."

"Of course, you are! You're the writer's agent. But tell me—what business do you have in Huntsville?"

Pharo spoke earnestly. "An unfortunate mistake by Sir Arthur required me to take the trip. You must hold this in the strictest confidence, but he left the draft of the latest Sherlock Holmes story at the fishing camp. When I went to make inquiries of his guide, I learned of Terrence's tragic accident."

"I'm haunted by the image of Terrence falling off his roof to his death. He was sitting in that very chair a couple of days ago. He'd come straight from the fishing camp and was downtrodden, his mood sullen. He told me that one of his guests, an executive in a railway company, was missing and presumed drowned. He blamed himself for not keeping proper watch. I tried to console him, but to little avail."

"Console him?"

"Yes, he was dabbing the tears on his cheek with a hankie."

"Did Terrence tell you anything more about this railway executive's disappearance?"

"Only that the police attended the camp and conducted a search of the lake. We both agreed to shut down the fishing camp for a few days and let the bad news pass. I'm not sure when it can be reopened now."

"Anything further discussed?" Pharo asked.

"As he prepared to leave, he made an unusual request for a loan of five hundred dollars. I asked him for a reason, but he refused to disclose it."

"Had he ever sought a loan before?"

"Terrence never asked me for an extra dollar. We had a business agreement about dividing the profits evenly from the fishing camp. I pressed him for a reason, but he wouldn't tell me what the five hundred dollars was for. I explained that such a sum was out of the question, and Terrence left without extending a farewell. One day later, he was found dead."

"And no mention of discovering a manuscript?"

"No, but let me assure you, Terrence always made a clean sweep of the camp before he left—even the fire pit. If the writer of the detective stories left it behind, it would be among Terrence's possessions at his house."

"I'll leave you my name and telephone number. Please contact me if you make the discovery." Pharo scribbled a random set of numbers on a piece of paper taken from her satchel bag and handed it to Cyrus. "I must be on my way," she said abruptly.

A moment later, Pharo related the conversation in the office to Booker as he leaned on an oak tree in the yard.

"We can eliminate Terrence as a suspect in the murder," she said firmly.

"Why is that?"

"Would a killer blame himself for not keeping proper

watch? I hardly think so. He'd distance himself from any responsibility for Mason's sudden disappearance."

"What of Cyrus?"

"I examined the stack of brogue Oxford shoes lined up against the wall. Not a speck of dirt on a single shoe. He's a money merchant who knows as much about canoes as I know about battleships."

"Then we're left with Rudolph Mulino."

"Unless someone was hiding in wait. We have those violent threats to Mason and his railway to consider."

"I don't understand why Terrence needed to acquire five hundred dollars."

"We stumbled on an important clue there. Terrence planned to make a quick getaway. He knew that someone was tailing him, and it was perilous to stay in this location—his life was in danger. A hefty sum of five hundred dollars would provide the means to move and establish a fresh start in another city."

"Who was on his trail—Rudolph Mulino?"

"The likely culprit, I surmise. Let's assume that Rudolph is Mason's killer. Terrence would be on the lookout for the missing canoe and observed Rudolph swim to shore. When Mason was discovered missing, it would be natural for Terrence to become suspicious and confront Rudolph. But Rudolph bribed him or threatened him and gained Terrence's silence. Rudolph needed to finish off his eyewitness to be certain that he didn't implicate him."

"We'll need to prove that Terrence was murdered and didn't just stumble off the roof."

"Correct, my esteemed colleague. But be certain that the trail to Mason Caulfield's killer is tightening. We're the hounds being led by scent to the shot peasant. Let's see where our investigation of Terrence's home leads us."

The bright yellow door of Terrence's house was easily spotted. Booker walked up the driveway of the adjacent house carrying the paint can. The smock would have suited someone twice his size. He knocked on the door and waited for it to open.

When a stooped, elderly woman answered, steam rising from the cup in her hand, Booker said, "We have a paint job next door, but no one is bothering to answer."

"Your timing is exquisite," she said eagerly. "I've just made a pot of tea. Would you care to join me in the kitchen?"

"No, thank you, ma'am."

"You're welcome to change your mind. My name is Mrs. Holcombe. I'm a retired schoolteacher. I miss my teaching days—I'm guessing that I taught half the people living in this town the alphabet. When I venture into town, I make a habit of counting the 'Good morning, Mrs. Holcombe.' I counted twenty-four one sprightly morning. Who is it you said you're looking for again?"

"The man next door—with the yellow door."

"Oh yes, silly to paint a door yellow. I told Terrence that, although he shot me a look to mind my own affairs. In my kindergarten class, the children used their yellow crayons to paint the sun. Not much good for anything else."

"You said Terrence lived there. Do you know him?"

"Is he the fellow you're looking to meet?"

"Yes, ma'am."

"I'm afraid you'll have to turn back," she said. "Terry has left us, and I pray his soul has gone to heaven. The poor man fell off his roof a few days ago. I was the one who found him lying on the ground. My window in the kitchen was open, and I heard a scream. It only lasted for a couple of seconds, but the sound shook me to my bones."

"Why was your kitchen window open?"

"You're a smart young fellow. I'd heard some shouting earlier."

"Shouting?" Booker asked. "And you opened the window to learn what it was about?"

"I heard voices, two men shouting. One of them was Terrence's. Can't tell you what they were saying. I'm not usually the nosy type, you know. But I never heard shouting like that before."

"Are you certain that Terrence was one of the men shouting?"

"I may be a crabby old woman, but I'm not daft as a bat. I heard two voices using words that aren't found in the dictionary—if you catch my drift. One of them was my neighbor and the second fellow was cussing like a pirate guarding his treasure."

"How long between the cussing and Terrence's scream?"

"Less than a minute, I guess."

"Why did you go outside?"

"I heard a loud, thumping sound right after the scream! So, I went to check on Terrence."

"Right away?"

"I was wearing a housecoat—I had to dress first."

"Did you tell the police about Terrence screaming and the thumping sound?"

"They never bothered to ask. I gave the police officer my name and told him I lived next door. The policeman seemed a lot less interested than you are." She sipped her tea and asked, "Any more questions?"

"Just one more. You've been very helpful."

"I'm community minded. I've voted in every election, and I volunteer at the old-age home by the river. I'm eighty-three and I'm helping folks ten years younger than me."

"What's your secret?" Booker asked.

"You've used up your last question," she replied tartly. "There's my secret—I like to joke a bit. I told Giselle at our bridge game that if she didn't stop frowning, I'd throw her out of our ladies' group."

"You seem like a most pleasant and cheerful lady, Mrs. Holcombe. Not crabby in the least."

"I'm only cross when the neighbor down the street walks his barking dog past my house whistling his army tunes. Sounds like my piano out of tune. What's your question, young man?" she asked, her rosy cheeks pink with interest.

"Did you know anything about the fellow who lived next door?"

"Terrence was a nice chap. He helped clear the snow from my front walk when it piled up. I'd offer him a cup of tea, but like you, he wasn't interested in tea. He wasn't around much in the spring and summer. He ran a fishing camp on Smoke Lake."

"Well, thank you for clearing that up for me," Booker said, smiling. "I'll be returning now to Bracebridge."

He went across the lawn to Terrence's front stoop and reported the neighbor's conversation to Pharo. "So, we still don't have real evidence that Terrence was pushed off the ladder."

"Let me ask you, Booker. If you were walking on the sidewalk and you watched someone tumble on the ice and hit their head, what would you do?"

"I'd try to help them, of course."

"And if they were unconscious and not breathing, would you leave the person lying there?"

"No, I'd bang on a neighbor's door and wait for the ambulance to arrive."

"When the neighbor found Terrence lying by the ladder, did she mention seeing anyone standing there?"

"No, actually, she didn't."

"That's our double killer, Booker."

Chapter Twenty-One

Mitchell Harris opened the door of the National Pencil Factory and stepped into a drab, murky lobby, like entering a grey cloud. The tall building across the street blocked any sunshine, and there was no electrical lighting to illuminate the lobby or hallway of the factory.

Mitchell had invited Willow Hooper to meet him at a soda fountain in a drug store across from the pencil factory. He wanted the *New York Times* reporter to have a first-hand look at the scene of the hideous crime.

"So, this is where the sweeper snatched Mary Phagan."

Mitchell agreed, and pointed a few feet ahead. "There's the hatchway leading to the basement."

Willow peered down and saw the first rung of a ladder. "It's pitch dark in there. Is that where Conley carried the poor girl?"

"He'd already strangled her with the cord. It would be impossible to get her through the small hole of the hatch if the girl was struggling. Mary Phagan came down the darkened stairwell after collecting her pay and passed near Conley in the gloom, a few feet from the hatchway. She would have been looking to exit by the front door, and wouldn't see the sweeper with a cord in his hand ready to pounce."

"It's like a monster tale, Mitchell."

"I'll leave you here, Willow. I have business to attend to upstairs."

On the fourth floor, Rabbi Marx waved Mitchell to follow him, and greeted the desk clerk. "We're looking for Alonzo Mann," he announced. "This is one of Leo Frank's lawyers," he said, indicating Mitchell with one finger. "It's quite important that we speak to Alonzo."

"Oh, how is poor Mr. Frank?" the clerk asked. "He was always the gentleman with me at the factory. Terrible lies they told about him at trial—making him out to be a skirt chaser! He never bothered any of the girls here, I can tell you. If he had, I'd be the first to know about it."

"Excuse me, what's your name?"

"Jezebel, Jezebel Walker. I gave my evidence at Mr. Frank's trial. My cousin Cassie was at the courthouse for the verdict. People were hollering and cheering like we won the Civil War. They were all mad, crazy, lifting that prosecutor in the air when he came outside—they passed him in the crowd all the way to the other side of the street. His feet never touched the ground."

The rabbi appeared crestfallen and struggled to speak. "Please, bring us Alonzo."

Several minutes passed before she returned. "I'm afraid you've wasted a trip this morning. Alonzo Mann reported sick today."

"Do you have a record of where he lives?" Mitchell asked.

"You'll have to promise not to tell. I can get in heaps of trouble for this." She turned to rummage through a wooden filing cabinet. "Here it is: 144 Miller Street."

"Can we see Mr. Frank's office before we leave?" Mitchell asked.

"Come with me." She led them to the end of the hall.

Mitchell peered inside. The office was unused. "What's this?" he asked, pointing at a window at the center of the office that opened with a latch.

"Oh, that's the pay window."

"When Mary Phagan came to collect her $1.20, was it to this window here?"

"Yes, certainly."

"So, when Mr. Frank handed Mary the envelope with her pay, he put it through the slot. He was never in her company."

*

As they departed the factory, Mitchell stopped on the sidewalk, deep in thought.

"What is it, Mitchell?" the rabbi asked, concerned.

"How old is Alonzo Mann, Rabbi?"

"Fourteen."

"Mary Phagan was three weeks shy of her fourteenth birthday when she was murdered. According to Leo's statement, Mary entered his office just after the office boy left. Alonzo must have passed Mary as he left—I'm certain of that. There was a Memorial Day parade on that Saturday afternoon. Alonzo could have waited for Mary to get her pay, to invite her to join him on the trolley to the parade. It's only a theory, but..."

"A theory that's entirely possible, Mitchell."

"And where would he wait for Mary Phagan?"

"At the front door to be certain not to miss her."

"The location where we're standing now."

"Mary fought back against the sweeper. That must have made enough noise to draw Alonzo to check inside the doors. He must know that John Conley killed Mary Phagan."

*

The screen door to the Mann house was rusted, and scrapes of paint chipped from the front door. Mitchell knocked softly at first, then resolutely, when no one answered.

Finally, the door creaked open, and a woman in a bonnet glared at the two visitors.

"What's your business here?" she demanded.

"This is Rabbi Marx, and I'm Mitchell Harris. I'm a lawyer representing Leo Frank. We'd like to speak to Alonzo. I assume you're his mother."

"You got that right," she shot back. "And I'm not letting you pass. You're trespassing on my property. Now get!"

"Please, Mrs. Mann," Rabbi Marx implored her. "We believe Alonzo has important information to help Mr. Frank's case. He may die if we don't have a chance to speak to your son. Please."

"I thought you fellows said you're his lawyers. Not very sharp if you are. The newspaper's reported that our governor stopped the killing of Frank. He's not going to the electric chair."

"What newspaper is that?"

"The *Atlanta Constitution*. Comes every morning. Go read it for yourselves. No need to speak to my boy now," she said, and she shut the door.

Elated, Rabbi Marx said, "We'd better return to Leo and share the good news! You don't seem pleased, Mitchell. What is the problem?"

"She seemed nervous to me, Rabbi—like a witness fearful that a lawyer might stumble on some uncomfortable truth. Did you see her hands trembling?"

"I didn't notice."

"Why is she protecting her son? If he has anything to add to his court testimony, let him stand before us and declare it. I'm more certain than ever: that the office boy is hiding the truth, and the truth supports Leo's innocence."

"But what choice do we have? It's the mother's right to refuse us. Quick, we must hurry to Leo. I'll purchase a newspaper to bring to him."

*

"Who was that, Mother?" Alonzo asked.

"Just some lawyers asking to speak to you."

"Maybe I should talk to them. I think a lot about what I saw. I can't sleep well. I keep seeing the janitor carrying that girl in his arms, Mother. I thought it was Mary—she had long hair like Mary—I saw it streaming down his back. I came back from the parade to go up the stairs to the office to finish my filing work, and there he was. He told me if I ever mentioned this he'd kill me, and I turned around and ran and took the streetcar home."

His mother shook her head firmly. "And what if that crazy man is telling the truth, and he comes after you? He killed once before, and he can do it again. I told you before, Alonzo, there's nothing you can do now. Keep to yourself what you saw. The jury found the superintendent guilty, but he isn't going to hang. He'll be all right in prison. I bet *his* kind get special treatment."

Chapter Twenty-Two

"The train leaves the Terminal Station to Macon in half an hour, Leo. I can only grant you a few minutes with the reporter."

"I'm grateful, Sheriff Donnelly. You're a good man. You didn't handcuff me once during the trial on the walk from the Tower to court." Leo Frank entered a room guarded by two police officers and stood a couple feet from Willow Hooper, notebook and pencil in her hand. "That's one of our pencils," he said.

"How are you certain?"

"The capital letters *NP* appear under the eraser. So, you're the intrepid reporter from the *New York Times*. Rabbi Marx has told me stories of your enterprising journalism. Mitchell praises you as well."

"I'm humbled by the compliments, but 'haggard and weary reporter' is a more apt description. I haven't slept for two days. I just returned in a cab from Governor Slayton's house. There was a crowd of at least one thousand people there hooting and hollering and hurling bricks, bottles and missiles at the second-floor window."

"I am grateful beyond words to the governor for the way he has disposed of the case. I just felt confident that I would not hang. Tell me, Miss Hooper, what are your impressions standing across from me?"

Willow stared at Leo's face. "You look to me like an astronomy professor."

"Astronomy!" Leo chuckled and continued. "I crave to see a night sky again. Shall I tell you what a reporter from the *Atlanta Georgian*, signing off as the 'Old Police Reporter,' described me as?"

"Please do."

"He wrote that if you see any good pictures of Leo Frank, you will understand what I mean when I say that he looks like a pervert. A pervert!"

"That is shameful reporting, Leo, not worthy of seeing print."

"No one can know what I have gone through. Of course, I am unsettled, as you see, from the nerve-racking experience through which I have been drawn, especially during the last trying hours of this ordeal."

A loud knock at the door followed. "One more minute," a voice bellowed.

"Tell me, Willow, have you ever been to Coney Island?"

"I'm from Flatbush—I take the motor car with my friends every weekend. One rule of caution. Always order your hot dog after the ride on the diving and climbing roller coaster."

The moment of frivolity passed with gay laughter, like a warm greeting of two friends on a park bench.

"I've told Lucille that when my freedom is gained, we shall travel to Brooklyn and walk, holding hands along the boardwalk, eating candy floss, and inhaling the salty air from the sea. I comfort myself with that dream every night."

Chapter Twenty-Three

Dear Pharo,

I'm eternally grateful that you are keenly pursuing the investigation of Mason Caulfield's death. I'm curious to learn if you made any unusual discoveries at Smoke Lake. It was the most heavenly place—although the memory is sullied by Mason's loss. I haven't fared well with my writing since my return to England. The European conflict looms larger every day. Our son, Kingsley, enlisted in the army with some of his chums from school. Lady Doyle tried valiantly to dissuade him, but fidelity to King and country prevailed. I admire the boy's spirit and patriotism, even if his good sense is lacking. It is a holiday month in Europe, the politicians nestled in country homes and villas while we move ever closer to conflict.

I traveled last week to a munitions factory being built near Gretna in Scotland. I had been invited as a distinguished guest and dressed in a velvet navy blue waistcoat and jacket, white trousers and my pocket watch and gold chain. Upon my arrival, it became clear that my visit was planned by a group sympathetic to the suffrage cause. The hangar for the factory, when completed, will be several miles long and will be perhaps the most remarkable place in the world. It was emphasized to me that the staff for this grand military venture will be twelve thousand munition workers, the vast majority, women. My opinion of suffragettes has softened like melting butter. I'm an ally and true advocate of your cause. Even all the exertions of the militants shall not in the future prevent me from being an advocate for their vote, for those who help to save the state should be allowed to help to guide it.

I do have some news to report that may benefit your investigation. My literary agent has a connection in Hollywood who checked out Rudolph Mulino for me. I dreaded the rascal's company on the fishing trip, and I assiduously avoided him whenever possible. But Lady Doyle chided me for being overly harsh, and it appears that she was the more astute. Mulino's reputation tells of munificence to the crew on set and acts of kindness to his co-workers. When a cameraman slipped during shooting and fell down a set of stairs, Rudolph sent a contribution of a hundred dollars— three months' wages!—to his family to help tide them over.

It is striking that the generous image portrayed is at odds with our experiences with Rudolph. There is something amiss, and we must strive to unravel the mystery.

One matter conveyed by the agent was of particular interest to me: Rudolph hasn't appeared in a film for a couple of years, since he returned from shooting a film in Rome. His upcoming film is being promoted as his comeback by the studio. 'The Heartthrob is Back,' runs the new ad campaign. I will investigate the whereabouts of our Rudolph during his two-year hiatus from acting.

Rest assured that I will not rest until Mason's killer is caught. Your assistance is duly noted and appreciated.
Sir Arthur

*

Pharo reread the cable and digested its contents. The news of Rudolph's charitable behavior did indeed clash with her impression of the man as ill-mannered and stuffy. She was familiar with divided personalities—her best friend, Marjorie, swung widely between moods of ebullient affection and bitter jealousy. After Pharo's car accident, Marjorie had remained at her bedside, pampering her with food and drink. The queen of misfortune, Pharo had named her close friend. Three husbands and each of them found dead during their marriage. The last fell down a spiral staircase, hitting his head at the bottom. Marjorie complained that no one would betroth her now, an assessment that Pharo shared. Marjorie became bitterly jealous of Pharo after attending her wedding and scoffed at her evincing affection for Burford. "He'll disappoint you one day," Marjorie admonished her.

But this shift in Rudolph Mulino's character was deeper and more mysterious. It strained credulity that the man she had encountered would part with a tidy sum of money in an act of beneficence. That news had a fishy smell. A robust investigation of Rudolph Mulino was required, and she and Booker would fulfill their part.

Pharo checked the chiming clock behind the counter at her hotel in Toronto. Burford was to call her at ten, but half an hour had passed since the sound of ten chimes rang through the lobby. She hadn't spoken to him in days—

how long would he be mired with Clarence Darrow for his upcoming trial in Los Angeles? Ah, there—she saw a clerk motioning her with a fluttering wave.

"Your call is ready, Mrs. Simmons. I will put it through to the telephone booth."

Pharo hurried to the bank of the booths and slid open the polished wood door of the first.

"Burf, you rascal. How is the trial preparation faring?" she said, holding the receiver.

"This is the greeting I get," he said, with a familiar loud laugh. "Clarence is as prepared a witness I've ever called to testify. I received a note that my judge for my next trial is bedridden with a bad case of the flu. He caught it from one of the courtroom clerks. We've been told that court is adjourned until next month. I'm taking an afternoon train to Buffalo, and Mitchell is arriving from Atlanta later this evening—we'll meet at the office. Mitchell is relieved that Leo Frank's life has been spared by the governor. He'll brief me tomorrow. When are you expecting to return, Pharo?"

"Our original plan was to leave tomorrow, but that's uncertain now. Booker sprained his ankle falling in the stairwell, so he's resting with ice packed in a towel to help the swelling. I have one more trip to make here, to see Mason Caulfield's wife. Sleuthing is a tiring business. But we're moving closer to solving the crime. Or should I say *double* crime? Two victims of murder."

"It sounds utterly dangerous to me. Two murders! I'm only concerned about you and Booker. Leave the murder investigation to the police."

Pharo snickered. "The police! They don't accept that any crime was committed. I'll have to hand them the case against Rudolph Mulino on a silver platter."

"He's your culprit? The film star?"

"Without a beaver's shadow of doubt. And I intend to prove it."

"I won't ask why you're certain it's Mulino. But if you're right, he will have every reason to harm you and Booker. You must return to Buffalo as soon as possible."

"Burf, Sir Arthur entrusted me to carry on the investigation of Mason Caulfield's murder, and I intend to see it through until a proper arrest is made."

"Please, at least take precautions. Any further sign of Hanus's henchman?"

"No sign of him. He's given up, I expect."

"Hanus doesn't surrender easily. We both know the depths of the man's resolve."

"The hotel clerk just knocked, Burf. That's my signal to end our call. I promised him that I'd be a minute on the call. There's a line of hotel guests waiting to use the telephone. I'll have to say farewell. Do you miss me?"

"Of course. When you return, we'll have a quiet dinner together and go to a film. We'll light a fire and snuggle up under a blanket."

"That is an enticing thought. We must plan a trip to New York to benefit from your postponed case—John Drew and Ethel Barrymore are appearing in a new play, *A Scrap of Paper*."

"Certainly, but a motion picture will be better suited for the moment, after all the scraps of paper that I've labored over in preparation for my trials."

"Any film not starring Rudolph Mulino, that is!"

Pharo left the hotel and stepped to the curb in search of a passing cab, seeing no doorman to do it for her. It was a brisk summer day, and she wore only a thin wool sweater knitted by her sister, Odette. But since she might have a considerable wait for Lilian Caulfield to return home, she had brought a bag with a notebook and pencil, and a banana and a bottle of chocolate milk for lunch.

Pharo didn't look forward to the visit with Lilian. She planned to be open with Lilian about her true identity and might be asked to leave, but she was prepared to persevere. A conversation with Lilian relating to the new findings at Smoke Lake was now vital to the investigation.

Entering the hailed cab, Pharo observed a man staring at her across the street. He was carrying an open newspaper, and as soon as he became aware of being noticed, he hid his face behind the pages.

Pharo recalled the description at her former hotel of the man carrying a gun: "crimson rounded jowls, trimmed beard and a ghoulish smile." His cheeks did appear round and reddish.

She resolved to confront her pursuer on her own terms.

"What's your name?" she asked the driver.

"Jimmy."

"All right then, Jimmy. Are you interested in making five dollars today?"

He turned and spoke earnestly. "Of course, Miss. It takes me a week to make that much."

"Do you know a hill overlooking a ravine that you can drive to?"

Jimmy paused to mull his answer. "Davenport Hill. Just past Casa Loma, the castle this rich architect just finished building. Took him three years. That road leads to a couple of factories. Hardly anyone travels on it."

"Perfect. I want you to wait until that man with the newspaper gets into a yellow cab. Then I want you to get ahead of his cab. The driver will be instructed to follow you, and I want to get at least thirty seconds ahead. Can you do that for me?"

"No one is catching me."

"Good, Jimmy. Now here's the five dollars," she said, handing him the bill. "After you drop me off, you're to return ten minutes later to pick me up. After that, I'll give you an address to take me to the east side of Toronto near the Scarborough Bluffs. Do you understand me?"

"I do, but that will be a long cab ride. And why is this guy chasing you around?"

"I believe he wants to kill me, but I don't have time to explain. And I don't want you to ask any questions of me. Look," Pharo said, turning back, "there he goes, he's stepping into a cab. Let's put your driving to the test."

Jimmy swerved his taxi from the curb and raced ahead. Pharo grasped the side of her seat, twisting to look back for the second taxi. It was almost out of sight.

"Faster, Jimmy," she urged him.

Minutes later, her driver pointed to a castle rising on a hill.

"There's Casa Loma," he said. "We're almost there, Miss."

A dirt road loomed ahead, and then a single-lane bridge. Jimmy stopped his car, and Pharo rushed out. "Ten minutes!" she shouted.

At the edge of the ravine ran a thin railing, about three feet from the ground on each side. Pharo placed her bag in front and draped her sweater over the railing. Trap set, she hurried to hide behind the girth of an oak tree.

A cab appeared and lurched to a stop. The suspicious figure who had been watching her exited and approached the railing. He picked up the leather bag and peered inside.

He lifted the sweater. On cue, he leaned his frame over the railing to survey the vast ravine below. Pharo gingerly began to stride across the street.

As she approached within a few feet, the stranger whirled around and faced her, smirking— he held a gun in his hand.

"You take me for a fool, Pharo Simmons. You thought I'd see your bag and sweater by the railing and assume that you had jumped. But of course, you were lying in wait. Why would a woman bother to remove a sweater before killing herself? I'm smarter than you think, and now you'll die for your mistake."

Pharo heard the shrill sound of a gun being fired and saw smoke rising above the shooter's gun. He reached back to grab her sweater from the railing. Pharo needed to react quickly. Her blood-curdling scream pierced the air— the bearded stranger froze, and the sweater fell from his hand.

Pharo reached behind her back and pulled a revolver, and pointed it at the stranger. "But not before you. You saw me barehanded with no bag and let your guard down. But I had my gun hidden in my waistband. It was I who laid the trap. Now drop your gun, or I'll shoot you."

The stranger let the gun slip from his hand to the ground.

"Now, let me assign you a name—Mr. Killer, do you read?"

"What nonsense is this?"

"Tsk, tsk...Never raise your voice to a suffragette pointing a gun at your chest. I asked about your reading habits because *Tarzan of the Apes* is on my nightstand, an admirable book by Edgar Rice Burroughs. In one chapter, Sabor, the lioness and wise hunter, lets out a fierce scream before she leaps—not to warn the little ape but to paralyze the creature with terror for an instant and hold it beyond hope of escape. You see the quaint similarity to the manner that I now hold you captive. My shriek allowed me time to grab my pistol, and you dropped yours. You have two options: surrender or hurl your body over the bridge."

"Do as you wish. Shoot me and be done with it."

"I am not the cold-hearted assassin of your ilk. If you advance, I will shoot you in each of your ankles to disable you. You won't be much use to Mortimer Hanus if you can't walk."

"You can shoot me," he said. "But Hanus won't relent. He's set his mind to get rid of you."

"He underestimates me as much as you do."

"You won't shoot me—you're a coward."

The man began to rush forward, and Pharo coolly fired two shots at his legs.

The first shot caused him to tumble backwards and the second to fall over the railing, down to the depths of the ravine.

His top hat lay on the ground, and Pharo picked it up. She put her sweater in her bag and carried the hat in her free hand, and walked to where Jimmy was to arrive.

Several minutes later, the cab appeared.

"Is everything in order, Miss? Your hands are shaking."

"I've had a bit of fright, that's all," Pharo said, getting in. "And remember our agreement— no questions."

"I'm curious, though. Just grant me this one question. Whose top hat are you holding?"

Pharo hesitated before answering. "It belonged to a professional killer who won't menace anyone again. I was his target today, and I'm the victor. He's the Roman gladiator with the sword plunged through his chest."

"All right then, Miss," Jimmy said, his voice quavering. "I'll be quiet now and follow your instructions. You don't have to worry—my lips are zipped shut."

"No one knows what happened at the bridge except you and me. I want it to remain that way, and I trust you. Let me ask you first—are you interested in making $20 for a day's work?"

Jimmy looked at her puzzled. "What's involved?" he asked.

"I've had enough excitement for one day. My plans have changed. You're going to drive to Buffalo and stop at an address that I'll give you after we get back to the hotel— it's the Parole Office. I will also write down a man's name, Mortimer Hanus. You'll drop the hat off at the front desk and let them know that you drove a fare there who forgot his hat in your cab—and you'll give them Hanus's name."

"That's all."

"Yes. I'll give you $10 now and the other half when you've completed the task."

"What for, Miss? That's a lot of trouble to go to, for a hat that doesn't even belong to the person."

"Precisely the point. Hanus will realize that I sent the hat, that I'm still alive and have vanquished his professional killer. I want to rattle him. He's an evil man, Jimmy."

"He must be, if he sent someone to kill you."

"If I allow Hanus to frighten me, I give him the upper hand. He needs to be wary of me. Many years ago, Hanus kidnapped my husband in Buffalo and took him to Canada. I led the police to his capture, so he blames me for sending him to prison for over a decade."

"When do you want me to take the trip?"

"After I'm safely back home."

"From your story, Miss, it doesn't seem that he'll stop pursuing you."

"Not to worry. I have an unpleasant surprise planned for Mortimer Hanus."

*

Back at the hotel, Pharo checked in on Booker. The swelling had subsided, and he'd be able to walk by the following day.

"We have one more stop—Lilian Caulfield's—in the morning," she said. "Here's your revolver, Booker. I borrowed it and fired two shots."

"Two shots! What happened, Pharo?"

"Fired in self-defense. You only need to know that I'll be safe walking the streets now."

Booker stared at her, perplexed. "Your over-blouse is ripped at your elbow."

"The bullet must have grazed me," Pharo said, checking her clothing.

"You were shot at? Mr. Simmons will be mighty cross with me when he's informed."

"Oh, shush, Booker—you're not assigned as my guardian angel, and I have no intention of spilling our secret to my husband. At least not until our investigation is complete. You will attend with me at Lilian Caulfield's house tomorrow. I asked the hotel to book our tickets on the four o'clock train to Buffalo. Burford and Mitchell are returning, and you'll have time to meet with them at your law office."

"And return to my legal work?"

"We're not quite done with our investigation yet, Booker.

And now, I'll get you fresh ice packs for your ankle."

"I'm glad you're on my side, Pharo."

"As your ally, I am seeking a couple of hours of quiet. I really must write a chapter of my novel. Today's excitement gives me abundant material to draw upon."

Chapter Twenty-Four

Booker gazed at Pharo in sheer wonderment, like the great pyramids of Egypt he had viewed in a travel book. He had never encountered anyone as brave or quixotic. Pharo had slain a hired gunman and not boasted a word about it; instead, she challenged Booker to three frolicking games of checkers, which she handily won.

Pharo now sat in the corner of the living room of their hotel suite, curling a red lock around two fingers as her fountain pen scurried across the paper, jotting her "bricks," as she described the sentences she wrote. His leg ached, the hour was late, and he was weary—yet he was drawn to the table where Pharo sat resolutely crafting her novel brick by brick. The story was shrouded in mystery; Pharo refused to reveal the plot until it was finished, blaming it on superstition. Her discipline was admirable. Each evening the hours between nine o'clock and midnight were set aside for her writing.

Booker imagined employing the same rigid approach to preparing for court. The key to winning at trial, Mitchell had taught him, was to prepare harder than your adversary to expose the cracks and frailties in his case. He remembered his first lesson. Mitchell had asked him to imagine defending a client charged with stealing a golden goose. The client was arrested, and the object was discovered by the policeman in his wagon. Mitchell stood at a blackboard as Booker recited the steps he'd take defending the case. At the end, Mitchell stood shaking his head in disapproval. The law student had missed a crucial step: to evaluate whether the goose was actually golden or just a gilded metal imitation of a golden goose. That single slip-up, he was admonished, could cost a man's freedom.

But it wasn't his gleaming future as a lawyer that dominated Booker's thoughts this evening; rather, Pharo's alarming admission that she'd fired his gun twice. He checked the cartridge and confirmed that two bullets were missing. Pharo had also been fired *at*—and a tragedy barely averted. He must report this troubling episode to Mr. Simmons. But would Pharo forgive him for betraying her? Would Mr. Simmons blame him for permitting Pharo to leave the hotel unattended? He didn't have the excuse that he was hobbled; he'd only suffered a sprained ankle.

Finally, Booker blurted out, "Are you planning to tell your husband about your narrow escape from death?"

Pharo turned her chair toward him and ignored the question. "Booker, I must send Sir Arthur a cable after we see Lilian Caulfield to update him on our investigation of Mason's murder."

"You're avoiding my question."

"Yes, with consummate skill." Pharo placed her fountain pen on the table. "I want to be open with Lilian about my suspicions of her nephew," she said.

"We still can't directly link Rudolph Mulino to his murder."

"True, but let's see what information we obtain at Lilian's house; I expect our meeting to be productive."

"If she agrees to talk."

"Yes, you're correct—she has every reason to be cross with us for deceiving her. We must impress upon her that our motive was laudable. We're pursuing her husband's killer, and making progress. The police certainly won't locate him."

"She may wonder why the police don't share your theory of a crime, Pharo."

"And I will be candid with her that as far as I'm concerned, the police are rank amateurs. They wouldn't even qualify as worthy members of the Sherlock Holmes Club. The most basic police procedures weren't followed in their investigation. A man goes out in a canoe on a lake without the ability to swim. Their simple conclusion, when he doesn't return, is that he drowned. This is flawed reasoning, Booker. There are other possibilities to consider, some sinister."

"But at some point, you'll need to persuade the police of the merits of your murder theory if you are to ensnare Rudolph or the real killer."

"An astute observation—I believe the police will have no choice but to act after Sir Arthur and I complete our work."

"Sir Arthur?"

"In my wire, I shall request his capable assistance. This is exciting, Booker. We are solving a crime with the creator of Sherlock Holmes! What an enchanting presentation I will deliver at the club's next meeting: 'Pharo, Booker and

Sherlock: Pursuing an Elusive Killer.'"

"But what of Mortimer Hanus? He won't rest after he learns the fate of his henchman."

"Hanus is like the speck of dirt that sticks in your eye. It's a bother, but you continue your day without interference."

"Specks of dirt don't shoot guns."

"I suppose." Pharo winked at her young colleague. "You mustn't say a word about this to my husband. He'll be furious with me."

"But I'm entrusted to report back to him," Booker said.

"I give you my solemn word that I'll tell him—I'll judge the appropriate time. Now let's get some rest. We have an important day ahead of us."

*

A cab dropped off Pharo and Booker outside the familiar home of Lilian Caulfield. In the front yard, a young man of perhaps twenty, in loosely fitting dungarees and a backwards cap, was swinging a baseball bat.

"Hello, Brian," Pharo said, recognizing him from the day of the memorial service.

"You remember my name, Miss?"

"Of course. I'm a friend of your mother's. This is Booker," she said pointing. "He's also a friend."

"I don't remember you telling me that you knew my mother. She doesn't have many friends. Even my stepsisters don't like her."

"I'm sorry about that. Can we be friends?"

"Sure! My neighbor taught me to hit bottle caps with my bat. Hey, Booker, want to see?"

"Certainly," Booker said, stepping back several feet. "Why didn't you come down to the service?"

The young man glowered. "My stepsisters call me 'dunce' and 'stupid.' I get upset and can't breathe—I hate my stepsisters. Here, I have five bottle caps. You go to the end of the yard and catch them if you can."

Brian waited for Booker to reach the fence and began to swing. The caps sailed over Booker's head each time.

"That's quite a swing you have there, Brian," Pharo said.

"My stepfather used to chase the caps for me. Now I have to pick them up myself. Will you and Booker come to my room after meeting with Mother? I have a book about insects and butterflies. I recognize the wings and colors of the butterflies. My stepfather liked to test me—I can show you the book."

"Of course, Brian, we can be your friends and look at your book. We'll see you after we finish with your mother. Is she at home?"

"She's home all the time, since my stepfather drowned. Mr. Cartwright from the railway came yesterday for a visit. He's the new president. My mom likes people visiting—it cheers her up. I can hear her crying at night and it makes me sad. I miss my stepfather too."

"I'm sure your stepfather was wonderful to you, Brian," Pharo said. "One more question, I promise. Do you know Rudolph Mulino?"

"I can't talk about him." Brian checked the surroundings, as if Mulino might be lurking under a bush, before rushing into the house.

Lilian opened the front door as Pharo and Booker reached the verandah. "Brian told me I had a couple of friends arriving. I'm happy to see you return for a visit. I'll get you a cup of coffee. Come sit down in the living room."

"Can we find a private area to speak?"

Lilian led them down the hall to a library. "It will be quiet here," she said. In a few minutes, she returned with a tray and cups of coffee.

"There's something that we need to tell you, Lilian."

Perched on a library bench, Pharo devoted the next quarter of an hour to revealing their true identities and the reason for their visit.

Lilian nodded along without interrupting.

At last, she spoke after a moment of pensive thought. "I'll be honest with you, Pharo. I'm happy to have some company. But your view that my husband was murdered has shaken me—the policemen were so certain he drowned. And you suspect the guilty culprit is my nephew, Rudolph Mulino? I simply can't believe it. Mason and I showed him nothing but kindness and generosity. I even lent him a pair of Mason's brand-new shoes for the funeral. What possible reason would lead Rudolph to kill my husband?"

"I haven't figured that out, Lilian. But when Booker and I solve that riddle, I believe that we'll have the evidence to prove that he's the killer."

"Rudolph returned to Los Angeles—he's acting in a new movie."

"Did he leave a telephone number for you to contact him?"

"I have it in my dresser. It's the movie studio's telephone number, but they can reach him. He made me promise to tell him if Mason's body was discovered."

"Yes," Booker said. "I'm quite sure that he'd be interested to learn about that."

"Why is that?" Lilian asked.

"Because the police will find evidence of a head wound that will lead to a murder investigation."

Pharo leaned forward. "I have a question for you, Lilian. After the commemorative service, I observed that Rudolph left alone. Why didn't the two of you leave together?"

"Let me pour another cup of coffee," Lilian said, lifting the pot from the tray. "Let's return to your claim that Mason was the victim of foul play. Mason and I had a long chat on the morning that he left for the fishing trip. He admitted to being nervous about a couple of threatening letters he'd received and that his life might be in danger."

"I'm aware of those letters," Pharo said.

Lilian stared at her incredulously. "I don't know what your source could be. But are you aware that a third letter arrived yesterday morning?"

"No, please tell me about it."

"It arrived by courier addressed to Mason, and his personal secretary opened it. Or should I say, *former* secretary? The letter contained a threat to blow up a piece of track outside Union Station. The police were notified, and the letter was traced to a young architect living on Euclid Avenue in Toronto. He confessed to the entire scheme, including sending all three letters. He claimed to be unaware that Mason was dead."

"What reason did he give for the threats?"

"The architect's father owned a pig farm in Chatham. It stood in the path of Mason's railway, and the farm had to be sold. One week later, the father shot himself in the head with his rifle."

"And this was the son's revenge?"

"Yes, the poor man. He never intended violence, only

to plant fear in Mason. I insisted that he not be prosecuted. I felt sorry for him, to be honest."

"That was an honorable thing you did, Mrs. Caulfield," Booker said.

"*Lilian*, please. You mentioned that you were both at Mason's service—I didn't see you there."

"We stood in the distance. Not far from Brian."

"I see that you met my boy."

"He asked to show us his book of butterflies and insects."

"That will have to wait for another visit. I heard his door bang shut. He'll come out when he's ready."

"He's a most impressive young man," Booker said.

Lilian nodded. "Brian has a few handicaps. I can't put him in school with the other boys. They make fun of him—he's a slow learner. A tutor comes twice a week with Brian's lessons. Mason was good with the boy, more patient than me. But right now, Brian's the only family I've got. My stepdaughters want nothing to do with me. They think I persuaded Mason to leave his estate to me—as if it wasn't natural that a man would leave his property to his wife! He never even discussed his will with me. But I haven't answered your question about Rudolph. He told me that he wanted to walk home after the service. When I returned alone, I found the rear window shattered, and I carefully checked the contents of the house. I discovered some jewels were missing from my bedroom dresser."

"Where was Rudolph?"

"He didn't return home until an hour or so later."

"Did you leave the house together for the memorial service?"

"Yes, I ordered a taxi. I recall that Rudolph forgot his

wallet. I gave him the key to the front door. But he was only gone for a few seconds."

"Less than a minute?" Booker asked.

"For certain, and he was carrying his wallet."

"Did you ask him why he needed a wallet? I assume that you paid for the taxi."

"Well, I don't know, perhaps he wanted to be able to pay for the taxi back. It's too far a distance to walk. You can both see that."

"Then he was already planning to return alone."

"Yes, that must be the case."

"Where had you kept your jewels?"

"Most of my jewelry was locked in a safe. I had a diamond bracelet and a few pairs of pearl earrings in a drawer in my bedroom, and a ruby bracelet too. When I came upstairs, the drawer was wide open, and the jewelry gone. Of course, the service had been written up in the newspaper. I was advertising my house for a break-in, I guess."

"I assure you that you didn't act recklessly, Lilian."

"What do you mean?"

"How many drawers do you have in your bedroom?"

"Six, including the one containing my jewelry."

"And were any of the other five drawers opened?"

"No."

"Which means that the thief who pilfered the jewelry knew where the jewelry was stored. He wasn't going to bother closing drawers as he searched."

"But this was the top drawer. He might have searched it first."

"If so, he wouldn't have stopped his search then—he'd have opened all the drawers. No, our thief knew precisely where to search because he'd searched there before."

The widow shook her head, unwilling to accept the answer. "Rudolph?"

"Yes, Rudolph Mulino." Pharo stamped her foot indignantly. "First, he murders your husband, and then he robs his widow."

"You must believe her, Lilian," Booker said. "Pharo is an accomplished sleuth."

"I don't disagree. It's just difficult to accept that Rudolph could act so wickedly."

Pharo looked across at Booker. "If you knew where to look, you could smash the window and steal the jewelry within a minute, couldn't you?"

"I agree, and you'd be sure to return later to deflect suspicion. And he nearly succeeded."

Pharo sipped the last drop of coffee. "Tell me, Lilian. Did you find Rudolph to be a quiet sort of fellow? Very withdrawn, even introverted."

"What rubbish! Who told you that?"

"It's information I received in a wire. Apparently, a Hollywood producer claims that Mulino has changed a great deal since he returned from filming a movie in Italy a couple of years ago. He speaks very little now."

Lilian shook her head firmly. "He's a chatterbox, that's for sure. Nothing like you're describing."

"How did he get along with your son?"

"He appeared friendly to him. Brian never mentioned a problem."

"Did Rudolph mention filming in Italy?"

"No, but on occasion he'd slip an Italian word into the conversation and then catch himself. I asked him to teach me a few Italian words. It's such a lyrical and expressive language. I asked him to translate the words he spoke."

"And did he?"

"Not a word."

Pharo mulled this over. "Interesting," she said.

"He might have picked up a few words while filming in Rome," Booker said.

"Very possibly. But if true, why catch yourself?"

"Because he knew his hosts didn't speak Italian. Only polite."

"Very good, Booker. You're testing my theory. This is helpful. And you may be correct."

"You don't seem to be persuaded though."

*

Lilian asked Mulino to tell her what he'd said. Correct?"

"Yes."

"But he never translated his words from Italian to English. Not very polite, do you agree?"

"I agree," Booker said.

"Perhaps there is a sinister reason yet to be uncovered. Come, Booker. Let's get back to the hotel. Please give my regrets to your son, Lilian —he offered to show us his book on insects and butterflies, and we'll be glad to see it on our next visit. The taxi will be waiting for us outside. I plan to send a wire to Sir Arthur before we leave for the train station."

Lilian looked bewildered. "Train?"

"Yes, Lilian. Booker and I are returning to Buffalo, our home city. It's been an eventful trip to Canada."

"Let's exchange telephone numbers. I'll let you know if Rudolph contacts me."

"I know it won't be easy, but please don't let on that we suspect him of killing Mason. He must be secure in the belief that his plan has worked."

"You've left me perplexed, Pharo. I'm to believe that Rudolph Mulino viciously killed Mason, disposed of his body and covered up his crime—but you haven't given me any reason why he did it. Mason was a gentle soul. I met him a year after he lost his first wife to breast cancer, and a finer gentleman I've never met. He cared for his employees when they were sick or suffered hardship and he was welcoming to anyone he invited to our home. And Rudolph was no exception. So please, I implore you, give me a single reason for this dastardly crime."

"I'm afraid I can't. Not yet. But you have my solemn word that I will provide you with that answer." Pharo took her sweater from a coat tree beside the closet.

"Oh, I didn't see this here before," Lilian said, pointing to a scarf on the tree. "That's Rudolph's scarf. He forgot it here."

On the way out, Booker stayed silent until they entered the taxi. Then he said,

"How can you make her such a promise? We're unlikely to scope out Rudolph's motive."

"I know some nefarious deed happened at Smoke Lake, and I won't rest until I uncover it. Poor Lilian, that heartbroken woman. I'd like to have a few moments with her stepdaughters, I'll tell you. A cruel lot they must be."

During the stop at the hotel, Pharo wrote out the cable to Sir Arthur—she had composed in her mind during the ride. She had a bold request to make of the world's greatest writer of detective stories.

Chapter Twenty-Five

"The third robbery in a month of Pickles Butcher Shop? I didn't know their pork chops were that tasty. Not that our kosher Chief Detective ever tasted one."

Ordinarily, Eli Jacob would join in the lively banter in the detectives' office at the end of a shift. It helped the camaraderie, and Eli delighted in taking the brunt of the humor. He had been a popular choice to lead the group of detectives at the station. He never forgot a birthday or missed a hospital visit for a close relative of the men he led. He had inspired an older detective with a degree in English Literature to bring Shakespearean plays to read at lunch hour and offered his own colorful insight.

Tonight, he merely smiled and bowed his head diffidently. He was preoccupied with a telephone call he had directed to be put through in a quarter of an hour. Rabbi Marx would be calling from Atlanta, and Eli had encouraging news to deliver. The American Jewish Committee was prepared to donate five thousand dollars to Leo Frank's defense fund. The governor had commuted Leo's death sentence, and all of his appeals were exhausted. New evidence must be uncovered proving Leo's innocence—with this tidy sum, the finest lawyers in the country could be retained. Mitchell and Clarence Darrow had signaled their desire to be involved in rectifying the injustice of Leo Frank's life imprisonment.

Eli tapped his foot impatiently, waiting for the last detective to leave.

Ormsby, a stocky former college wrestler with a tattoo of a mermaid on his wrist, whistled gaily as he shuffled papers into a file folder.

"Working late, Detective Jacob?" he asked.

"I'm organizing the shift schedule for next week. If you're gone from the station within five minutes, I'll give you the morning shift."

"I'm leaving now." One minute later, Ormsby raced down the stairs, police jacket and cap under one arm. "Goodnight, sir," he shouted before exiting.

The detective placed the letter from the American Jewish Committee on his desk. He planned to read it reverentially for the rabbi, like a covenant of peace. It read:

"We, the undersigned, are steadfast in our belief that Leo Frank is innocent and his continued imprisonment in the state of Georgia a travesty of justice. We cannot stand idly by when a member of our community is vilified as 'a Jew Sodomite' and falsely convicted of the murder of a young girl in the name of placating a frenzied mob. The Board of our Committee has unanimously resolved to offer our financial support in the amount of $5,000 to the Defense Fund for Leo Frank. So be it ordered."

The telephone rang, and the detective picked up the receiver. "Rabbi Marx, how are you faring this evening?"

A barely audible whisper followed. "Hello, Eli."

"Is there something wrong? You don't sound well, Rabbi."

"He's dead."

The statement jarred Detective Jacob, and he stood up. "Who is dead?"

The rabbi began to sob. "Leo. They've killed our Leo."

Eli allowed a minute to pass, but the sobbing grew louder, unabated. "Please, Rabbi Marx, tell me what happened," he pleaded.

Rabbi Marx composed himself and spoke slowly. "A group of men stormed the prison at Milledgeville State Farm where Leo was being held. They abducted him and drove seven hours to Mariota and then tied a rope around his neck and lynched him from a tree. They kept his wedding ring and left it at the doorstep of the Mariota Police Station. A sergeant called me from there."

"That is terrible news, Rabbi. It's an act of murder."

"I'm afraid that the perpetrators will be celebrated as heroes. Oh, Eli. What words can I muster to comfort Leo's distraught wife? It's an unspeakable tragedy. First the trial, then the jury's verdict and now this."

The rabbi gave in to sobs again, and Eli hung up the phone. His hands trembled, and his body winded as he absorbed the news like a boxer's sharp body blow.

The mob had emerged victorious. They had their glorious pound of flesh. A man's life needlessly sacrificed as the outcome.

"*Mon Dieu*, I should have been at the prison protecting him. I could have saved him."

Even as he remonstrated with himself, Eli accepted that his self-doubt was unwarranted. No human being could have saved Leo Frank's precious life. It was like resisting the force of an oncoming tidal wave.

Eli sat silently for several minutes, reflecting on the grim news. It would be shared with the world soon. Many would be gleeful and celebrate. The detective quoted a passage from *Julius Caesar*: "The evil that men do lives after them. The good is oft interred with their bones."

He decided that he must telephone Mitchell at his home. Mitchell deserved to know. He'd made the lengthy trip to Atlanta to meet the beleaguered client, and Rabbi Marx had described their meeting as uplifting to Leo, who expressed delight at having Mitchell lead his legal team. And the governor had spared Leo's life. Mitchell had called the detective as soon as he arrived back in Buffalo, elated that Leo's life had been spared, but called it only the first step to achieving real justice.

The telephone rang again, and Eli picked up the receiver.

The Rabbi had himself under control this time. "I'm sorry, Eli. The news has been jarring. The newspapers are already telephoning me for a comment. I've restrained myself from sharing my true thoughts. It would be helpful if I might direct the reporters to Mitchell. Do you think that would be all right? He truly impressed me and I'm confident that he'll express our collective outrage."

"Of course, Rabbi. I'll let him know. Tell me, where is Leo's body?"

"I spared you the details earlier. He was left for hours tied to an oak tree, so passers-by could pose triumphantly for pictures beside his corpse. One newspaperman asked me to comment. What words are adequate to counter such acts of treachery? Eli, I fear for humanity—I confess that my faith is being severely tested."

"Be strong, Rabbi Marx. Leo's family needs your *grand soutien* and your spiritual guidance. There is the funeral and the week of mourning to plan for. I leave you to your work."

After putting down the receiver, Eli shouted, "*Les batards!*" He pounded his fist on a desk, his rage boiling over.

*

Alonzo Mann stepped down from the trolley and began the two-block walk to the National Pencil Factory. Everywhere, buoyant strangers were greeting each other with broad smiles and handshakes. "We got him," he heard one man say as he passed.

Alonzo approached a police officer with a broad smile perched on a bench.

"Excuse me, mister. Why is everyone happy this morning?"

"You didn't hear the news? They hanged Leo Frank. He finally got what was coming to him. They pointed him to Mary Phagan's home where she grew up when they strung him up."

Alonzo's face turned ashen. "Who did this?" he asked.

"I don't know, and I don't care to either. They deserve medals, I tell you. Where you heading?"

"I'm the office boy at the pencil factory down the street."

"Isn't that the place where Leo Frank murdered the girl?"

Alonzo hesitated before answering. "Yes, it is. I was there in the morning, but I left for the parade."

"Good thing. He might have killed you too. The world's a safer place today. One less killer walking around."

Alonzo nodded. "Yessir, sure is safer."

Chapter Twenty-Six

Dear Sir Arthur,

We have narrowed our list to one viable suspect, and it is Rudolph Mulino!

Our wily killer is elusive and is making a splendid effort to cover his tracks. We must be diligent and calculating in our pursuit. It is vital that Rudolph Mulino believes the chase is over, and that he can resume the next chapter of his life without a shadow of suspicion shrouding him. I am convinced that the key to solving the riddle of Mason Caulfield's murder lies in the city of Rome. It is as if a different Rudolph emerged from that city after the filming in the Colosseum. The name of the film company that produced 'Roman Holiday for Two' is Case di Produzione Bologna. I telephoned the American distributor of the film and learned that the company was originally based in Bergamo, near the city of Milan. It moved last month to Bologna and changed its name.

Your connection to a Hollywood director may be helpful to the investigation. I wish to conduct a careful review of Rudolph Mulino's films. There are five in total. If you are able to acquire them for me, I will reimburse the director for the costs involved.

I will be prudent and not share with you in a cable all of the findings of my investigation at Smoke Lake. I will only pique your curiosity by venturing that Sherlock Holmes would praise my methods. I benefitted greatly from a visit to the home of Lilian Caulfield and her lovely son. Such a gracious woman; she resists casting her relative as the killer. We will need to supply her with the proof. She conveniently solved the mystery of Mason's threatening letters: they are wholly unconnected with his murder.

I read the stories in the newspaper, the drums of war banging more loudly on the European continent. What a shambles such a needless war would bring. My thoughts are with you, Lady Doyle and your family.

Pharo

*

Pharo rushed into the boardroom of Burford's law office, where he sat with Mitchell and Booker. Hugging him tightly, she cried, "Burford! Oh, how I missed you."

"I missed you as well, Pharo."

"I'm very sorry to interrupt your work. My apologies, Mitchell and Booker."

"None necessary, Mrs. Simmons," Mitchell said. "We were just discussing my trip to Georgia."

"I read the news about the dreadful tragedy, the mob stringing that poor man up to a tree like that."

"I spoke to one of his trial lawyers this morning. Leo Frank's body hung on the tree for a day before it was cut down. People drove to Mariota to pose for pictures with the noose still around his neck. I hear they were selling the pictures for a nickel. Someone recovered the noose and wants a dollar for it. He's bragging about the rope, which was tied in a Gallows Knot."

"Say that again, Mitchell," Pharo demanded.

"That they were selling pictures of the dead body?"

"No, the part about the knot."

"It was tied in a Gallows Knot."

"Burford, who would I turn to for advice on knots?"

"Well, I expect someone experienced with sailing boats would know about tying knots. I'd go down to the marina and start your search there. Why the sudden interest in knots?"

Booker spoke. "I know where Pharo is heading with this, Mr. Simmons. We discovered some tied rope on the shore of Smoke Lake. I kept it back at Mitchell's apartment."

"And did it have a knot?"

"Yes," Pharo said. "An unusual one. Lilian Caulfield showed me the scarf Rudolph Mulino left behind, also tied in a knot."

"And don't forget the new shoes," Booker put in. "Lilian let Rudolph borrow a pair of Mason's brand-new shoes for the commemorative service—might be worth a look at those shoelaces."

"Brilliant observation! Booker, you're a true sleuth. We must make a comparison."

"You're not returning to Toronto, Pharo."

"I have no intention of going back, Burf. I have a rather unpleasant memory of that city. But I put a taxi driver in Toronto on retainer. He'll deliver them. I'll need to make a telephone call to Lilian Caulfield after I get home."

"So much for our dinner and a film."

Pharo shrugged and smiled. "What type of witness will Clarence be, Burford?"

"A terrible witness. Clarence is irrepressible—more stubborn than a resting mule in the desert sun. I've expended countless hours trying to persuade my good friend that he fumbled by hurrying to the scene of the blackmail exchange. He foolishly walked right into a trap set by the police. Clarence prefers his truer version that describes an anonymous telephone call warning that his investigator was about to bribe a juror, followed by his chivalrous rescue of a man he employed. A jury will view his righteous account uncharitably."

"Then what can you do, Mr. Simmons?"

"You'll learn in time, Booker, as you develop into a fine lawyer, that you can't mold or shape your client's explanation to a jury. That is as dishonest as taking a man's wallet as he shuts his eyes in prayer at church. But you can persuade a witness that his story has as many holes as a target sheet after shooting practice. Still up to the witness to fill the holes, though. Not the lawyer. When we arrive in Los Angeles, Neeru will be running Clarence through a searing cross-examination to prepare him. If our client survives it intact, he'll be ready to testify."

"I'll leave you men to your work. All these sheaves of paper on the table."

Booker accompanied Pharo to the hallway.

"What is it?" she asked.

"Have you told Mr. Simmons that you fired my gun?"

"He'll just become inquisitive, and want to know who I shot."

Booker stared at her, puzzled. "That's the point, isn't it? I suspect it was Hanus's main henchman. Who else can it be? You've stepped on the paw of a rabid dog."

"I agree with you. Hanus needs to be finished off."

"Please, Pharo! You're a novelist, not an assassin."

"Of course. But Hanus is like the battered fighter who refuses to stay down for the count. The moment will arrive when I must resort to violent means to defend myself, and I'll be prepared. I have a surprise planned for that villain!"

*

Lilian Caulfield was delighted to hear Pharo's chipper voice. "I'm keeping myself occupied," she said. "Card games with my friends, tending to the budding tulips in my garden and walking to the shops with Brian. You made quite a positive impression on my son. Brian asks for you and Booker every day."

"Tell Brian that we miss him too. I need a small favor from you, Lilian. I'll be sending a cab by your home in the morning to pick up Rudolph Mulino's scarf and the shoes that Rudolph wore to Mason's service."

"I'll bundle them in a bag and have them ready by the door. I assume that this has some connection to your ongoing investigation of Rudolph. I received a letter in the mail from Rudolph that may interest you."

"Please tell me more," Pharo said.

"He says he is planning to travel to Canada next summer, and asked if he can count on my hospitality for another visit."

Pharo's mind churned as she considered Rudolph's intentions. "It seems he has unfinished business at your home, Lilian. You must send him a warm response, welcoming his return."

"*Unfinished business*? Am I in danger?"

"Please trust me, Lilian—no part of my plan involves any possibility of harm to you or your son."

"Brian frowned when I mentioned that Rudolph might visit again."

"That's curious. Did he give you a reason for his displeasure?"

"He became quiet when I asked if there had been a problem with Rudolph. Perhaps you can ask him another time. He's outside playing with his caps and baseball bat."

Ending the call, Pharo jotted a note: "Why is Brian upset with Rudolph Mulino?"

Chapter Twenty-Seven

On his thirtieth-eighth birthday, Mortimer Hanus presented his trusted worker, Draper, a felt bowler hat, purchased at a milliner's shop on a business trip to Dublin. Instructions had been left with the milliner to add to the lining—a pouch where one might safely store a pocketknife. For a professional killer, an extra knife might be handy. Hanus had watched a sampling of his own victims, their bodies riddled with bullets, regain a modicum of strength, and fight back. He would finish them off, when required, with a deft poke of a knife to the neck.

Draper, unsentimental and gruff in manner, who commemorated each killing he performed for Hanus by hammering a silver nail into his bedroom wall, grabbed the gift and asked,

"What am I supposed to do with my old hat?"

Draper knew he would be forgiven by Hanus for the slight. His unique brand of service was valued by his employer. He was like the principal dancer of a ballet, chosen from the rest for an exquisite pirouette only he could perform. Draper's specialty was to commit the messy act of murder without leaving a scrap of evidence tracking back to Hanus. He calmly wiped away any smudges of bloody fingerprints or footprints before departing the victim's abode; he resisted pilfering items from his target, regardless of value. Draper performed adroitly as the executioner of choice tasked to dispose of the various enemies of a vengeful Mortimer Hanus: the bar owner skimming Hanus's share of profits; the boyfriend of his younger sister, Sally, who slapped her in an argument; the bribed city councilor who turned his vote against Hanus.

Receiving a steep fee from Hanus for each of his killings, Draper could have retired to a peaceful life in the countryside, but he relished his work. He had hunted with his father as a boy, but hunting and killing humans was more gratifying than animals. He liked humans to display fear when he stalked them. His dreams were filled with images of stark fright and despair and whimpering pleas to be spared.

The assignment for Draper to dust off Pharo Simmons had been conveyed over a hearty breakfast of bacon and toast and hash potatoes. Hanus brought out a recent photograph of Pharo from a Buffalo newspaper. Draper was familiar with Pharo's role in foiling her husband's kidnapping by Hanus. As they feasted, Hanus highlighted his desire that Pharo's death should not be swift as was customary; he wanted it to be painful and drawn out.

"Let her linger with her wounds and remind her who sent you," Hanus said, smiling.

"I can do that." Draper bunched his fists together, the tattoo of a shark and a tiger displayed on each wrist. "She's only a woman."

"I warn you, she is wily. Do not underestimate Pharo Simmons. And bring me proof that you've killed her!"

Having thus warned his colleague and knowing his efficiency and skill, the discovery of Draper's bowler hat at the Parole Office startled Hanus.

At first, he ascribed it to misguided humor on the part of his subordinate, but Draper didn't possess a drop of jocular spirit. He was as cold as a frosty wind, just as Hanus had groomed him to be.

At length, Hanus accepted the fact that Pharo Simmons had soundly defeated his chief gladiator—and he was livid. He'd cautioned Draper not to be outwitted by his foil. Draper had followed Pharo to Toronto on the train and stalked her to her hotel—what could have gone awry?

Electric with rage, Hanus imagined Pharo's gloating smirk, contemplating his retrieval of Draper's hat at the parole office. Urgent action to avenge Draper's killing was necessary.

He summoned his new deputy, Tommie, to gather his closest confederates at his office for a midnight meeting.

Now Tommie, part-time errand boy, part-time enforcer and trusted bodyguard for Mortimer Hanus, took his seat at the back of the empty room. Hanus had taken a shine to Tommie from the moment he'd picked him up outside the prison gate. Tommie signaled to Jakesie and Mills, a couple of Hanus's armed personal guards, who hovered by the front door brandishing pistols to thwart any intruder. The invited guests were set to arrive.

Hanus soon entered the room without a greeting. Radish-colored cheeks beaming like a blazing lantern, Mortimer Hanus knocked his knuckles on the brass table and surveyed the seven senior members of his organization.

"Draper is dead," Hanus declared, fists clenched like a

boxer ready to pounce.

The group of men exchanged bewildered looks.

"Who could get to Draper, Boss?" Milkins, rakishly thin and with the strength of a couple of elephants, pulled a toothpick from his lips, waving it like a baton. "He bragged to me about his seventeen kills. Even I admit to being frightened of Draper."

Tommie spoke assuredly, "Must be a gang that ambushed him. One man couldn't get the job done."

"You're right about that," Hanus answered. "One man couldn't—it was a woman. And not just any woman—Pharo Simmons."

Hanus didn't need to elaborate on the identity of Pharo. Everyone in Hanus's inner circle knew that she was their boss's bitter nemesis. His spittle flew as he cursed her name.

Archie Mills, the bookish man seated closest to Hanus, hooked his thumbs around his suspenders and spoke: "If word gets out that Draper was done in by a woman, we'll look weak and lose business. We have to keep it hush."

Hanus peered at his accountant, entrusted with checking the tally sheet of revenues every day. "Archie is right. We need to pretend Draper never existed. Everyone understand? I don't ever want to hear his name mentioned again."

The men nodded in unison.

Tompkins asked, "Do you want to send a couple of guys to knock her off? I just read somewhere that her attorney husband is defending some big shot lawyer from Chicago."

"You read the papers, Tompkins?" The room erupted in laughter until Hanus spoke sternly. "Burford Simmons is busy defending another creepy lawyer. I wish all those rats were dead! I hate the bunch of them."

"Let me send some of my boys to clean up the mess."

"We have to be careful, Chubby. We'll need to wait for her to be alone—no witnesses—and it needs to be clean. If anything happens to her, the police will pay me the first visit. I'll be their prime suspect, maybe the only one. Draper was planning to visit her in her hotel room and make it look like an accident. I told him to make it look like she slipped in the bathtub and hit her head."

Mortimer Hanus had called his team to the late-night meeting to check for nervous tics, but was so far disappointed. He studied each of their shocked faces in turn, certain that one of his men had betrayed him and was working for Pharo Simmons and her lawyer husband. He could not accept that she could outsmart his top enforcer without inside help. Who had delivered Draper's bowler hat to his parole officer's office, he wondered.

"Boss, can I say something?"

"Sure, Fenton."

Fenton Smith, Hanus's new second in command, had helped run the business while Hanus served his prison sentence.

"We have to snuff out Pharo, but also protect you. It needs to happen when you have an air-tight alibi. Like a time when you're at the races and you keep your betting tickets and we take your picture."

Tommie interrupted, "Leave it with me, Mr. Hanus. I'll finish off the problem. Let me take one of your guards with me. It'll be a clean hit. Just like Draper would—sorry, boss... I forgot. Just like I was trained to do."

Hanus mulled the offer. Pharo Simmons's imminent death appealed to him. Even the mention of her name drove him to a boiling rage.

"You have my approval, Tommie. I was planning to go

to the races on Saturday. I'll bring a couple of the boys as company. They'll be my witnesses. But sending you across the border to nick her is risky—I need you back here. You're a smart boy, Tommie, so finish her off quick and make your escape. Do not tell me your plan, just let me know that the job is done. I will be able to sleep again. That wretched woman!"

*

Willie Hornsby opened the curtains of his *villa al mare* and stepped onto his veranda, breathing in the salty air of the coral sea. A plush, hilly path was carved through the rocks and linked the villa to the beach at the Grand Rimini Hotel. Willie sipped on his double espresso and ate the freshly baked cornetto on his gold-trimmed plate. The English newspaper, nestled in his lap, contained bold headlines about the dreaded war looming closer on the horizon. Serbia had rejected Austria's over-wrought ultimatum, and countries around the continent, including Italy, were mobilizing for armed conflict.

Willie pondered the somber prospect of war. No one had adequately explained to him why Europe was consumed by brinksmanship because of the shooting of an obscure Austro-Hungarian archduke, whose virtue was limited to pomp and prattle.

The war in Europe strayed from Willie's thoughts as he watched a child and mother splashing merrily in the calm sea, throwing a stick for their golden retriever to chase.

Sir Arthur Conan Doyle had sent a telegram the day before seeking a favor. Willie hadn't seen Sir Arthur since the yearly dinner party at their publisher's palatial home.

It had rained heavily in London that day, and Sir Arthur and Willie had taken cover in their soaked overcoats under a Corinthian-columned arcade.

Willie had since decided to retire from publishing the *Encyclopedia Britannica*, leaving the business to his two sons. The combination of his savings and a hefty inheritance from his mother, permitted him to enjoy a restful retirement on the coast of Italy.

But the sedate lifestyle, consisting of ascending the hilly terrain, reading in bed late in the morning, indulgent lunches of linguini and gnocchi with aromatic sauces, and long afternoon siestas had caused Willie to become restless and lethargic. He pounced on the opportunity that Sir Arthur's note presented—a chance to get involved in a murder investigation with the world's greatest writer of detective mysteries. "Oh, the intrigue!" Willie exclaimed.

"I need you to gain all the information you can about a film actor, Rudolph Mulino," Sir Arthur had requested. The actor's last film, he was instructed, had been produced by a studio in Bologna, *Case di Produzione Bologna*—a street address was included.

Willie's response was to unreservedly agree. Such was the regard that Willie had for the famed author that if Sir Arthur had asked him to boat along the Tiber River dressed as a pirate, smoking a pipe and shouting, "*Buona giornata a tutti*," he would have booked his seat on the next train to Rome. The Sherlock Holmes author's request was more modest: "Confidentially, there has been a suspicious death in Canada of an acquaintance of mine—murder?—RM may be the culprit. All I can say at present. Your assistance will be most gratefully received. A.C. Doyle."

Refreshed from a quick dip in the Adriatic, Willie dressed

and set out in his open-top car for the half-day trip to Bologna. He rehearsed his lines for the unscheduled meeting, between intermittent bellowing of Enrico Caruso arias. As the road signs marked his entry to the city, Willie pondered the likely success of his mission. A total stranger, an Englishman, speaking only choppy Italian, marching into a film studio to garner details of a silent film actor. "I don't want to disappoint Sir Arthur," Willie mused.

In the studio lot, he straightened his hazy blue ascot and combed his wavy hair. He entered the main building and approached the receptionist.

"My name is Willie Hornsby, and I'm looking to speak to the president of your film company," he announced.

"Just a moment, *signor*."

One minute later, Willie was ushered into an office at the end of the hall with the name of Domenic Vincenzo on a plaque on the door.

"Come in, *Signor* Hornsby. I have been expecting you." A hearty handshake followed. "Please sit. I am the owner of the film studio."

"Expecting me?" Willie asked. "I haven't announced the purpose of my visit."

"Please say no more, *signor*—you are representing the world's greatest writer, Arthur Conan Doyle. I've read all his books—I am honored that he is considering my film studio to produce his next film. You must tell me more about the project."

Willie instantly grasped Doyle's wily plan. "May I ask for a glass of water before I begin?"

"Of course!"

Sipping his drink, Willie hatched his story. "Sir Arthur and I discussed Italy as a proper venue to film *The Sign of*

Four, and your film studio seemed perfectly suited. We're thinking about the right casting for the film. What would you think of the actor you engaged in your film at the Roman Colosseum, Rudolph Mulino?"

"Mulino?" Domenic stood upright, mouth agape and eyes glowering. "This is not possible. I will not work with this actor again."

"Was there a problem?"

"Not with Rudolph Mulino. But his brother Luigi showed up on the set every day and pestered the film crew and me. I wanted to throw him out, but Rudolph insisted that his twin brother remain."

"Twin brother?" Willie digested every word to be relayed to Sir Arthur.

"Not merely a twin, *signor*, an identical twin. It was a challenge to set the pair apart."

"Sir Arthur was keen to have Mulino starring in the film. What kind of problems did his twin cause?"

"He was rude to the crew and flirted with the actresses. At the picnic we held at the close of filming, he showed up drunk, cursing—then I did order him to leave. He refused and shouted insults at me in Italian as he was carried out. He scraped the security guard's arms with his nails as he clung to him. I remember that Rudolph once told me that his brother had a flower stand in Bologna when we were looking to purchase bouquets for the set. Rudolph had a kind soul—too kind if you ask me."

"Have you encountered his twin here?"

"Not yet—I rue the day when I pass him in the market."

"Ah well, I'll convey your concerns about Rudolph Mulino to Sir Arthur. Perhaps you give me your list of recommended actors for the film after you've read the script."

"Please deliver the script to me—when will it be finished?"

"Hard to say," Willie said. "I don't govern Sir Arthur's timetable. But I give you my word. You will have the film rights when my client's decision is made—we'll only negotiate a deal with your studio."

The meeting concluded, and his task completed, Willie set off again to return to Rimini.

*

Clarence Darrow followed Neeru out among the crowd at the LaSalle Theatre. Neeru had stayed in Chicago an extra day for some final trial preparation. A few patrons recognized the famed lawyer, shook Darrow's hand and wished him good fortune at his upcoming trial.

As they plotted their way through the aisles, Darrow recited lines of dialogue from the play they'd just attended.

"How do you remember all that?" Neeru asked.

"It's a habit I developed in my youth. It keeps my mind razor sharp."

Neeru was set to return to Buffalo in the morning, and she had convinced Darrow that a night out to watch a play would be a useful distraction from the tribulations of his upcoming trial. Burford had suggested a comical farce for their play.

"A rather silly plot, don't you think, Neeru," Darrow said now, crossing the street. "Two business owners quarrelling over who devised the idea for their purple digestive pill. In my experience, capitalists are only interested in the pursuit of profit and the bottom line. They aren't soft and sentimental about the origins of their product."

"Yes—but you'd agree the lawyer for the company devised

a brilliant solution to the problem. A poker game with the loser confined to the role of a butler to the second partner for a year."

"I'm afraid I'd renege if I lost a card game to a pair of sixes. I don't succumb to orders easily, as you've discovered. The first mention of fetching the floppy slippers or opening the lace curtains would be more than my constitution could tolerate."

"And what if you won?"

"Even worse, my dear counsel. I could never ally myself with any form of servitude. My proposed solution would have been markedly different. Walk out onto the street and offer the running of the company to the first stranger that passes by. A real lesson in humility that would be. These titans of capitalism deem themselves indispensable. But every electric light loses its current and is replaced. We're all merely temporary custodians of our fate. And if I can mend a few peoples' misfortune on the journey, I'll leave content."

"You must avoid your stuffy soliloquies when you testify, Clarence. You're sure to offend at least one member of the jury by pontificating about the virtues of life. We can't assume that risk. Keep your answers simple and direct. And avoid lectures to the jury filled with fury about the grave injustice you've suffered."

"I shall be as sweet as the dew of the melon. I shall make you proud, Neeru. Even the sharp tongue of an irascible prosecutor will not tempt me to retort in anger. Can any reasonable man think that I'd dishonor my career, purge my reputation and lose my liberty to gain the possible vote of a single juror? A preposterous allegation, mounted against me. You must make that clear to these jurors, Neeru."

"And we will, Clarence, with your able assistance. Burford intends to ask you about your career successes as a lawyer. Don't be humble—we must establish the motive of the police to trap you and thereby rid themselves of the chief unraveller of their investigations."

"Humble, Neeru? Has anyone since law school attributed such a foreign label to me? I boast about my striking court triumphs from morning until the night's last shadow. You should see my performances at parties, with a couple of sherries in my belly. Sound the bugles. I will be eloquent in self-praise."

Sensing her client's weariness, Neeru sat on a bench and motioned Darrow to follow her.

The moon shone a spotlight on his downcast face. She leaned back to watch the constellation of stars beckoning on the horizon.

"My bones are weary," Darrow said in a quivering voice, wiping the cowlick from his forehead. "A false claim is the mightiest conqueror a man may face in his lifetime. You and Burford are the strong columns supporting me. I trust you know that."

Neeru measured her words, having detected her companion's watery eyes and a tear flowing down his rotund cheek. "I've encountered a legion of folk in my lifetime, Mr. Darrow, but you stand out as the most impressive. You're a hero to many people. Soon you'll be restored to your vaunted status. But once you've laid out your bona fides, leave the rest of it to Burford and me. This is not your moment to inspire; it's the time to persuade. Promise me you'll resist the platform of the witness stand to vent your rancor. Of course, you are bitter— they want you that way. The prosecutor will bait you to spill your anger on the courtroom floor."

Darrow's frame arched upright. "Enough about my trial! Have you heard how Mitchell is faring, after the lynching of Leo Frank by that vicious mob?"

"Luckily, he's preoccupied with a trial to prepare for. I called Mitchell last night--we are close friends and colleagues. The lynching of an innocent client jolted him. He worries that if he hadn't rushed back to Buffalo, he might have saved poor Leo."

"There would be two innocent souls lost if he'd tried. He will understand that after some time passes. A Southern mob encountering a Negro protecting a Yankee Jew? There would be a race to string them both up. Burford was right to bring Mitchell Harris into his firm. He's developed into a superb trial attorney. I'm enormously proud of the progress he's made."

"And he's expressed his gratitude to me for your steadfast support. There's some resentment that a Negro lawyer has risen to the top echelons of the Bar."

"A *Negro* lawyer! Whatever happened to describing someone as simply a damned fine lawyer? It's almost fifty years since the Civil War ended. When are folks going to come to their senses?"

"There will always be the boisterous haters in our profession, I fear."

"My approach to lawyering is that the more rancorous my opponent, the firmer is my handshake when I whip them in court."

"My handshake will be feather light after we win your trial."

"A bear hug is assured, Neeru. As tightly as my arms can clasp around you and your esteemed co-counsel."

"Thank you for warning me," she said. "I must return

to my hotel. Mitchell has a pressing matter about his case that he wanted to discuss."

"No bribing of jurors, tell him."

"He'll need to excel defending this client. A steep uphill climb to an acquittal if he stumbles on the witness stand. Now come, let's be on our way. I want you to have a good night's rest before you testify."

"Little chance of that. My nerves are as jumbled as a cat playing with a ball of thread. I have never had the vantage point of the witness box in the courtroom. It presents an entirely unique experience for me. But the moment does carry an advantage."

"What's that?" Neeru asked.

"I'll have a ready response next time a client complains that I have no idea of the challenges of testifying in a courtroom."

They reached Neeru's hotel a few minutes later, and the lawyer turned to wish Darrow goodbye.

*

Pharo telephoned Burford at his law office. The lawyer had devoted the evening to reading the stack of letters on a pile on his desk and preparing to interview a new client. He had contacted Mitchell and Booker to arrange to meet in the morning to discuss the new file.

"Is there a problem?" he asked. "It isn't customary for you to call at this late hour."

"Release me from my promise to you not to travel to Toronto," she declared.

"Why, Pharo, must you go to Canada *again*?"

"It's not another bumpy train ride to Toronto that

I'm pining for. A fresh matter arose in my call with Lilian Caulfield. It concerns her son. I believe that he may have crucial information about Rudolph Mulino."

"Then speak to him on the telephone," Burford urged her.

"It must be in person, Burf—trust me. The boy won't open up to me otherwise."

"Well, if you must go, please take Booker as your companion. He'll need Mitchell's permission, of course."

"Booker is not just my companion; he possesses the faculty to solve deep mysteries," Pharo said warmly. "Let me give you one shining example. Mason received a threat delivered to his office after the report of his presumed drowning in Smoke Lake. The story was carried on the front page of the newspapers in Toronto. The police apprehended the culprit, and he admitted his involvement."

"And you still wonder why he made a threat against a dead man. Perhaps he didn't read the newspapers."

"I wondered if that was true too. But my suspicions lingered, until Booker devised a clever scheme. He found the telephone number of the arrested man listed in a directory at the hotel. He called and, posing as a clerk for a local newspaper, inquired about the quality of delivery. A woman answered and complained about the delivery being missed on a couple of days."

"And one of the dates missed might have contained the story of Mason's tragic outcome."

"Yes, exactly—all attributable to Booker's quick thinking."

"Still, I'd much prefer that he spends his summer in the training of law."

"You and Mitchell are doing a splendid job grooming

him for his legal career. I won't stand in your way. It will be a quick turnaround and return to Buffalo in a day."

"I'll hold you to your word."

Chapter Twenty-Eight

"Pharo!... Booker!"

Brian Caulfield dropped his bat and rushed to the curb in front of his house. "Mother didn't say anything about you visiting today," he said.

"It's a surprise visit. I brought you a present." Pharo opened her bag and pulled out a book. "I found it at a shop at the train station. It has illustrations of different butterflies."

Brian, elated, took the book and flipped the pages. "Look, there's a monarch!"

"Want to hit some bottle caps with me?" Booker asked. "Pharo has to speak to your mother, and we can play outside."

Brian eagerly accepted the invitation, and Pharo left the pair and walked to the front door. Lilian had opened it and welcomed her inside. She had two chairs set up on a patio overlooking her garden with a tray of fresh fruit. After Pharo was seated, Lilian requested an indulgence— no conversation about Mason or his suspected murder.

"Do you like the opera?" Pharo asked.

Lilian beamed. "Mason and I attended a performance of Tosca on a trip to Sydney, Australia. I was rivetted by Tosca's courage to resist the Chief of Police."

"Tell me about the operas you attended with Mason," Pharo said eagerly.

A couple of hours later, Booker and Pharo were sharing a first-class carriage on a train returning to Buffalo.

"What did you learn from Brian?"

"I asked about Rudolph Mulino, and Brian frowned when I mentioned his name. I asked if there had been a problem with the house guest, and he nodded his head, but said that he made a promise not to tell."

"That's certainly curious. Was it Rudolph who made him promise?"

"Yes, but he refused to explain why the promise was made. We went up to his room and looked at the book of illustrations that he'd wanted to show us. He told me he was sorry that he wasn't on the fishing trip to protect his stepfather. He had asked to join the trip, but Rudolph had protested that it would pose too much of a burden for Mason. Brian was angry at Rudolph and refused to speak to him. Now I come to the interesting part of Brian's account—he snuck into Rudolph's room and searched it. He told me that he found a book under a pillow and ripped a page out."

"Did he keep the page?" Pharo asked anxiously.

Booker reached into his jacket pocket and pulled out a folded paper. "He let me bring it to show you."

Pharo opened it. "Oh, my God!" She spread the page across her lap and read it. The title at the top read: 'The Investigation of the Cause of a Fire.'

Booker looked ponderous. "Why would Mulino be interested in reading a book about fire investigations?"

"There can be only one plausible explanation. He's an arsonist plotting to make his crime appear as an accidental fire."

"We now know why he insisted on visiting the Caulfield home next summer," Booker said.

Pharo spoke resolutely. "We won't give Rudolph Mulino that opportunity."

"What does he gain with a house fire?" Booker asked.

"Who inherits the Caulfield fortune if Lilian and her son perish? Lilian isn't bequeathing it to her stepdaughters. Those ornery girls are not Lilian's daughters."

"Rudolph Mulino?"

"Mulino is her blood nephew, so might he not be her legitimate next of kin? I'll check with Lilian, but I won't be surprised if his name appears as the first rightful heir—and that he devised that change to the will when he was a house guest."

"This is a diabolical plan, Pharo."

"Indeed, now let's make our way back to the train station. If we're lucky, we'll catch the night train to Buffalo."

*

Pharo jotted a few notes in her diary as the train chugged through the night air, Booker, her silent companion. He'd fallen asleep before the whistle sounded as the train departed from Union Station. Booker's conversation with Brian Caulfield gave them new fodder for their investigation. Rudolph had discouraged Mason from bringing his stepson on the fishing trip. What was the true reason?

Was Rudolph concerned that a doting father in the constant company of his son might intrude on his plans? Had Rudolph plotted to murder Mason at Smoke Lake? Was it part of a grand scheme to knock off Mason, Lilian, and Brian to secure the Caulfield inheritance? Pharo would check with Lilian to see if Rudolph had approached her about being included in her will.

There would be a second trip Rudolph planned to the Caulfield home, and he'd wait for his opportunity to maneuver his way into the will at that time. The next step would be to set the house ablaze and make it appear like a tragic accident. A drowning in a lake and a house fire and the Caulfield fortune would be bequeathed to him.

The pieces of the puzzle were connecting. But Pharo would foil Rudolph's dastardly plot.

*

Pharo greeted the man in dungarees, holding a shovel, in her front yard.

"I'm with Cooley's Construction Crew. We're here to dig the fox trap you wanted."

"Those pesky foxes have been trampling in my garden searching for food. I'm taking the drastic step of capturing them in the act. I'd like the hole placed a foot or so in front of the garden bed."

"It will take us a few hours to get the hole dug. What do you want us to cover it with?"

"A cloth to cover the hole covered by dirt to camouflage it. I'd like the hole to be deep and wide enough to catch a couple of foxes."

"How deep, Ma'am?"

"Eight feet. The word will spread through the fox family to not tangle with Pharo Simmons."

Later that morning, a manila box arrived by special delivery. Pharo carried the heavy parcel in and laid it on the kitchen table. Inside, sheathed in cotton padding lay fifteen spools of film encased in round aluminum cases. Sir Arthur had performed his magic—his contact in California had sent the movies.

Five films starring the actor, Rudolph Mulino, with titles printed on each cover: *Emma the Adventuress, Roman Holiday for Two, The Mystery of the Juggler's Pin, Fantastic Slide* and *Beggar to Riches*. She'd leave *Roman Holiday for Two* to the end. It was clearly Rudolph's last film at the Coliseum in Rome.

Hearing a knock on the door, Pharo went to the front to see Booker standing in front on the steps holding a piece of rope.

"Oh! I forgot you were dropping off the rope from Smoke Lake today. Come in, Booker, and I'll make you a fresh cup of coffee."

Pharo placed the rope in the hallway beside the bag containing the shoes and Rudolph Mulino's scarf, and led Booker into the kitchen.

"I can only stay for a few minutes. Mitchell is meeting me at the office with Mr. Simmons before court today. I'm excited to work on a new case with Mitchell." Booker pointed at the table. "What are these?"

"I'll move them aside. It's a collection of Rudolph Mulino films. Sir Arthur arranged for them to be sent to me, and I've paid the owner of the Oliver Theatre to let me use his theatre to watch them. I shall let him know that I'll require the theatre tomorrow morning. A movie projectionist will be along to run the films."

"What are you expecting to find?" Booker asked, puzzled.

"A clue to the murder, I hope. It's a bit of a treasure hunt, but it keeps me occupied. I've made no progress in my writing since my sojourn in Toronto—I'm not accustomed to violent episodes and gunfire, and that encounter with my pursuer shook me."

"That is understandable, Pharo. Do you have any fear of being followed now?"

"It's not foremost on my mind—but I'm certainly watching my steps. I swing around on my walks before every turn to check. Anyone watching me from a distance must surely think I'm mad with my constant pirouettes. Burford has admonished me to be cautious." She giggled. "If my dear husband only knew the extent of my danger. I found a boot print in the garden in the backyard with a few broken twigs surrounding it. It's a larger size than Burf's, not that there is any chance of him strolling through my garden."

"How long has the boot print been there?"

"I did some watering in the garden the day before we left for Toronto. I'm quite certain it wasn't there—it's a prominent print. Something else: the boot is pointed away from the house. It indicates that care was taken to avoid an impression on the approach. A measure of care taken initially, but sloppy in the final execution. Probably not a professional killer."

"Did you check with your neighbor?"

"The sprightly Mrs. Turner? She's up at the crack of dawn and off to the market to do her shopping. She picks up groceries for her elderly father, who lives alone and relishes her visits. My neighbor doesn't return until much later in the day. She brings me some glossy red apples or brown sugar cubes after some of her trips."

"It's still worth checking with her," Booker said. "Do you have a revolver in the house?"

Pharo shook her head. "I've fired a gun for the very last time."

"This footprint is cause for dire concern. Let me speak to Mitchell—we must get a Pinkerton guard over to the house. You need protection, Pharo. It is sheer folly to ignore the further risk to your life."

"Thank you for your genuine concern, young man. It is heartwarming to know that you sincerely care. Oh! Your coffee." Pharo turned to brew the coffee. "And thank you for bringing the strand of rope. I now have the complete set of Rudolph's knots. Lilian couldn't have been more cordial when I spoke to her. She called me a master sleuth. That will impress Sir Arthur. I am a rival for his Sherlock."

"I bought Sir Arthur's latest book, *The Hound of the Baskervilles*. I'm quite enjoying the suspense of a detective story."

"I will invite you to join our club. Will you be able to finish the trial with Mitchell before you return to your studies at law school?"

"Mitchell asked me to sit beside him at the attorneys' table. He said that it wouldn't impress the jury if I had to dip out a few days early. I assured him that I would remain at the trial until the jury reaches its verdict."

"It will be excellent experience for you to learn at Mitchell's side." She paused, placing a steaming cup on the table. "I worry, Booker, that Mason Caulfield's murder may go unanswered. The only one concerned with the wicked deed is me—and Lilian, of course. Absent a confession from

Rudolph, what good am I doing harnessing the case against the culprit? The police view me as an eccentric American woman off on a frolic of fantasy. My work on behalf of the suffragette movement is further cause for the police to discount my contribution."

"I've a suggestion if you're interested."

"Please do share it."

"Mitchell taught me that to persuade the jurors, you must trick them into thinking that the solution is their own creation. You can employ that strategy with the police. Bring your findings to the police in Huntsville and tell them you're struggling to piece it together. Lead them to the trough, and they'll do the drinking. If you come to the station displaying how brainy you are, they'll resist. But if they own the idea, you may find the police energized."

Pharo considered Booker's tip.

"I'm still some distance from making my way to Huntsville. Perhaps my trip to the movies will be fruitful."

*

Pharo waited for the projectionist to start the first film. She had chosen *Emma the Adventuress*, thinking an overseas adventure suited her mood. The movie's exotic tale didn't disappoint her. Played by an actress close to Pharo's own age, Emma received an inheritance from a rich uncle and decided to take a trip to a Greek island. At a club there, she met a flamenco dancer, played by Rudolph Mulino, who taught her to dance, and to love. Emma stumbled through her dance steps, gracefully guided by Rudolph's character.

Her attention suddenly focused, Pharo recalled that the man she had met at Lilian Caulfield's house was bereft of charm or grace.

The next film selected was *Beggar to Riches*, a fable of the fickle fate of fortune. Rudolph Mulino's hobo character lived in a crowded tenement in the Bowery, where he one day discovered a bag of gold coins secreted under a stairway outside his home. He used the gold coins to purchase a clock factory, which over time, he built into the largest clock company in the state of New York. One day, a former friend from the Bowery appeared at his office seeking a job, but was brusquely turned away. Disgruntled, the bum returned that night and set the factory on fire. The business was ruined, and Rudolph had no insurance policy in place to recoup the losses. Forced to return to the Bowery, he received a hostile reception from the community that he'd turned his back on. He walked into a neighboring alley, never to be seen again.

Pharo pondered the accidental discovery of the gold coins in the film. Had Rudolph Mulino stumbled upon some fortune at the Caulfields? There was the break-in and theft of the jewelry, but that had occurred after Mason Caulfield was dead and at a time when Mulino was present at the commemorative service. Perhaps Rudolph planned to pilfer boxes of jewelry before setting the Caulfield home ablaze.

She called for the projectionist to play the next film. *The Mystery of the Juggler's Pin* had an intriguing plot: Rudolph was the juggler in a travelling circus that visited towns and villages dotting the country roads. He juggled cans and balls as a dog pulled at his pants until they slipped down, and the audience howled in laughter at his misfortune. Rudolph did not enjoy the humiliation. One day a salesman approached him at the end of a show and offered him a magical juggling pin to purchase for his act. The salesman demonstrated its magic by making the pin, hurled into the air, stay afloat for several seconds until it landed back in his hand. The trick was that the pin was attached to a long invisible rubber band tied around the salesman's wrist and tucked under his jacket sleeve. The flying pin became a mainstay of the juggling act, and soon Rudolph's juggler became the main act at the circus. No one laughed at the act again.

Fantastic Slide was a children's adventure. Pharo imagined the theatre filled with mothers and their children. Rudolph's character sold playground equipment and brought wagons filled with swings and teeter-totters to city parks. The main attraction was a slide that twirled in circles on the ride to the ground. One night, Rudolph's purveyor character devised a special slide, twice as high, with perches for the children to stop at intervals on their way down. He imagined that at each interval, the enthralled child would step out and enter the world of a fairy tale. On one level, it would be Jack and the Beanstalk, at another, Humpty Dumpty, until the child passed through them all and reached the ground.

Pharo waited for the projectionist to start *Roman Holiday for Two*, Rudolph's most recent film.

In the city of Rome, Rudolph's character was the tour guide for a couple of wealthy American tourists. Touring the Colosseum, Rudolph stumbled, hit his head on the ground, and lost consciousness. He awoke to find himself centuries earlier, in a cage waiting to battle as a gladiator on the grounds of the Colosseum.

At the end of the film, Pharo asked the projectionist to replay the final scene, a sword fight in the Roman Colosseum.

"Stop there!" she shouted.

Rudolph's character, the warring gladiator, had raised his arm with a sword clenched in his hand in victory. A ring could be clearly seen on the screen, a crest with the initials 'BFC' in the middle.

Pharo was certain that Mulino had not worn a ring in the Caulfield house. She had checked to see if he wore a wedding band. What did the initials 'BFC' stand for? The letters weren't chosen randomly. Pharo imagined Sir Arthur with a silver pocket watch with the letters 'ACD' inscribed on the back. Could the letter 'C' represent Lilian and Mason's surname? She recalled that her Aunt Sally wore a pin with a monogram with the initial 'T' for her married name of Tucker, placed in the middle. Pharo had no answer to the meaning of the initials 'BFC,' but she was certain that it was a clue worthy of being added to the investigative bin.

Chapter Twenty-Nine

Pharo returned home with the mystery of the initials of 'BFC' dominating her thoughts. She surmised that the letters were three initials of the name of the owner. Rudolph was Lilian's cousin. On the assumption that the letter 'C' represented the surname Caulfield, could the ring have been stolen? And what had happened to the ring? Why wasn't Rudolph wearing it at Lilian's home? The ring was a clue she ignored at her peril. She'd raise it in her next cable to Sir Arthur.

Back at home, Pharo left the cab at the curb and approached her front porch. The distinct sound of a man's shouts for help could be heard—becoming more pronounced with each step.

"The hole!" Pharo cried. "He's fallen into my trap."

She scrambled up the porch steps, ran along to the open sitting room window, and peered down over the porch railing into the deep hole carved into the ground below.

"Greetings," she called down.

"Help me," the man below her pleaded. There were

specks of dirt mixed into his chestnut hair.

"Why should I?" Pharo asked. "You arrived at my home with intent to shoot me. You couldn't believe your good fortune when you found the window wide open. You didn't count on me setting a trap for you with a carpet covering this hole, did you? Like your predecessor, you foolishly underestimated Pharo Simmons. On my life, I can't understand why women are deprived of the vote. Women are obviously brighter than men, based on your current predicament." Pharo stared down into the hole and noticed a gun pointed at her head. "You won't be wise to shoot me," she said firmly. "I'm the only person who can rescue you."

The stranger moaned in pain. "I broke my leg in the fall. Please—just help me out of here."

"The hole was designed for you to break some limbs. I don't want you climbing out and finishing your task." Pharo stared at the man's face contorted between unremitting fury and an abject plea. "What's your name?"

"Tommie."

"Tommie what?"

Some hesitation before the answer was forthcoming. "Tommie. Tommie Hendry."

"How old are you?"

"Twenty-six."

"Well. Mr. *Hendry*. I suppose you aren't likely to shoot me now, are you? I'm the only one who can save your life. I will call the police. But you'll have to tell me who sent you to kill me before I ask the police to pull you out of the hole. Of course, you may choose to stay here. I suppose we'll be neighbors in a way. Your gravesite in my front yard."

"I'm not saying anything."

"Suit yourself. You may have gauged my character correctly. Perhaps I would never permit a man to languish in agony and slowly starve to death. Or perhaps you underestimate my cruel nature. It's quite a risk to take, don't you think?" Pharo flashed a gloating smile.

Her ploy succeeded.

"Please, I'll do anything you ask. Just get me out!" The anguished voice told of a hired killer ready to succumb and meet his captor's demands.

"Tell me who sent you," Pharo demanded, and she kicked some dirt down the hole.

He wheezed as he choked out the name: "Mortimer Hanus."

"Hanus spoke to you directly, did he?"

"Yes, a few days ago. I've done some work with his organization."

"Where do you live?"

"In Toronto—in my mother's apartment. She'll be worried that I didn't get back."

Pharo detected a discordant gentleness in the young man's voice. "What organization do you work for? You must tell me."

Tommie's resistance had waned. "We're mostly involved with the rackets and gambling. We do some protection for shops in businesses—collect a fee to keep the riffraff away."

"You get a fee because you extort the shopkeepers to pay you. I know a lot about the universe that criminals inhabit. Tell me, have you been ordered to kill before?"

"No, and I wasn't going to kill you either."

"Why should I believe you?"

"I was only going to frighten you—I'm no killer. Please," he begged, "get me out of this hole."

"Tommie, I'm keenly interested in the involvement of Mortimer Hanus in your current assignment. I'm going inside to get a notepad and pencil. Mull your options as you wait."

Moments later, Pharo returned. "Speak," she demanded.

"Hanus knew that I was coming to Buffalo, and he called yesterday. He wanted the job done and your husband to find you dead. He used a few curse words when he mentioned his name."

"His name is Burford Simmons, and he outwitted Hanus in the past—a sore memory for the loser."

"Hanus wanted me to bring back proof you were dead. He described you as wily and sneaky."

"You might have heeded his advice. What precisely were your orders?"

"To come into your bedroom while you were sleeping and shoot you in the chest."

"A charming thought. What if I had held a pistol under the covers waiting for you?"

"He didn't say anything about you having a gun."

"Where is Mortimer Hanus now?"

"Back in Toronto. He runs a legitimate export-import business as a front. His gang is one of the most powerful in the northeast. Even the big players in New York City are afraid of him. He's crazy, you know. I heard he threw his wife off the roof of his building because she complained about his stinking cigars."

"Do you know where he was when he called you?"

"No, but likely his office on Temple Street. He was expecting some deliveries. Guns and dynamite. They hide the explosives in coffee bags."

Pharo underlined her note.

"How are you supposed to report that the job is done?" she asked.

"Ahhhh..." The man moaned in pain.

"We'll get your leg attended to in a hospital shortly. Just answer my question."

"That's just it—Hanus will be angry that I didn't call in already. I'm going to have some explaining to do. But I ain't telling him about falling into this hole. I'd be signing my own death warrant."

"Tell him that I left early before you arrived. You had to wait until I returned. How is Hanus supposed to pay you?"

"Half the money upfront, and the other half when the job is finished."

"Job? Is that how you describe your occupation? Hanus dispatches his underlings to travel around murdering innocent people. How many victims, Hendry?"

"Look, just get me out of here. I did what you asked of me."

"*Part* of what you need to do, Hendry. I believe you're telling the truth, though. I'll go inside and telephone the police. We'll be standing right beside you when you speak to Hanus from my home. You'll tell him there's blood all over my pillow and sheets, that you've made a real mess in my bedroom. You kept a framed photograph of me smeared in blood to bring. Then you'll tell Hanus you found a piece of paper on the dresser beside my bed with a list of initials and symbols next to them and a dollar figure of $1,500 at the bottom of the page. At the top of the paper is written "*Mortimer Hanus*." He'll want details, but you'll say you need to be paid first. Suggest meeting at a restaurant, because it isn't safe to go to his office. When you get your money, you'll turn over the list."

"Hanus doesn't take orders from anyone."

"He'll agree to meet you--Hanus will be eager to get the list if he believes that there are traitors working for him."

"You had this whole plan to get back at Hanus when you dug this hole."

"Precisely—and you're the lucky fellow who fell in."

"All right, I'll do it."

"Wise decision, Mr. Hendry. You rolled the dice and they came up sevens. I'm in a grumpy mood this afternoon. The fresh violets I was promised at the garden center haven't arrived yet."

While waiting for the Buffalo police to arrive, Pharo checked her mailbox. The groaning from the hole grew louder. She reminded herself to waste no pity on the ambushed hitman Hendry. In different circumstances, he'd now be exulting over her murder. He hadn't travelled across the border to yell 'boo' at her under her blanket.

She pulled an envelope from the mailbox, a cable from Sir Arthur. She rushed to the kitchen table and sat down, eagerly waiting to receive the latest update from England and read the cable:

Dear Pharo,

I congratulate you on possessing the traits of a worthy sleuth. Your premonition about Rudolph Mulino is accurate. As soon as I received your last cable, I contacted a former colleague from my publishing house, retired and living at an Italian villa by the sea. He was most accommodating and agreed to meet with the head of the film studio that produced the film, Roman Holiday for Two. From the information gleaned from his interview, he learned that Rudolph has an identical twin, living in the Italian city of Bologna. His name is Luigi and he operated a flower stand in the city.

As similar as the two brothers were in appearance, their character was opposite. From a variety of sources, my friend learned that Rudolph Mulino was a delightful actor to work with, dedicated to his craft, affable, prompt, gentlemanly, collegial and above all, charming. Luigi, in turn, was rude, disruptive and scheming.

When this was reported to me, I assured my contact in Italy that the man I met at Smoke Lake was as much a charmer as I am a singer. And I can't sing a bar in tune. I urged my friend to probe further.

Here is where the account takes a sharp turn of intrigue: the flower stand in the market of Bologna has been abandoned. My man found no sign of Rudolph's brother anywhere. He has simply vanished, the flowers left on his stand to wilt. Willie was able to pinpoint the exact date that the brother vanished to the end of the filming of Roman Holiday for Two. There it is, the puzzle almost solved.

My friend interviewed the shopkeepers around the flower stand. One young woman who worked in a cheese store had a vivid memory of Luigi. He pestered her to join him for dinner —her protests that she had a fiancé went unheeded. Luigi boasted about his career as a professional athlete. He played for the Bologna Football Club in 1909 and 1910. He showed her the ring that the club gave *to all its players in its inaugural season. Luigi told her that he wore the ring as a cherished memento and a good luck piece.*

I recalled Rudolph being rather adept at kicking around an empty can of beans at Smoke Lake. He juggled the can from foot to foot without it once dropping to the ground. Rudolph easily climbed the hills that we hiked and was a strong paddler in the canoe.

One further illuminating fact. My friend learned that Luigi Mulino spoke in a high pitch. Mason Caulfield's guest at Smoke Lake spoke in a distinctively high pitch. An actress who worked with Rudolph Mulino, described a deep, warm voice. The contrast in voice between the brothers is the difference between a bass and a tenor in a choir.

The contact in Hollywood who sent me Rudolph's films told me that Rudolph has been behaving strangely on the set of his new film. He presents as unusually reserved and quiet, and is reluctant to socialize with the cast and crew.

The man who appeared with Caulfield Mason and the Doyles at Smoke Lake was an imposter. I believe he had already murdered his identical twin and assumed the role of the star actor, with the riches and fame that followed. He knew his true voice would betray him in Hollywood; therefore, he learned to disguise his voice and rarely spoke a word. His films were silent, so the viewing public would never know.

It was a brilliant scheme if the brother had even a modicum of acting skills. But judging from the time we spent at Smoke Lake together, the brother must be a consummate actor. Lady Doyle, an astute judge of character, has watched all of Rudolph's films and never detected the difference.

I confess to you, Pharo, that I feel as if I have arrived near the conclusion of one of my novels, where the killer is identified by my master detective—but the body of the novel is missing. Why did the imposter murder Mason Caulfield at Smoke Lake? Why did he make the lengthy journey to the Caulfield home? How can we establish beyond any doubt that this twin brother of Rudolph is Mason's killer?

I owe it to Mason to return immediately to Canada and assist you with the investigation. Unfortunately, we have been warned that any crossing of the ocean is perilous at present. Submarines prowl the ports of Europe. Danger is lurking everywhere on the continent. I, therefore, am indebted to you for carrying the burden of investigating this dastardly rogue further.

He must be held accountable for two murders. Luigi (I shall not credit my companion at Smoke Lake with the name of Rudolph any further) likely sent his twin's corpse to the bottom of the Tiber River, as Mason's body is at the bottom of Smoke Lake.

But he shall not elude our grasp. Duty beckons us to mete justice to the perpetrator.

Sir Arthur

Pharo sat at her table transfixed by the content of the cable. The mystery of the initials 'BFC' had been solved:

Bologna Football Club. Credit to Sir Arthur for propelling the investigation forward. Rudolph Mulino was murdered after the filming of *Roman Holiday for Two*.

But one mystery lingered. The real Rudolph wore the ring with the insignia in the film, while the imposter didn't wear his ring at the Caulfield home. The ring appeared to be missing. The only plausible explanation that Pharo could muster was that Rudolph borrowed the ring and was killed still wearing it.

Pharo felt certain that she would be in a position soon to answer one of the questions posed by Sir Arthur: *Why did the imposter murder Mason Caulfield at Smoke Lake?*

Just then, the shrill noise of sirens summoned her from her absorption. Police cars were approaching, and Mortimer Hanus must be her first priority.

*

Mitchell was bounding up the steps to the courthouse when he heard a shout from beyond:

"Mitchell Harris, hold up there!"

He turned to see Detective Eli Jacob running toward him and waited for the panting detective to approach.

"Yes, Detective Jacob—is there a problem? I only have a couple of minutes to spare."

"No, Mitchell. I'm aware that you're in court for a trial today. I won't keep you occupied for more than a minute or two. But I have a surprise visitor for you. Look down there." Jacob pointed to a man ascending from the bottom of the stairway.

"Rabbi Marx!"

"Yes, the rabbi and I will attend your courtroom this

Steve Skurka

morning. He is in Buffalo for a couple of days. The rabbi will explain the reason. Come, Rabbi Marx, and greet Mitchell."

"Hello, Mitchell." The rabbi stepped forward. Tears streamed down his pallid cheeks as he continued. "You left an indelible impression on the family of Leo Frank. His wife asked me to convey her sincere gratitude. You gave Leo hope in the last days of his life. It is all so tragic. The lynching must stop. Another man was lynched the same day as Leo, in the city of Mariota."

"Please tell Mitchell the reason for your visit."

"Yes, thank you, Eli. We are raising money to set up an Anti-Defamation League to combat the scourge of antisemitism and hatred in the country. I will be speaking at a synagogue in Buffalo this evening."

Mitchell grasped the rabbi's hand. "I think of Leo every day. Our law firm will donate to your worthy cause. I'll address it with Burford upon my return to the office. But I must leave you now. I cannot be tardy for court. My associate is inside."

Chapter Thirty

Mitchell presented the case to Burford and Booker in the boardroom of the law firm. Booker had been instructed to take notes.

"The client's name is George Ducharme," Mitchell began. "Upon graduating from Fordham Law School, George opened a law office with a specialty in an emerging area of law: torts. To give his practice a boost, he affixed flyers to lampposts in his neighborhood reading: 'Fall on a sidewalk borrowing a cup of sugar? Foot run over by a runaway carriage? Poisoned by stale milk? Then I'm your lawyer for hire. Contact George Ducharme.'"

"My jug of milk was rotten this morning. Do I have a proper case to sue?"

"If you woke up in the hospital, you might. Remember that the key to torts is damages. Without harm or injury, there can be no civil claim."

"Listen to your mentor's advice, Booker."

Mitchell continued, "Alas, the business of torts didn't bring a flourish of new business. George waited idly by the telephone for his first prospective client. Finally, after laboring through two wasted months, George was introduced to his first client. A neighbor's son was arrested on a charge of murder and asked George to handle the case."

"Had he defended a criminal case before?" Booker interrupted.

"There's the nub of the problem. Without a drop of experience, he told the neighbor that he was the lawyer for her son, and he negotiated a moderate retainer. Within an hour, George arrived at the jail and was ushered in by a prison guard to meet his client. He was informed by the stern, wiry man in drab prison garb that his name was Clive Scully, and that he'd fired his first two lawyers before accepting his mother's recommendation. The client then informed George that he needed a lawyer to pass messages to his buddies."

"And George agreed?" Burford asked.

"The client assured him that he'd passed messages through his lawyers before. Scully proceeded to tell the lawyer the reason for his murder charge. The police accused him of killing a man in a bar with a pool stick—the victim was found on the floor in a pool of blood with the pool stick protruding through his heart. One customer in the bar, Johnny Curtis, came forward and identified Scully as the culprit. Scully had claimed that the victim owed him money."

"Only one witness?"

"The prosecutor's case relied on a single eyewitness."

"An eyewitness who gained no advantage from coming forward and implicating Scully," Burford added.

"Precisely," Mitchell said. "After reciting the story of his charges, Scully instructed George to write a message on a piece of paper. 'I want to be home for Christmas. I want a special tree with a present from the guys in a red box.'"

"What was George to do with the message?"

"He was told to take the note to a diner at Mercantile and Michigan Street and to sit at the third table from the door in the window seat. He'd be approached by a guy who said he was Jimmy. George was to give him the note."

"And did he take the note?"

"Yes, Booker, and as soon as the note was passed, three men in suits seated at the counter rushed to the table with their revolvers pointed at George. They hauled him from the table, checked the note and then handcuffed him behind his back and arrested him for conspiracy to commit murder."

"I don't understand," Booker said.

"It was a message for Jimmy from Clive Scully to have the witness in a coffin—the red box."

"Did someone tip off the police that red is the color for Christmas?"

"Booker has a valid point—that's the entire case against your client, Mitchell?" Burford asked.

"The police arrested a couple of members of Scully's gang who were informed of the meeting in the diner. They're co-operating and will testify that George Ducharme told the pair he was waiting for a signal from Scully to take care of the government's main witness."

"But both are plainly lying. George was meeting with Scully for the first time. The jail records will surely back that up."

"The prosecutor will regret bringing such a tepid case... Now tell me, Booker, what current escapade is my dear wife involved in?"

"She's solving a murder for Sherlock Holmes."

"The famous Sherlock Holmes!" Mitchell exclaimed.

"The *writer* of the Sherlock Holmes stories. We're close to solving it too."

"So Pharo tells me," Burford said. "And you share her conviction that this railway executive was murdered on Smoke Lake?"

"Yes, sir, I do."

"My wife is planning yet another trip to Toronto to solve this mystery of a railway executive's disappearance. I trust my wife to know if she's on a frolic of her own design."

Booker replied earnestly to his principal. "I can assure you that it's not a frolic, sir."

Chapter Thirty-One

Herb's Diner was renowned in the city of Toronto for its wondrous hash, scrambled eggs and a crisp slice of bacon. In the morning, especially on the weekend, a line of customers waited on the sidewalk for a table. Herb Solway, the affable owner, ran the cash register and handled the steady stream of customers as if he was greeting old friends on a street corner.

The diner was located one block from the office of Mortimer Hanus on Jarvis Street, and Hanus was a regular customer. In the odd moment when the restaurant was half full, Herb called over, and saved Hanus's customary corner booth for him until he arrived. The servers competed to serve Hanus's table because of his generous tipping. Hanus relished watching the waitresses' radiant eyes as he pulled out a wad of bills to pay for his meal.

On this misty morning, Hanus telephoned ahead and requested a table in an hour, noting that he would be accompanied by a guest. Herb knew his corner booth was a priority, and that he didn't like to be disappointed.

The slated guest, Tommie Hendry, arrived on crutches five minutes early for the meeting. He mentioned Hanus's name and was escorted by Herb to the back, where he sat and asked for a glass of water. He recited his instructions from the detective in a faint whisper one final time: "Stay calm. Ask for your money at the outset and be firm about getting it. Let Hanus volunteer the details of the hit job on Pharo Simmons."

Tommie looked around the restaurant to see if anyone looked like a policeman. He'd been promised protection, in the event that Hanus became violent. A couple of older men stooped over their plates, and there was a table with a boisterous family of four including two young children. Two youthful Negro men at the next table were dressed in black suits with thin bowties.

One of them looked back and smiled at Tommie.

"Can you recommend anything on the menu, sir?" he asked. "We're missionaries passing through the area on our way to Montreal. Passing the good word of God."

"It's my first time here too. I can't help you—and don't bother me again."

"That's fine. Good luck," he answered with a wink.

"Good luck with what?" Tommie demanded.

"Don't take my friend too literally," the second man at the table said. "He's only wishing you good fortune in your future." He picked up a black book. "It's all here in the Bible, sir."

Minutes later, Mortimer Hanus entered the restaurant and sauntered to Tommie's table. A ham sandwich was on a plate, as he'd requested.

"This better be worth it, Hendry," he said, flopping into his seat and leaning back. His mouth quivered, and his fists were clenched as he stared across the table at the crutches. "What happened to your leg?"

"I fell down the stairs. Had to spend a few hours in the hospital, but they patched me up. I wasn't going to miss this trip, though. I want my money, Hanus. Think I'd waste my time if I couldn't deliver the goods? Remember, I'm doing *you* a favor by coming here."

"We'll see about that, Hendry. I don't want to be disappointed. You won't need to bother with a return trip if I leave this diner unhappy. Give me the list."

"Why, so you can take it and leave me stranded here? Pay me what I'm owed first. The job is done."

"A smart guy. I'll pay you as soon as you provide me with proof that Pharo Simmons is dead."

"Here is the proof." Tommie pulled out a framed photograph of Pharo covered in dry chicken blood. "I found this on the dresser after I shot her."

"I checked the newspapers. There's nothing about her being dead."

"Of course not—she told me her husband is out of the city on a trial. He'll be surprised at what he discovers in the bedroom when he returns."

Hanus pulled an envelope from his pocket and handed it to Tommie. "Fifty dollars, as I promised you for the job. Well done. Now give me the list."

Tommie placed it on the table. Hanus studied it, shaking his head as he read each entry.

A waitress appeared at the next table to take the orders of the two missionaries.

The first one said, "I'm sorry, my friend is a mute. Can you lend us a pencil, and my brother will write down his order?"

"Here," she said, leaving a pencil and turning back to the kitchen.

Tommie stared at the men in bewilderment—both the men had spoken to him moments earlier. He returned his gaze to Hanus just in time.

"I can't believe these guys are traitors!" Hanus shouted. He slammed his fist on the table, making Tommie's glass fall to the floor and shatter.

Tommie nodded solemnly. "I knew it would upset you—men on your payroll, betraying you to Pharo Simmons."

"I'm going to slowly strangle every one of them with my own hands."

"Do you want me to go now?" Tommie asked.

"No, I want you to tell me how you killed Pharo Simmons."

Tommie could see the missionary begin to write with his pencil as he replied, "I got in through an open window in front of her garden. I went upstairs and took off my shoes. The hallway was wooden, and I didn't want my shoes to squeak. She was sleeping with her head facing the door, so I figured I better be quick. I lifted up her blanket…"

"Did you shoot her twice in the chest like I told you?"

Tommie lowered his voice again. "Yes, after she awoke and begged for her life. She squealed like a pig about to be roasted."

Hanus appeared pleased.

"Her blood splattered everywhere. It got on my pants and belt. I burned them in the fire when I got home."

"Better lie low for a while when you return home. Help your mother with her chores. You've done excellent work, Tommie. You'll go places in my organization. I need workers I can rely on and trust."

"That's me, Mr. Hanus. You won't find a more loyal soldier."

"Call me Mortimer. Take care of your leg. Let me know when you're ready for an assignment, and I'll bring you back to replace Draper. Draper used to count his victims by hammering a nail on a board for every kill. Enjoy your breakfast." He dropped a wad of bills on the table. "This will take care of breakfast and the server," Hanus said.

He abruptly stood up, put the list in his jacket pocket, and shouted to get Herb's attention. He pointed at the stack of money and raised a thumb before leaving the restaurant. The pair of missionaries stood and hurriedly moved to the door.

"They're coppers?" Tommie asked out loud.

*

Willow Hooper sat across the desk of the publisher of the *New York Times*, reporter's journal and pencil in her lap.

"Your interview with Leo Frank impressed me," he began. "I'm not prepared to drop the story now with his lynching by a mob. There hasn't been a single arrest. How do you manage to enter a guarded and locked prison facility and grab a prisoner in the middle of the night? *The Atlanta Constitution* was correct to describe this sordid episode in an editorial as Georgia's shame. Well, it will be our shame, too, if we permit this travesty to fester without any accountability."

The door to Adolph Ochs's office opened, and the associate editor of the newspaper, John Short, entered.

"I made it clear that I wasn't to be interrupted."

"I apologize to you Mr. Ochs, but I felt that you should

hear the news we just received."

"What news, John?"

"Austria has declared war on Serbia by telegram. We're on the path to a major international conflict."

"Will America be drawn into war?" Willow asked.

"Inevitably, yes."

"Send me there as the newspaper's war correspondent."

"We have reporters stationed in London and Paris, Willow."

"A handful of reporters can't adequately cover this war."

"What do you say we need?"

"I think we'll need a team of journalists standing by in Europe. The continent is about to blow up."

"America can't stand idly by. Willow, I want your story on Leo Frank's lynching written before I change your assignment."

"I'll make my arrangements to travel to Buffalo to interview Frank's lawyer."

"That is Mitchell Harris, isn't it?" the associate editor asked.

"Correct."

"His law partner is Burford Simmons. We heard from a police source that the Toronto police just arrested the fellow who kidnapped him a few years ago."

"Mortimer Hanus?"

"That's his name."

"I covered that story when I worked for the newspaper in Buffalo. What is he arrested for now?"

"He was caught plotting to kill Simmons's wife."

"Pharo Simmons—I'll have another reason now to meet with Mitchell Harris."

*

"A hit man trapped in our garden!"

Pharo gulped before answering. She had been dreading the moment she'd have to explain to Burford about her travails with Tommie Hendry, the hole and his arrest, his co-operation with the police and the arrest in Canada of Mortimer Hanus for hatching a plan to murder her.

"Yes, Burf," she said glumly.

"Don't bother telling me what happened. Eli Jacob told me the whole story at court this morning. I dropped in to watch Mitchell's trial and sat beside the detective in court. At the break, he asked to talk with me privately, and what a tale he spun. Hanus sent a professional killer to our home, and you dug a hole to ensnare him—have I got that right? Now I understand why you cautioned me to stay out of our garden."

"Yes, and I confess that wasn't the first killer he dispatched—but he's behind bars now, so the danger has passed!"

"What happened to the first killer?"

"He's dead."

"How can you be certain of that?"

"Because I shot and killed him in Toronto."

"Oh, Pharo! What life in the shadows are you not sharing with me? You killed Hanus's hit man! Hell hath no fury like a scoundrel scorned. Hanus will redouble his efforts to harm you, Pharo. You'll need to report the account of your shooting to Detective Jacob?"

"Will I be in any trouble, Burf?"

"The police will be sympathetic to your plight—I'm certain of it. You were targeted by Mortimer Hanus and took the necessary steps to defend your life. I'm only cross with you that you didn't share any of this with me. I'm your husband—I'm surely entitled to know that my wife is in grave danger."

"I didn't want to disturb you, Burf. Clarence needed your attention directed to his case."

"I'm aware of it now. We must take immediate steps to ensure your protection. I've arranged for Detective Jacob to meet privately with you. He's most grateful for my law firm's work on behalf of Leo Frank. He claims that he will be forever indebted to Mitchell and me."

"I'll be pleased to take direction from the detective. I'm leaving now, however, for a meeting of our local suffragettes. We're organizing a protest march for next Saturday in front of City Hall."

Burford knew that it would be a wasted effort to dissuade her from attending. "Please be careful," he said.

Pharo leaned forward eagerly. "You haven't told me your thoughts about Mitchell and Booker's trial."

"I focused my attention on the jurors as they were chosen. A plumber and an owner of a toy store were the first couple of jurors selected. It isn't easy finding a jury sympathetic to a lawyer charged with a serious crime. We're a despised profession."

"That is, until you're needed."

Burford had once explained to Pharo his theory that jurors could be divided into useful categories. There are the mayors, the boisterous type, who try to govern the group with an iron fist but fail miserably in the end. The tourists are attentive to the dramatic and exciting parts of the trial and disinterested in the rest. The salesmen make their emotional pitch in the jury room with flair and panache but little substance. Then there are the teachers, who echo the judge's instruction on the law as Biblical scripture. And there are the plumbers, Burford's favorite jurors, hardworking, industrious and prepared to grind through the evidence until the correct verdict is reached.

"How is Booker faring?" Pharo asked.

"Very well. He's been a great asset to Mitchell. He's helping to prepare the client to testify. I feel sorry for the chap. I spoke to him briefly in court. He looked as pale as a bedsheet, and his hands were shaking. Booker has been cheering him up."

Pharo stood, pushing in her chair. "I'm planning to travel to Toronto one last time," she said.

"When will you be leaving?"

"The timing is uncertain."

"I insist that you meet with Detective Jacob before you depart. He'll ensure that you're adequately protected. You're marching right into the hornet's nest. He'll arrange for you to meet with the Toronto police. I'll retain a local lawyer to assist you."

"You have my promise, Burf, and I'll provide the detective all the information he seeks. I'm waiting for you to inquire about my progress with the Mason Caulfield investigation."

"You haven't given up solving it, I see."

"Not at all. I've been in regular contact with Sir Arthur. Our agenda for tomorrow's session of the Sherlock Holmes Club will fill them in on my meeting in Toronto with Arthur Conan Doyle. I'll discuss the fascinating content of the recent cable I've received from London. The case has taken a peculiar twist."

"Well, keep me in suspense until you've nabbed Mason's killer." Burford smiled as he spoke.

"You're mocking me now, are you? A retainer to defend America's most famous advocate and you come back with an overstuffed ego. I'll permit no gloating in our home."

"My humble apology to you, Pharo."

Pharo had misgivings about telling her husband a fib about her plans for the afternoon—but there was no choice. It was inconceivable that, had Pharo informed Burford of her appointment with Neeru Sharma, he wouldn't press for an elaborate explanation. She needed Neeru's advice about a private matter connected to the Mason Caulfield investigation.

A few hours later, Neeru ushered Pharo into her office and led her to a comfortable padded chair.

"What is the problem?" Neeru asked.

"I need to get a will prepared."

"I've drafted a few wills, and I can help you with that. But it will be beneficial if you and Burford prepare a joint will. Have you discussed this with him?"

"It isn't a will for me, Neeru?"

The lawyer appeared perplexed. "Then who is it for?"

"It's for someone who is dead. His name is Mason Caulfield, and he owned a railway in Canada."

"There is an issue of jurisdiction. A Canadian lawyer needs to draft the will. But if he's dead, the only will to prepare will be for the heirs who inherit his fortune."

"It's not a real will," Pharo said.

"Pardon—did I hear you correctly? It's not a real will?"

"I'm trying to trick some fellow into believing that he's the beneficiary of Mason's will. It's vitally important that I persuade this man to return to Canada, and this is the surest way to do it."

"So, you think by creating a fictitious legal document, you'll entice this man to appear in Canada to collect his fortune."

"I knew you'd understand, Neeru."

"Understanding your plight and the execution of a legal document are two separate matters. If I create a bogus will, Pharo, I can lose my license to practice law and possibly go to jail. I'll need to hire Burford to be my attorney... Tell me, what is this about?"

"A man has escaped justice for a murder he committed, and I'm trying to correct that."

"Surely it's a matter for the police to investigate."

"At one time, I believed that too. The police are convinced that the cause of death was drowning—all an unfortunate accident. We are in the process of collecting evidence to prove that it was a premeditated killing."

"*We?*"

"Yes, me and Sir Author Conan Doyle, the author of the vaunted Sherlock Holmes series of books and stories."

Neeru shifted the subject. "Burford has no idea that you're meeting me, does he?"

"No, and you must not tell him. He'll be livid with me for consorting with a murderer."

"Your secret is safe with me. I'm duty-bound to keep it confidential between us—but please reconsider, Pharo. It's folly for you to be involved in police business."

"Can I ask you this, Neeru? Is there any law that prevents me from misleading someone about an inheritance?"

"I don't see a crime being committed there."

"That is most helpful," Pharo said, stepping out of the office, ready to implement her plan.

Chapter Thirty-Two

The Sherlock Holmes Club convened as usual on the third Tuesday of the month. All seventeen members of the club were in attendance in the ballroom, eager to listen to Pharo speak about her encounter with the venerated author of the Sherlock Holmes detective novels. A surprise guest was announced by Pharo for the evening, Detective Eli Jacob.

"A *real* detective?" Tory Bumpkins asked after introducing himself.

Jacob rose and faced the questioner. "*Oui, Monsieur*. I am a senior detective and most interested in attending your club this evening. *Madame* Simmons has shared with me her efforts to solve the murder of Mason Caulfield."

"Murder?" Tory's voice was raised in befuddlement. "Pharo has sent our club correspondence complaining that the police aren't treating it as a crime."

"I do not wish to speak badly of another police force, but in truth, I must. The Canadian policemen who investigated this man's disappearance are *imbeciles*! The clues they choose to ignore are ready to be plucked as easily as the petals of a tulip."

Pharo strode to the podium, interrupting the detective. "You'll have an opportunity to speak to our guest at the cocktail reception. First, let me bring you up to date on my investigation, guided expertly by Sir Arthur."

"Did he spill any secrets about his next story?" Marjorie Wilkins asked.

"No," Pharo answered with a broad smile. "But he did mention that he's already plotted the demise of Sherlock. His curiosity in ghosts and spirits piques his interest."

"I dare say that Doyle's book sales will drop like a rock plunging off a cliff if he abandons Sherlock Holmes," Godfrey Hines interjected, startled. "*Séance on the Seine* won't jump off the bookshelf."

"I suggested that he retain Dr. Watson's character to assume Sherlock's role."

"What was Sir Arthur's response, Pharo?"

"Out of the question," he said. "Watson lacked the eccentricities and guile of his mentor. When has Watson ever solved a crime? The point was made emphatically, and of course, he was quite right."

"I will miss this club," Godfrey said. "Perish the thought that we've seen the last of the great consulting detective."

"Perhaps I should write a book of my own exploits."

"Yes, Detective Jacob, and you can start with Burford Simmons's kidnapping."

"*Mais non, Monsieur* Tory, the credit is owed to the president of your club for solving that sordid crime. *Madame* Pharo Simmons!"

The club burst into applause. "We've heard quite enough about ancient business," Pharo said blushing. "There's an important matter on our agenda this evening, and I'm seeking your advice."

Pharo continued to speak to a hushed room.

"There are a couple of new members to the club, and I shall start at the beginning of my adventure. I travelled to Toronto to interview Sir Arthur Conan Doyle—and I must report to you that I failed miserably at my task. The interview is promised still, and we shall see if Sir Arthur honors his word. When we met, Sir Arthur had just returned with Lady Doyle from a fishing trip at a campsite in northern Ontario on the shore of Smoke Lake. A member of his party, Mason Caulfield, the head of a railway company, had gone missing and was presumed dead. Naturally, Sir Arthur was distracted by the pressing matters of a companion's sudden death. The local police presumed that Caulfield, the genial host of Sir Arthur and Lady Doyle, had drowned. Sir Arthur disputes this theory. There was one additional guest at the Smoke Lake camp, an actor by the name of Rudolph Mulino. Rudolph's connection was his relationship as a nephew to Lilian Caulfield, Mason's widow. Sir Arthur disputes the conclusion of the police and steadfastly believes that there was foul play involved."

"*Bien sûr!*" Eli Jacob shouted.

"As is evident by the detective's outburst, he shares Sir Arthur's suspicions."

"Sir Arthur and Lady Doyle sailed for England on a steamship on July 11, and Sir Arthur entrusted me to carry on and solve the sordid crime. He was resolved to assist, and his cables have benefited my investigation significantly. I have also been ably assisted by a student at my husband's law firm. I am confident that I shall ensnare Mason Caulfield's killer in the coming days. The trail is getting closer to the target."

Marjorie Wilkins cried excitedly, "You're like a real-life Sherlock Holmes, Pharo."

"I'm a novelist, Marjorie, and a rank amateur as a sleuth. But I must confess to you, my friends, that the chase is invigorating. I wait for the moment that the police clasp a set of handcuffs firmly around the killer's wrists."

Godfrey asked, "Do you have multiple suspects?"

"One suspect—and I'm certain that he's the killer."

"Then take your evidence to the police if you're sure," Godfrey advised.

"I must first satisfy the police that a murder occurred, and the perpetrator is my suspect."

"How do you propose to do that?"

Pharo smiled. The speaker, Mark Miller, a bookstore owner in Buffalo, had also been skeptical that Doyle would devote the time to meet with her.

"By collecting irrefutable evidence and presenting it to police on a silver tray," she said calmly. "The murder investigation is tied up in knots, but I have a meeting with a knot expert in a couple of days. I'm also planning another trip by train across the border to Toronto. I've befriended Mason Caulfield's widow, Lilian, and I keep her updated on my progress. I'm hopeful that my next trip will wrap up the mystery of her husband's tragic passing."

"Please take me with you to your meeting with the knot expert, Pharo. I've been trained in shorthand." Sally Timkins was a retired bank manager who customarily spent her summers in a cottage in Provence, but those plans had been postponed with the brewing European war.

"I'll welcome your company, Sally. Booker is occupied with a trial with my husband's partner, and a skilled note-taker will be useful."

"May I be heard?"

"Yes, Miller."

"If there is, in fact, a murderer out there, isn't there some urgency to apprehend him before he strikes again?"

"It's a fair point because our killer did strike twice before. He killed a witness to his misdeeds at Smoke Lake. He also murdered his twin brother."

At the mention of the twin brother, there were gasps heard around the room.

"Please tell us the full story, Pharo. You have our attention now," Sally said.

Pharo devoted the next hour to giving the complete account of her investigation, including the latest cable from Sir Arthur.

"How do you propose to get Rudolph Mulino to return to Canada? If the culprit murdered Mason Caulfield as you suggest, Canada is the last place he'd venture to."

"I've thought about that, Godfrey, and you may be able to help bring him here."

"Me? What can I possibly do?"

"You're a master of disguise. You portray the roles of the characters in the Sherlock Holmes stories with exquisite finesse and aplomb. I will pay your way to visit Rudolph in Hollywood and convince him that you are the representative for Mason Caulfield's estate. You'll tell the scoundrel that he is a beneficiary of Mason's will and give him a date when you'll be announcing the details of the estate. You need to have him present to hand him his considerable share."

"I don't know, Pharo. I'm not sure that I can pull that off. Isn't it dangerous?"

"Very dangerous—I will understand if you decline."

"When do you propose to send me to California?"

"In the next couple of days, I expect."

Godfrey gathered himself together. "All right, Pharo. I'll do it," he said.

Chapter Thirty-Three

Burford Simmons's plan to secrete himself in his law office to review a pile of missed correspondence, read law reports and schedule meetings with clients and prosecutors was interrupted by a telephone call from Detective Jacob. The detective was unusually abrupt as he requested an urgent meeting with Burford; he apologized for being discreet.

Burford arrived at the Merchant Street Police Station about an hour later and was ushered directly to Detective Jacob's office, where he found the detective pensive and pacing the floor.

"I'm pleased that you're here Mr. Simmons. Please have a seat." Eli moved to his desk across from Burford's chair.

"I spoke to Clarence last night. He was full of *joie de vivre*, good spirit and preparing for trial. He invited me to be his guest in Chicago in the autumn, and I readily agreed."

Burford smiled. "He'll take you for long winding walks along the Chicago River. I should warn you that with his lanky legs, he insists on keeping a brisk pace. I always enter the office behind him panting and short of breath."

"I shall bring my swimming trunks then," Eli said with a mischievous smirk, "and challenge him to a race in the river. None of the other *gendarmes* in my unit could keep up in our training sessions in the river Seine." The detective leaned back in his chair and grabbed a framed photograph of Jacob with an arm draped around Darrow. "A memento from your solved kidnapping investigation. *Mon Dieu*, such a marvelous mind Clarence Darrow possesses! I was bestowed with the honor of working beside the master attorney. He expressed to me that he is most grateful for the stellar defense you and Neeru are preparing. *C'est magnifique!*"

"I doubt he used that French expression, but I'm grateful for his praise. It's an arduous exercise preparing Clarence to testify. Lawyers make terrible witnesses most of the time. Too haughty for their own good."

"That is my impression of *les avocats* in Paris and here. You and Mitchell are notable exceptions."

"I'm ferocious and hard as a steel beam in the courtroom, Detective Jacob. My duty to my client is to furnish a shining light in the darkness and guide the jury to the tunnel's light at the end."

"You will emerge victorious at Clarence's trial."

"Let the trial unfold first—I've been admonished before about gloating too soon."

"By Mrs. Simmons, I assume. She is the reason that I summoned you on such short notice. I attended her meeting of the Sherlock Holmes Club last night. I have decided to take some time from my official duties to assist your wife."

"Is she grateful for your offer?"

"I've kept it a secret—Madame Simmons will accuse me of meddling in her affairs. I will be guarding her safety and watchful from a distance. I am trained to conduct surveillance without being observed."

"This is most generous of you, Eli."

"I will never forget your efforts to help Leo Frank. I'm indebted to you and Mitchell."

"It was our solemn honor."

The detective dabbed his eyes with a hankie. "I am certain that you have discussed with your wife, the arrest of Mortimer Hanus."

"I am aware that Hanus was stopped in a plot to kill Pharo. We agree that Hanus is exactly where he deserves to be. In a prison cell."

"*Mais oui.* Pharo spoke candidly about her deadly encounter with another of Hanus's men in Toronto. I have informed a senior detective in Toronto, Detective Sperling, and he would like to meet with Pharo *tout suite.* The detective assured me that she has nothing to fear."

"What can you share with me about the case against Hanus?"

"The case against Hanus is strong. His admission of the plot to kill Pharo was witnessed and recorded on paper by a police officer seated a few feet away."

"And yet I haven't seen anything in the newspaper about Hanus's arrest?"

"The police didn't want to hamper their ongoing investigation into Hanus's associates. But Hanus will be appearing in court tomorrow, and *voila*, his sordid deeds will be known. The newspapers will connect the murder plot to your kidnapping as soon as Pharo's name appears."

"An episode of our lives that I fervently desire to put

behind me. It is like a deep bruise that never fades from the skin. The evil of that wretched man Hanus knows no bounds. I sincerely hope that he's locked away for life this time."

"*Bien sur*. We share the same goal. Detective Sperling also indicated that the threat to Mrs. Simmons's life is a major concern for the police. Mortimer Hanus is blaming his arrest on your wife."

"Of course, my crafty wife is responsible. What choice did she have? She's thwarted him again. Surely you didn't need to beckon me to your office to expound on Hanus looming as Pharo's chief adversary. What are you hiding from me?"

"You are very astute, *Monsieur* Simmons. Indeed, that wasn't my purpose. Your attendance is related to a discovery that the Toronto police made after Hanus's arrest. In his jacket pocket, they found a scrap of paper with the address of your law office. Underneath was printed a name: Booker. A student in your office, *je comprends*."

Burford leaned forward and pounded the desk.

"If Hanus harms that young man, I'll rip him in half."

"I understand your rage, Mr. Simmons. But Hanus is not my present concern. I sent an officer to locate Booker as soon as I was informed of this note. He isn't at the apartment that he is renting. An officer checked your office: it was locked, and the lights were out inside. He watched you arrive."

"Booker must be with Mitchell, Detective. He is assisting him with his trial."

"I'd be obliged if you'd telephone Mitchell and make an inquiry."

"It's Saturday, and he's likely at the law library at the courthouse."

"We will go together. Permit me to drive you."

Detective Jacob escorted Burford to the front door.

They were halted by a wave of the desk sergeant.

"Sorry, sir. One of the detectives asked to speak to you before you leave."

"Certainly, we can wait."

Seconds passed before an officer appeared, frantic. "Detective Jacob," he said, panting.

"Yes, Fryer. What is it?"

"The downtown precinct just called. They were advised that anything connected to the Mortimer Hanus arrest was to be passed on to you immediately."

"Yes, what has happened?"

"A typed note was dropped off at the front desk. No one saw who left it. The note says that if Mortimer Hanus isn't released from prison within forty-eight hours, Booker's body will be dumped on the side of the road."

"Call them back and get every detail you can—I want the exact wording of the note. I need a team of officers and detectives assigned to this investigation. The rotation is marked on the blackboard. I'll meet everyone upstairs in a couple of minutes. Get moving!"

In tears, Burford looked at the detective. "It's my fault. I failed to protect Booker. He was entrusted to my care."

"Nonsense. You did nothing wrong. I must ask you to leave now but to be available for questioning. Locate Mitchell and return to the station in his company. He may have useful information about Booker's last location."

"Please keep me updated, Eli. Please..."

Chapter Thirty-Four

An hour had passed since Booker was abducted, and there were no further messages relayed by the kidnappers. Detective Jacob had alerted the station that he was to be notified at his home as soon as word was received. He'd assigned a team of four detectives to work around the clock on the investigation.

Detective Jacob telephoned the Detective's Office at the downtown precinct to receive an update from one of the detectives on the team.

"Any progress, Jameson?" he asked.

"Just a visit from a snoopy reporter from the *New York Times*. Her name is Willow Hooper."

"I am familiar with Hooper. What information was she seeking from you?"

"She isn't aware that the law student is kidnapped. She was asking about Mortimer Hanus's arrest."

"*C'est catastrophe!* You said *rien* about the investigation, of course. Did she tell you where she is staying?"

"No, but she assured me that she'd return to the station later today."

"I am leaving shortly and will be there to greet her. Listen, Jameson; I'm relying on you to convince the Toronto police to hold back the story from the press for as long as possible," Jacob urged. "The kidnappers must believe we're serious about an exchange between Booker and Hanus. They will accuse us of planting the story in the press if it's reported. Waiting under the cover of silence is the only possible way to keep Booker alive."

"I've talked to Detective Sperling, and I'll follow up. He told me that Hanus had no visitors or telephone calls since his arrest. He must have issued the order to seize Booker before his arrest."

"Mortimer Hanus prepared for all possible contingencies and left instructions to kidnap Booker to use as a pawn for his release from jail. Booker must have been seen by his men in Toronto together with Pharo. Hanus is a madman, but he is not prone to leave idle threats. *Je comprends tout*. I understand the way he thinks."

"Well, the Canadian police aren't about to set Hanus free, are they?"

"*Non, non*, the idea is preposterous. But I have a plan that I will share with our team. I had a case like this in Paris once, and to my genuine surprise, it worked."

"I'm listening, sir."

"Hanus's lackeys will contact the police station again. It will surely be soon, as they are serious about brokering a deal. We will let it be known that we are prepared to meet their demands, but we first require assurance that Booker is alive and in good health. Unless we hear from him directly, there will be no deal. We will give them the senior detective's telephone number in Toronto, and he will make it clear that he is waiting to receive word from a prosecutor to authorize the deal for Hanus to be freed. You must brief Detective Sperling, Jameson. He must be firm that no exchange will occur unless I have an opportunity to speak to Booker first and am satisfied that he is in good health."

"How will you find our victim, Detective Jacob?"

"Our young victim is clever. We can hope that he will manage to pass on some piece of information with a clue to disclose his whereabouts. We must record every word spoken by Booker, as the clue will be in code."

"We'll need a backup plan."

"There is no backup plan, Detective. The kidnappers are planning to kill Booker. He can identify them. One day longer, perhaps two—that will be all the time we have."

*

Burford Simmons entered the courthouse library. The librarian directed him to an octagonal window next to a stack of Supreme Court Reports, where he found Mitchell Harris's head buried in a book.

"Mitchell," he whispered.

The lawyer looked up.

"Perhaps we should leave the library to talk more freely."

Mitchell surveyed the face of his alarmed partner. "Tell me now," he said.

"Was Booker working with you this morning?"

"Yes, he left a couple of hours ago. What's wrong?"

"He's been taken by Mortimer Hanus's men."

Mitchell appeared startled. "What? I can't believe it! Why Booker?"

"Hanus was arrested in Toronto. They're trying to

exchange Booker for Hanus's freedom."

"What can I do to help?"

"Detective Jacob is handling the investigation. I'm taking a cab to the police station as soon as I leave here. The kidnappers may be in contact."

"I'm joining you." Mitchell began assembling his books to return them to the desk. "Have Booker's parents been notified? They live in Ithaca."

"The police will arrange to speak to them. I haven't told Pharo yet. She will be devastated. She is fond of Booker."

"We all are...Oh, this is terrible news. We don't have any time to spare, Burford."

Fortunately, a cab passed by just as they reached the street in front of the courthouse. They reached the Merchant Street Police Station a few minutes later.

Detective Jacob rushed to greet them after being advised of their arrival.

"Quickly, we must hurry! The kidnapper called, and I explained my terms. He was unhappy, but I told him I must speak to Booker and satisfy myself that he hasn't been harmed. He hung up on me, but I'm certain he'll call back. He declined my offer to contact the Toronto detective on Mortimer Hanus's case. I've evidently satisfied him that my offer is sincere. Come, there is a telephone in my office that I'll use. I want you both there. *C'est tres important.* You may be able to assist with deciphering Booker's code."

"Code?" Mitchell asked.

"Your young associate will send us a helpful message—mark my words. Take a piece of paper from my desk and a pencil."

Half an hour passed, and then an hour—still no call.

At five minutes before noon, the phone rang.

Jacob calmly answered. "Hello?"

"I have your man here. He'll let you know that we're treating him fine. Live up to your part of the bargain and let Hanus go, and you'll see him today. Otherwise, two shots to the head, and I'm not bluffing."

"I know you are telling the truth. It is good to deal with another person with a sense of honor. And I must tell you, *Monsieur*, that as we speak, the prosecutor's office in Toronto is preparing the documents for Hanus's release from jail. It will take some time, so please be patient."

"I don't have patience, you fool!" the man shouted.

Jacob heard static—the caller had a poor connection.

"Look, you can kill the young man in your company, but then you will have no leverage. I will not negotiate further, *Monsieur*. Mr. Hanus will be most unhappy if he learns that we were negotiating his release in good faith, and you acted hastily to prevent his freedom. Let's be real here— you have as much interest as the police do in waiting. Not for long, I promise you that. Now, please put Booker on the telephone."

A gravelly voice was heard next. "Hello."

"Hello, Booker. My name is Detective Jacob. I'm the detective assigned to bring you home safely, and I promise you that I will not fail. Please tell me how you're being treated by your captors."

"They have treated me well. I'm given my water and ham sandwich on the floor in a locked room. I have a blanket and towel and a sink and toilet."

"Were you beaten?"

"No, not at all. Can you let Mitchell Harris know that I'm sorry that I can't be at Mr. Torak's trial? I am sorry that I will miss it."

"Not to worry. I promise to let him know. He's standing beside me, with Mr. Simmons."

"Sorry, but they're motioning for me to end the call. Please do what they say, Detective Jacob. These men can be relied upon. Just follow their instructions."

"We are, Booker. Be strong."

The kidnapper returned to the line: "You have one hour, Detective. I want to hear Mortimer Hanus's voice, and I want to hear him say that he is being released. If not, we'll have to shoot Booker. It'll be a darn shame. He's such a polite and respectful lad."

Mitchell became excited as Eli related his conversation with Booker. "He was regretful that he had to miss my trial."

"I was surprised that concerned him," the detective replied.

"Yes, but our client's name isn't Torak." He printed the name in large block letters on his paper.

"This is the clue you've been searching for, Eli."

Eli, Burford and Mitchell studied the piece of paper.

"A young man's life is depending on three of us solving Booker's clue," Jacob announced.

"I believe I may have something," Burford exclaimed. 'Torak' spelled backwards is 'Karot.'"

"But how does that offer us a lead to Booker?" Mitchell asked.

Burford's shoulders sagged, and he sighed. "I agree that it's an unhelpful epiphany."

"*Mais non*, you are both incorrect—a carrot is a true clue," the detective said, excited. "What hidden message is Booker sending us? Can it be a street name? Let me check my road map." Eli opened a drawer, placed the map on the table and studied it. "I can find no road or street with that name."

"Could it be a grocery store selling vegetables?"

"Possibly, but that doesn't narrow our search. There must be hundreds of them spread across the streets of Buffalo. Come, gentlemen, our time is short. The code must narrow our search, or it is useless. Booker must be guiding us to his location." Detective Jacob paused. "But I admit that I'm puzzled. Of what possible assistance is the word 'carrot'?" He snapped his fingers. "Unless it refers to a shape—some kind of tall building, or better, a tower! But where?"

Mitchell pressed his palm against his forehead, deep in thought. "What about a silo, Detective?" he asked. "It's long and protruding and rounded at the top."

The detective considered the comparison. "*Je ne pense pas*. The shapes are not the same. The carrot is pointed at the top."

"But a silo and carrot have two common features: long and cylindrical."

The detective shrugged his shoulders. "*Je suis sceptique*."

"But we don't have any other options, Detective Jacob. Please consider that Booker is held in a silo," Mitchell implored him.

"There is no other building structure that resembles a carrot," Burford said.

"*Je me souviens maintenant*." Detective Jacob paced the floor. "There is an old silo on a farm on the outskirts of the city," he said. "I've passed it a couple of times."

"I know exactly where it is," Burford added. "I recall observing that the field appeared brown and patchy, as if the farm was abandoned."

"I'll check the silo thoroughly, but I'll need to be most discreet. I can't risk alarming the kidnappers with a large police presence. I'll bring one detective with me. Both of you can wait in my office until we return. I hope that I will be accompanied by young Booker. Let us pray."

*

Detective Jacob paused behind a tree to survey the farm and silo with his binoculars. He was joined by Detective Gilchrist, who parked the police car on a deserted strip of road. The pair of detectives walked through thick brush and a barren field to reach the farm. Jacob searched for tire tracks in the muddy road leading to the silo but found none. There was no car in the vicinity. He checked his watch. Thirty minutes had passed since the phone call. Time was running out for Booker.

Suddenly, a door to the silo opened, and a bulky man in a plaid shirt and bushy beard stepped outside the silo and lit a cigarette.

Jacob motioned to Gilchrist to peer through the binoculars.

"*Voila*," he whispered. "This is our *grand* chance."

Jacob walked back about a hundred feet, with the second detective following suit, and began to crawl through the field. His knees hurt, and an occasional brush slapped across his face, but Jacob moved unimpeded and at a brisk pace. He could hear Detective Gilchrist struggling behind him.

Eli stopped when he reached the edge of the cleared area around the silo. He reached for his gun and continued to crawl forward. The man peered ahead, staring into the sunlight as Eli approached from the side. Eli motioned to Gilchrist to stand against the curvature of the silo as he edged closer.

The man stomped on his cigarette butt and turned toward the silo door, and Eli planted his gun firmly against the man's cheek.

His voice was barely audible. "One word, and I blow your face off. Do you understand?"

The man nodded, his body shaking.

"Lie down on the ground with your hands behind your back," he ordered in a whisper. "Gilchrist, stay with him. I'm going inside."

Eli gingerly entered the black shaft of the silo. The darkness provided cover. He could see a candle burning, and, in its light, a young man on the floor covered in a blanket with a hankie across his mouth.

The young man noticed the detective and moved his head sharply to the left in a gesture of warning.

Eli held his revolver out as he stepped forward.

The second kidnapper, a revolver tucked into his waist, had his back turned. Eli ordered him to freeze and raise his hands, but the man reached for his gun. Eli fired twice and watched the kidnapper slump to the ground.

The detective went to him, and the man looked up— then his eyes shut, and he slumped again.

Eli moved to Booker, untied his hands and removed the hankie.

"Thank you," Booker said, his voice shaking.

"Let us leave, young man. A lot of people are worried about you."

Outside, Detective Gilchrist held the handcuffed kidnapper. They marched to the detective's car. Eli instructed the detective to remain at the silo and secure it until a team arrived to collect evidence. An ambulance would be called to pick up the dead kidnapper's body.

"How did you find me?" Booker asked inside the car.

"The round carrot, *Monsieur*, was a crumb of a clue."

"I had to be creative," Booker said with a faint smile. "To be honest, I didn't believe that you'd figure it out."

"You can credit Burford Simmons and Mitchell Harris for cracking your code. It was not the finest code I've witnessed in a police investigation." The detective paused in mid-sentence at an obvious point that had eluded him until this moment. "But from where did you telephone?" he asked. "There was no telephone in the silo."

"I was blindfolded and driven to another location," Booker said. "I didn't know if they intended to return to the silo, but we did so shortly before you arrived."

"Then there must be a third party to the kidnapping. There is no sign of a car here. You surely met him on the road. Did the voice of the man who spoke to me sound familiar?"

"Yes, it was the man you shot."

Detective Jacob parked his car at the police station and walked with the handcuffed prisoner.

"What is your name?"

"Barney."

"Barney, you have one opportunity to help your *tres mauvais* situation. If you assist me, I give you my sincere word that I will inform the prosecutor, and your sentence may be reduced. Perhaps by years of your life. I believe you were not in charge of this young man's kidnapping."

"You're right."

"Were you present when Booker was moved for his

phone call with the police?"

"Yes."

The detective pressed Barney for details of the location. "When is the fellow in charge checking back with you?" he asked.

"He's supposed to drop by tonight in his car."

"To the silo?"

"Yeah."

"What about Booker?"

"He said he'd deal with him. Our job was just to stay in the silo while he negotiated with the police."

"Then I must return *tout suite* to conduct the negotiation of Mortimer Hanus's release. We will have a surprise for our master kidnapper when he arrives at the silo tonight. Booker, we must keep your safe release a secret. Your parents must be notified, of course, and Mr. Simmons and Mr. Harris are waiting at the station."

"But Mitchell!" Booker cried. "I must get back to court to assist him with his trial. He depends on me."

Impressed by Booker's determination, Eli Jacob said, "The trial is not your priority right now. We'll arrange for a doctor to check you out. And I will be occupied with one final task in this investigation."

"What is that, Detective?"

"At the appropriate time, I shall convey to Mortimer Hanus, *avec plaisir*, that his plan to gain his freedom has been foiled. Now we must make haste, Booker. We don't have a moment to spare."

At the station, Detective Jacob stood back and watched Booker embrace his two principals. Mitchell held him tightly, tears streaming down his cheeks.

Burford clapped Booker on the back. "We've agreed

that you will live with Mitchell for a few days. You're not to leave his sight, Booker, not even for a moment. For your own protection."

"Yes, Mr. Simmons."

"We need to let your family know you're safe."

"I will provide Booker with a telephone," Jacob interrupted. "I would desire everyone to remain at the police station for now. We're planning to apprehend the third member and possibly the leader of the kidnapping team."

"Detective Jacob?"

The speaker was an officer carrying a loop of keys around his belt.

"You've left the cells, Greenfield?"

"Yes, sir. Holtby replaced me. I need to speak to you in your office."

"Speak here. These gentlemen are to be trusted, and will be discreet."

"It's the prisoner, Barney. He refuses to disclose his surname. When I passed him his dinner tray, I observed him shaking like a leaf in the autumn wind. I asked him if he was ill, and his answer puzzled me. I felt it was important to share it with you."

"Well, what did he say?"

"That he was afraid he was going to die. He's not sick, but he fears death. That's odd, don't you think, sir?"

"Take me to this Barney fellow at once. I want you to open his cell, and I will enter. We are not to be disturbed until I call for you. Unfortunately, I understand perfectly what is troubling our prisoner. Move, Greenfield, *vite!*"

*

Barney appeared relieved to see the detective as he entered the cell.

Jacob pressed him for more information about the third kidnapper: his physical description, his habits and mannerisms, and the location of the meeting. Barney was sparing in his answers.

Jacob turned to the reason for his visit. "All right, *Monsieur*, speak. What did you fail to tell me?"

"How do you know that?"

"Because I am not an *imbecile*. You are afraid of the death penalty, although I promised you assistance with your sentence if you were forthcoming. No more *charades*!"

"You must believe me, Detective. I wasn't trying to hide it. I simply forgot. The third guy isn't local. I never saw him before. When he met with us to plan the operation, he gave us a yellow cloth. We were instructed to always leave the yellow cloth in the door when we closed it. It was a signal to him that there were no glitches."

Jacob recalled seeing a yellow cloth on the ground as he left the silo. It had meant nothing to him at the time. "*Mon Dieu*," he said. "If he passes the silo, he will know the police are present."

Barney nodded.

"Gilchrist!" the detective exclaimed. He had been left alone inside the silo, awaiting the presence of more officers. "I must return to the scene at once."

Jacob banged on the cell door, and Holtby returned with dispatch to unlock it. The detective flung the door open and raced up the stairs and walked briskly to his office.

"I will return soon, *Monsieur* Simmons," he said as he passed. "I must attend to a most urgent matter."

As Detective Jacob rushed back to the silo, he pondered the ruse of the yellow cloth. The third kidnapper was crafty and could not be underestimated. This would not be the tidy end to his investigation that he expected. Gilchrist was in grave danger, unaware that his presence had been exposed to one of Booker's kidnappers.

When Jacob reached the silo, three police cars were in the driveway. He observed a couple of officers milling about, and stopped his car in front of them.

"Where is Detective Gilchrist?" he asked.

"We're waiting for the ambulance to arrive. There are two bodies inside the silo."

"Two?"

The man nodded grimly. "Gilchrist was shot in the back of his head. We found him near the entrance with a pool of blood around him."

"And the shooter?"

"Gone by the time we came by. Sad to lose one of our men. We were all shaken when we found him."

"We can be certain that our killer will not be returning here again. He is on the run now, making his escape. We must foil his plans."

One part of the discussion in the cells with Barney lingered with Detective Jacob. Barney had described the train rumbling by during his time with the third kidnapper. He described the house vibrating and the shrill sound of the train's whistle. The whistle was blown to warn ahead that a train was rapidly approaching a street intersection, where a warning light and railing were located.

Jacob determined that he needed to find a house or apartment with a railway track adjoining it and a nearby intersection where the train passed. But where? Suddenly, a bold idea came to him. He would need the cooperation of the head of the railway, but he would obtain that.

A police officer was dead, and his killer was on the loose.

*

One hour later, Detective Jacob led a procession of four police cars along a section of railway track that crossed into part of the city. All trains had been halted until the police investigation concluded. As the cars rumbled over the tracks, Jacob surveyed his surroundings. Houses and apartments crowded the whole perimeter of the tracks. It was an impossible task to pinpoint a single location.

Then, all at once, the railroad tracks curved into a section of the city where a row of houses abutted close enough to the track that Jacob could see the bewildered faces of residents peering out their back windows. At one house, Jacob observed, the drapes were closed. He counted the houses in the row: it was the sixth from the end. One block later, Jacob stopped his car and waited for the group of officers to congregate around him. In the distance, a lifted railway guard was visible at a street intersection.

Jacob told the men he believed he had found their suspect. It was only a hunch—there was no discernible evidence that the killer was in the house he'd identified. But if it was Gilchrist's killer, he would not surrender easily. He faced a certain death sentence for his crime. The police must assume that he would return fire.

"We must outsmart him and catch him with his guard down," Jacob explained. "I shall stand in his backyard and fire my gun into the air. He will be alarmed and peer through the split in the middle of his drapes. I will be hiding under his window. I will then fire a second time. The shot will undoubtedly confound him, and he will be unable to resist coming outside to check its origin. We shall be ready for him."

The twelve officers took up their locations in the adjacent yards to the house, secreted behind fences and posts. Jacob raised his arm in the air and fired his revolver once. The blast pierced the air.

Moments later, Jacob heard running footsteps. As the man entered the backyard, he was greeted by the detective's gun pointed at his chest.

"Get down on the ground," Jacob ordered.

The man began to flee and reached for his pocket, and Jacob fired once more. The man fell to the ground as the other officers hurried to approach.

"A revolver tucked into his belt. McIlroy, turn him over. I want to see his face."

The stocky man was turned over. His singlet was soaked in blood. Jacob stooped over and peered at the dead man's mouth. "There it is, the mole over his lip. Barney described this mole to me. We have our culprit. He thought he could outwit the great French detective." Jacob peered down at the limp corpse. "*Mais non, Monsieur*, you mistook my sense of decency for weakness. A fatal mistake on your part."

Chapter Thirty-Five

Booker heard the rustling sound of a key unlocking the front door of the apartment. The door opened, and a stranger entered, smiling.

"Don't be alarmed, Booker. My name is Neeru Sharma—I'm a close friend of Mitchell's. He gave me an extra key. I thought you might be hungry, so I brought a pot of curry stew that I cooked and fresh naan bread."

"Mitchell is in his room napping—he said he'd make me a sandwich with some biscuits for dinner."

Neeru took the pot to the kitchen and returned. "You'll enjoy my stew more, Booker. I put carrots and potatoes in and my own secret sauce."

"Carrots!"

"Yes, Booker. It's a recipe that my mother taught me in India before we settled in America. Are you allergic to carrots?"

"No, your timing is odd, that's all."

Neeru stared at the young man, perplexed.

"Why did you come to live in Buffalo?" Booker asked.

"My father was a banker with an English bank. They asked him to relocate to America, and our family moved when I was ten."

"I'd like to travel to India one day. Mitchell has copies of the *National Geographic Magazine* that I'm reading. I enjoyed seeing the photographs of the Chicago World's Fair."

"I just returned from Chicago. I'm preparing to defend a trial with Mitchell's partner, Burford Simmons."

"Then you must know Mr. Simmons's wife."

"Pharo, of course I do. A firecracker that never fizzles, that's Mrs. Simmons. Oh, please don't tell her I said that, Booker. I meant it as a true compliment."

"I give you my word," Booker said, winking. "Pharo and I are working together to solve a murder case."

Neeru appeared flummoxed. "Can you repeat that, please?"

Booker's expression turned exultant. "Pharo and I are setting a trap for the murderer, and in a few weeks, he'll tumble into the net."

Just then, Mitchell entered the living room. "I heard your voice, Neeru. You've been chatting with my house guest. He's been through an exhilarating adventure. The scent of your delicious curry wafting through the apartment is most welcome."

"Let's eat dinner! Booker, you must be starved."

Over the course of a hearty dinner, Neeru and Mitchell laughed and told stories, as Booker listened raptly. He watched as Mitchell affectionately brushed his hand against Neeru's and fondly kissed her cheek. It was indeed a close friendship.

Mitchell stared into Neeru's sparkling eyes every time she spoke.

"I'm weary and need my sleep," Booker said, rising from his chair. "Thank you for the delicious dinner, Neeru." Out of her line of sight, he signaled thumb-in-the-air approval in Mitchell's direction before leaving the kitchen.

Neeru took Mitchell's hands and held them in her lap. "Would you like me to stay?" she asked.

Mitchell spoke in a whisper. "I need you to hold me in your arms, Neeru. I just need to be held. Twice now, people I care deeply about have been hurt, and I've been a helpless bystander. My vigor is whittled to nothing, and my spirit weak. I'm haunted by a single nightmare—the hangman, bloated with evil, holding the noose, and Leo Frank staring at that roused mob, haggard and beaten but still defiant in his innocence."

"Come, Mitchell darling," she said softly. "Let's sit together under the blanket in the living room. When this trial is over, we'll take a holiday in a log cabin in a forest and count the raindrops trickling down the window."

"That will be sublime," Mitchell said.

Chapter Thirty-Six

Willow Hooper had a front-page scoop for her newspaper. Arriving at the Merchant Street Police Station, she was immediately ushered into the office of the familiar detective, Eli Jacob. After reminiscing briefly about Burford Simmons's kidnapping, Jacob asked her to take her notepad and pencil and record the story of an investigation that had concluded successfully only moments earlier.

And what a story Detective Jacob had to tell. The arrest of Mortimer Hanus for conspiring to kill Pharo Simmons; the abduction of a law student at Pharo's husband's law firm; the ploy to secure Hanus's release and the foiled plan of the kidnappers—leaving two of the kidnappers and a policeman dead.

Detective Jacob gave her an office to write her story and permitted her to use the wire service to ship it off to the *New York Times*. He beseeched her to devote as much space in the story to the sordid ploy of Mortimer Hanus—and his plan to destroy Pharo. Jacob planned to take a copy of Willow's story with him when he visited Hanus in his Canadian prison.

The detective had another pungent surprise to present to Hanus. Tommie Hendry, a co-operating witness, had given the Toronto police a journal he discovered in Draper's apartment. Tommie had been tasked by Mortimer Hanus to search Draper's home after his untimely death, and to gather his guns and knives and pack them in a suitcase. Tommie turned over the suitcase but kept the journal. It detailed every killing ordered by Hanus, forty-two in total. Detective Sperling shared the journal with Eli. There was one page that merited special attention for the detective. Draper described his target as Benjy Mills, a member of Hanus's gang. Hanus's purpose for the hit was made clear in Draper's journal. Benjy's killing was blamed on a rival gang and then used as an excuse by Hanus to start a brutal gang war.

Detective Jacob planned a message for the prisoner. If there was one further attack on Pharo Simmons, the page in Draper's journal detailing the order for Benjy's hit would be turned over to Hanus's gang. A bleak outcome for Hanus would be assured.

*

On her way back to her hotel, Willow asked her taxi to stop at a newspaper stand to pick up the latest edition of the *New York Times*. Inside the cab, she read the bold-lettered headline: 'War in Europe Imminent'. The reporting on the newspaper's front page portrayed a large-scale war on the tip of erupting:

"The sudden call-up of reservists in Austria has almost brought the harvest to a standstill. The trains in France are overflowing at night with soldiers returning to their regiments. All airplane factories are placed under military protection. The wireless station at the Eiffel Tower is under military guard.

The ships of Germany's Baltic Sea fleet returned to their base in the morning. Cadets at the Russian naval school were, in the presence of the tsar himself, promoted to the rank of officers. The British First Fleet sailed past Dover during the night, heading to the war stations in the North Sea.

The Austrian shelling of Belgrade commenced late last night and continued for hours."

Willow folded the newspaper, her mood turning sullen. A monumental war, as close as her shadow, was set to begin, and she'd soon be close to the front lines covering it.

*

"Oh, Pharo, this is so exciting. A string expert. Marvelous! We undervalue string, you know. It plays such an intrinsic part in our lives. It keeps our shoes tied, permits virtuoso music to be played on the violin and guitar, and lets our clothes dry after a wash."

"Yes, Sally, but Max Winter is not a *string* expert. He is proficient in *knots*."

"Strings, knots, what is the difference, really? Rope is just a thicker version of string."

Pharo already regretted honoring her promise to bring Sally along.

Sally Timkins, a longstanding member of the club, had moved with her family to Buffalo from England. She claimed to have been an official organizer of parties for Queen Victoria in the last years of her reign, and to have assumed the same responsibilities for her son as King. Sally bubbled with enthusiasm and indulged in hyperbole to describe the most rudimentary of tasks. Assigned to start a library of Sherlock Holmes books and short stories, she prepared a column for the Buffalo Morning Express comparing her task to the librarian of the Vatican. "Sherlock Holmes is the Moses of our generation," she wrote. "Holmes has liberated our minds. Scientific reasoning is, to the rigid mind, the land of Canaan."

Pharo and Sally had travelled to Rochester to meet Max Winter, who owned a marina on Lake Ontario and was highly recommended by Burford after he testified as an expert in one of his murder trials.

"Look, Pharo, the Kodak plant." Sally pointed to the large plant as their cab passed by. "I must stop by there and let them know how impressed I am with their camera. We used it for our son James's christening. We have the most incredible photographs to cherish. Bless the inventors of Kodak!"

"Convey your gratitude in a letter, Sally. Now remember, it's important that we have a record of everything Max Winter tells us. I intend to follow up with the Huntsville police about his findings."

Slightly subdued, Sally said, "Yes, I perfectly understand my role, Pharo."

At the marina, they were directed to a kiosk on the water's edge.

Pharo knocked.

"Mr. Winter?"

The door opened, and a man with a long grey beard, whiskers and a cane appeared. "Mrs. Simmons?" he asked.

"Yes, and this is my friend, Sally, who is assisting my investigation."

"Come in. Call me Max. You're both welcome—but unfortunately, I have only one chair. The office is compact. I don't usually have visitors from out of the city. When I testified for your husband, I came to his office."

Sally burbled, "What an impressive area of expertise, Max! I'm an expert on china—I studied it at Buckingham Palace."

"I don't know much about China except that it's a country," Max chuckled. "But I know everything about the science of knots and the tying of knots. I've studied books on sailing and fishing knots, knitting, surgery, scouting and camping."

Pharo opened her satchel, and spread a piece of rope, a shoe and a scarf across the desk, saying, "These are the items that I mentioned in my letter, Max."

"And you want to know if I can connect them to the same source? Let me examine the knots." Max picked up each item separately, studying it from different angles. He carefully examined the bow in each knot and the width of the knot and loosened the knots slightly. "Very interesting," he said.

Sally blurted out, "Did the same person tie all three knots?"

After a scornful look from Pharo, she returned to her note-taking duties.

"I'll get to my opinion—but I'll begin with a brief lesson about knots. We develop similar tying habits, which become as natural as the way we write our letters. Each person's handwriting is unique, from the curl in the letter 's' to the lines in the letters 'l' and 'n.' The more unusual the tying habits are, the more likely we are to make a match. But knot evidence is group characteristic rather than specific to a person like fingerprints." Max picked up the shoe from the desk. "Let's look at the shoelaces first," he said. "The shoelaces, like the rope, are of considerable length. Shoelaces are typically tied with a Bow Knot, which contains two simple Half Knots. The bows on these shoelaces are tied together with a third Half Knot. We call this overall configuration a Shoe Clerk's Knot. However, all three Half Knots are doubled, which is unusual. They're Double Half Knots with a tying sequence of LH, RH and LH. This enhanced Shoe Clerk's Knot is very secure and cannot come untied easily. The rope and the scarf you've presented are also tied with three Double Half Knots. There is not enough scarf length for a bow. But the rope does have a bow and is also tied in a Shoe Clerk's Knot followed with Double Half Knots."

"Please tell us, Max," Pharo said anxiously. "Can you say for sure that the same person tied all three knots?"

"My conclusion is that the rope and shoelaces are tied in a highly unique way, and the knot was likely tied by one person—I'm prepared to testify to that in a courtroom."

"Oh, this is all so exciting," Sally exclaimed. "I feel like I'm living in a detective novel."

Pharo ignored the comment. "This is most helpful, Max. I will detail your findings to the policemen in Huntsville. It relates to a man's murder. Unlike my husband's chosen vocation, I'm assisting the police with solving a murder."

Sally could not resist boasting, "And Sherlock Holmes—I mean Sir Arthur Conan Doyle, is working with Pharo!"

"Really?" Max asked. "I'm a big fan of the Sherlock Holmes stories."

"With good cause!" Pharo approved. "May I ask the Huntsville police to contact you?"

"Of course, I'm happy to help. And please pass on my regards to your husband. He paid my fee promptly, which I appreciated. And now, if you're hungry, we have a restaurant on the marina that makes the best fish and chips."

"Yummy," Sally said. "We haven't eaten lunch. That sounds splendid."

Pharo returned the items to her satchel.

Sally followed her out of the office.

"You appear pensive, Pharo. What deep thoughts are churning in that wonderful mind of yours?"

"The rope is tightening around Rudolph's neck. I dare the police to ignore this expert's findings. But we're still missing one key element, Sally."

"What's that?"

"*Why* was Mason Caulfield murdered? This wasn't a random killing. And if I'm going to confront him, then I need to fill in the missing link."

"What? You're confronting the killer? You must let me accompany you, Pharo. The excitement is unbearable. Oh my. I never experienced such a sensation in the palace. There was an occasion when a silver fork went missing—that caused quite a stir, until it was discovered under a chair pillow."

"Let's enjoy our fish and chips. I'm famished too. Did you record everything Max said?"

Sally held up her notebook triumphantly. "Every word, Pharo."

Chapter Thirty-Seven

Judge Cokley Carmichael came from a long line of police officers. His father had been a patrolman, his grandfather a sergeant and his great-grandfather a chief of police in Rochester. Carmichael's own effort to join the force was spurned after a medical checkup. He had a bad case of blurred vision that prevented him from discharging a gun. "You'll end up shooting one of your own," the doctor told him.

The dispiriting news that he could never wear a police uniform led Carmichael to search for an alternate career. He specialized in shielding insurance companies from frivolous lawsuits. He'd hire retired policemen to follow the various plaintiffs claiming serious injuries, to catch them in strenuous physical activity. One litigant, claiming his back had been shattered in an accident with a horse and carriage, was seen moving furniture from his tenement. Carmichael excelled in his work, and when the president of an insurance company he represented was elected to Congress, he marshalled Carmichael's appointment as a judge.

Never overcoming his failed desire to become a police officer, Carmichael settled into the doldrums of judging and devoted his evenings at the shooting range. The staff rang a bell on the rare occasion that he hit the target.

Life as a judge bored Carmichael. With drooping eyes half shut, flopping ears and a sullen expression, he appeared to be napping during a jury trial. On occasion, he'd be drawn from his perennial slumber by the lawyers in his courtroom to rule on an objection or to call for a luncheon recess. Otherwise, he appeared as animated as a piece of timber adorning a ceremonial room.

Cokley Carmichael's stalwart admiration of the police made him a favored draw for the prosecutors at the Buffalo courthouse. Woe to the attorney defending a case where the victim of the crime was a police officer. The judge ruled his courtroom like a captain of a vessel, steering the jury's verdict to his bearings.

Mitchell Harris returned to Judge Carmichael's courtroom and took his seat beside his client, George Ducharme, with Booker on his other side.

Burford sat in the front row of the gallery, one eye following the proceedings and the other watchful of Booker. Burford had first-hand experience of being the victim of a kidnapping.

Bartholomew Hopkins, the prosecutor trying his first case, approached Booker and shook his hand.

"We're glad to have you back with us," he said, to a smattering of applause in the courtroom.

The clerk announced the judge's entry into the courtroom. Judge Carmichael placed his books on the dais, peered with drooping eyes at the crowded courtroom and sighed. Another day was set to begin. The jurors shuffled into court and took their seats.

The judge guzzled a drink of water from his glass, opened his trial book and began to read out loud:

"I wish to say a few words at the outset of today's proceedings. We have all read the newspapers and are aware of the death of a police officer in our community, Detective Gilrich. Police officers keep our communities safe, and we value their contribution. I salute this brave officer, and every police officer wearing a badge protecting the citizens of this city. We all mourn the loss of this officer. Are we ready to proceed, Mr. Hopkins?"

"Yes, the witness is standing outside the courtroom."

Mitchell rose sharply. "There is a matter that I want to address first, Judge." At the judge's nod, Mitchell continued. "The name of the police officer killed in the line of duty was Detective *Gilchrist*."

Judge Carmichael fumbled through his trial book. "Is that not what I said? Thank you for bringing the matter to my attention, Mr. Harris. Now call your witness, Mr. Hopkins."

"I'm not quite finished, Judge," Mitchell said. "You are aware that the next witness is also a police officer. He is an important witness for the prosecution. It is, therefore, inappropriate for you, as the presiding judge at this trial, to declare in front of this jury that you salute every police officer carrying a badge in this community. In effect, you have vouched for the next witness's character."

"Now listen here, young man. I will not permit you to speak to this court in that surly tone."

"I'm not a young man, Judge. I'm an attorney and I ask you to address me accordingly. And as for my tone—my tone was neither surly nor disrespectful, but pitched with the requisite passion for ensuring that my client receives a fair trial. Let him be tried on the evidence alone. That is all I am seeking."

The judge stared down at the lawyer and paused for several seconds before continuing. Then he turned toward the jurors.

"Gentlemen, my earlier comments in this courtroom were not intended to support the veracity of the prosecutor's next witness. You will assess his credibility strictly on his testimony." He turned back.

"Does that satisfy your concern, Mr. Harris?"

"Yes, Judge, I'm grateful."

"Get the officer on the witness stand," the judge declared in a huff.

Burford was displeased with Mitchell's exchange with the judge. He was correct, of course, but a police officer had been killed in the line of duty, and his rebuke of Judge Carmichael might be viewed by the jurors as insensitive. He should have asked that the jury be excused before he made his point.

The police witness wore a red ribbon on his lapel. Pointing to it, the prosecutor asked about the purpose of the ribbon.

"Sir, it's in support of a..."

But Mitchell jumped up to object.

Judge Carmichael spoke first. "Mr. Hopkins, let's get to the reason the witness is here."

Burford brimmed with rage at the prosecutor's tawdry stunt. What was Mitchell to do now, ask the officer to remove the ribbon?

The officer, P.J. Tuff, had ruddy cheeks, hair parted in the middle, and a propensity to lard every sentence with the word "sir." He described in detail the arrest of George Ducharme at a restaurant. He had followed Ducharme from the jail to the café where he'd met with his client, Clive Scully.

The prosecutor asked the officer about the piece of paper Ducharme was found with at his arrest.

"Please read to the gentlemen of this jury the content of the note."

The man read out, "I'd like to be out of here by Christmas. There will be red gifts around the Christmas tree."

"Did the note concern you when you read it?"

Mitchell rose to object. "The witness's concern is irrelevant. It's up to the jurors to decide whether it's significant."

Hopkins responded quickly, "I disagree, Judge! Officer Tuff has vast experience with the codes that criminal gangs use to communicate with each other. The jury will benefit greatly from his insight."

"I agree with the prosecutor. The question will be allowed."

Now Burford could relax. Everything was unfolding, he thought, just as they had planned at the office meeting. The trap was set.

The officer steadied himself, speaking in a clear voice: "The message in the coded note was that Clive Scully wanted to escape from jail by Christmas, and the *red gifts* meant that blood needed to be spilled against his captors."

Gasps came from the courtroom as the officer spoke.

The prosecutor sat back in his chair with a look of a first-trial victor.

"Any cross-examination, Mr. Harris?"

Mitchell rose. "Yes, Judge, I do have questions for the witness." He glanced at the officer scornfully, being certain to be noticed by the jurors.

"Is Christmas an important holiday to you, Officer?" he began.

"Yes, it is, sir."

"A day you like to spend with your family?"

"Yes, sir."

"You buy gifts for your family?"

"Sure."

"You sing festive carols over the holiday?"

"Yes."

"If you were stranded overseas for Christmas, might you write a letter to your wife, wishing that you could be home for the Christmas holiday?"

"I suppose I might, sir."

"What color is Santa Claus's suit?"

"Red."

"Red is a color associated with the Christmas holiday?"

"Yes."

"And it is consistent with the holiday spirit that Christmas gifts be wrapped in red paper?"

"I agree."

"So being stranded overseas, you might ask your wife to wrap the gifts in red paper."

"Possibly, sir."

"Officer, I'd like you to suppose for the purpose of my question, that you're stranded in the port of Lisbon, and you won't be home for Christmas. Read the note again that you found in George Ducharme's possession."

"I'd like to be out of here by Christmas. There will be red gifts around the Christmas tree."

"Could that possibly be a note you might write to your wife?"

"If I wasn't able to make it home for the holiday?" The witness paused, before continuing, realizing the trap door he was about to fall into. "I don't believe that I would write such a letter."

"Why not?" Mitchell asked incredulously.

"I don't care about the color of the wrapping, sir."

Mitchell observed a couple of jurors smirking. "But many others might stick to the color of the holiday and use red wrapping, you'd agree?"

"I guess."

"Red packaging for their gifts."

"Yes."

"Now my client, George Ducharme, represented a man, Clive Scully, who isn't in the port of Lisbon but rather in a prison cell."

"Correct."

"There is nothing unusual about Mr. Scully wanting to be home for Christmas?"

"I can't say there is, sir."

"Let's assume for my next question that his taste in Christmas gifts is similar to the many who prefer red wrapping."

"Yes."

"Please read again for the jurors the note you retrieved from my client."

Judge Carmichael interrupted. "The jurors heard the note the first time, Mr. Harris. I see no purpose in having the officer read it again."

"The benefit is that there may be a second way to interpret the note." Mitchell stared briefly at the jurors and sat down. "No further questions," he declared.

Burford smiled at his law partner as he turned to face

him. Mission accomplished: the message for the defense conveyed. He stood up to leave the courtroom and was greeted outside the door by Detective Jacob.

"*Monsieur* Simmons," he said. "Can we speak privately?"

"Yes, of course."

Jacob led him to a corner of the hallway.

"I thought you were following my wife."

"*Mais oui.* I will return to my duties shortly. There is a matter of importance that I must discuss with you. The kidnapping of Booker opened a channel of communication for me with the Toronto Detectives' office. I had a long conversation with Detective Stokely about the death of Mason Caulfield. I convinced him to speak to his police colleagues in Huntsville about reopening the investigation."

"A murder investigation?"

"Yes, Mr. Simmons."

"Then Pharo was right all along."

"Yes, and that brings me to the second reason I need your attention. Pharo explained to me that she has solved the crime. She is certain of the reason Rudolph Mulino murdered the railway executive, but she refuses to tell me."

"Why not?"

"She has set a trap for the killer at the home of Lilian Caulfield in a couple of weeks. I am invited to attend as a spectator. *Mon Dieu!* Your wife is treating this as a cat-and-mouse game."

"And what do you expect me to do about it, Detective Jacob?"

"Persuade her to turn over her information to the police. I will ensure that the Canadian police treat it seriously."

"You're setting me an impossible task. My powers of

persuasion with Pharo are fleeting."

"I must go," the detective said, stomping his foot. Without another word, Jacob turned and strode down the hallway.

*

At dinner that night, reminding Burford that many days had passed since their last dinner alone together, Pharo made him promise: no conversation about Booker's recent travails or Mitchell's trial.

So, as he sipped his Chablis, Burford asked, "How is your Sherlock Holmes Club faring?"

"Splendidly. The members of the club are intrigued by my investigation of Mason Caulfield's murder. I shall solve it soon."

"You seem rather confident."

"Attribute that in part to your knot man, Max Winter."

Burford nodded. "An excellent witness. He cracked open a case for me. My client was in a struggle with her parents' insurance company. They had been found hanged in their homes, and the life insurance policy was invalidated if there was a suicide involved. The company insisted that it was a murder-suicide."

"Foolish, really," Pharo said. "Who bothers with a hanging to kill themselves? Poison is much simpler and less painful."

"Max compared the knots in the ligatures of the nooses and found them to be entirely different from the knot the father had used on his sailboat. Max's testimony carried the day in court."

"Why was it assumed that the husband must be the killer?"

"Good thing you weren't on my jury, Pharo. I never even considered that possibility."

Pharo shook her head disapprovingly, then said. "I'm planning one final trip to Toronto to visit Lilian Caulfield. I will witness the denouement of the investigation—the apprehension and arrest of Mason Caulfield's killer."

"Detective Jacob stopped by to chat with me about your investigation."

"This case needed a policeman with Eli Jacob's acumen and skill," Pharo said resolutely. "But the investigation is over now. The net is cast to ensnare the true killer."

"And you'll say nothing more?"

"Only Lilian Caulfield and I share the secret."

"I expected nothing more. Please consider inviting Booker to join you on your Canadian trip."

"I will—but I thought he was assisting Mitchell with his trial."

"The trial is finished," Burford said with quiet gratification. "The prosecutor waved the white flag and surrendered, after the collapse of his case. He was crestfallen to lose his first trial."

"I expect Booker has had sufficient excitement for a while. I won't be disappointed if he declines my offer. I'm tying up a few loose ends. I haven't heard from Sir Arthur for some time—the rumblings of war in Europe are growing, and that surely must preoccupy him. But I'll relay the outcome to him in a cable. I must keep my solemn promise."

Chapter Thirty-Eight

The man in the white seersucker suit, wearing a Panama hat and carrying a brown portfolio, stood out on the Hollywood lot. After checking his name on the approved guest list, the security agent allowed him to pass.

His listed name was Whitaker Chambers, and he carried a business card for the Chambers Life Insurance Company with a portfolio inside his briefcase titled: The Life Insurance Policy of Mason Caulfield. The folder was thick, but it was filled with plain white paper without a word typed or printed on a page.

Chambers carried his wallet with his true identification in his inside jacket pocket, along with a slip of paper containing Pharo's instructions. He'd studied the page on the train ride from Buffalo and could recite the contents by heart.

"Rudolph Mulino is in studio number ten. They usually break around this time. You'll have to wait outside the set while there is filming going on."

Chambers nodded at the agent and continued to walk,

breathing a sigh of relief that his identification hadn't been checked at the gate. He had discovered a couple of spelling mistakes when he perused the document the previous evening.

Arriving at studio number ten, Chambers observed a piece of furniture being wheeled out of the door on a cart.

"Excuse me, young fellow," he said, "I see that you've come from number ten. Are they still filming inside?"

"Just wrapped up for the day. I have to get this table clock to a set across the lot. I'm late already."

"You've been most helpful," Chambers said.

He caught the studio door before it closed, and slipped inside. A couple of women dressed in sequined dresses adorned with chains of beads passed him at the exit, already smoking cigarettes in holders. An older man with a grey beard and megaphone sat at a table scribbling notes.

Chambers approached him. "I'm looking for Rudolph Mulino, sir. He's expecting me today. Would you be good enough to point him out to me?"

"I'm the director here. Who are you?"

"A business associate of Rudolph's. He's expecting me."

"He's likely in his dressing room. He likes to wash off his makeup as soon as I call it a wrap for the day. I've never met an actor who seems to hate his job before—that is until I met Mulino. Never smiles. I'm not sure why the ladies are crazy about him. He's handsome, of course, but he has all the charm of a rattlesnake. Don't worry about quoting me. I've said it to him myself."

"Yes, well, thank you kindly. I'll be meeting with him for only a short time."

"Take all the time you need. We're finished for the day. One of the actresses broke her leg in a fall. Now it's in the producer's hands to find a replacement. We'll stop filming until he does."

"Will that take a couple of weeks?"

"At least. The new actress will need to study her part before filming can start again."

A stroke of good fortune! Chambers thought to himself. Their most daunting problem—convincing Rudolph to leave the film set for Toronto—was removed. Now the work of luring the film actor, or more correctly, the impostor portraying the film actor, fell to Chambers.

He knocked confidently on the dressing room with Rudolph Mulino's name on the door.

"Who is it?"

"It's Whitaker Chambers. You're expecting me—the insurance agent from Toronto."

"Come in. The door is unlocked."

Mason watched the actor wipe smudges of makeup off his face with a wet cloth.

"This dreaded stuff, I hate it. It's already ruined the collar of three of my shirts. I'll be glad to be done with this film. I've already forgotten the title."

"*The Swashbuckler and His Dwindling Fortune*," Chambers reminded him.

"Yes, that's it. I had prepared for a film about a cowboy drifter, but I'm rehearsing for the role of a pauper begging on the streets. Such a dreary existence. I'd be dead before I permitted myself such a fate."

Mulino reminded Chambers of a curmudgeonly uncle who spread misery to everyone he encountered like a cloud of dust in the wind. Still, Chambers stayed in his cheery role, saying, "Well, that presents a perfect introduction for my purpose here!"

"In your letter, you wrote that Mason had made me the beneficiary of a portion of his life insurance policy. Sporting of the fellow to be so generous to me. I still think about his head bobbing under the water. What was that dreaded lake called? If only Mason had asked me to join him on his jaunt in the canoe. Oh well, no sense worrying about that now. Whatacker..."

"It's Whitaker, and the lake is called Smoke Lake."

"The only smoke I saw on our trip came from our guide's pipe."

"Terrence—I assume you're aware of his untimely death—fell off a ladder."

"I never cared for the fellow. Tumbling off a ladder, you say. Now that's an embarrassing ending."

"I'll leave you to do your grieving privately," Whitaker said with a smirk. "Let's move on to the purpose of my trip."

"You're here to deliver a cheque from that briefcase you're carrying. Let's do our business, and you can be gone. I appreciate the effort you made to deliver the cheque in person. You're welcome to stay for lunch on the studio lot. I'll get them to send me the bill. No alcohol, though. Or, as Lady Doyle called it, spirits." Spirits was uttered in a mocking tone.

"Generous of you to offer me lunch, but I'm not here to present you with a cheque, Mr. Mulino."

The actor folded his arms. "What do you mean, you don't have a cheque? Then what are you here for?"

"No point raising your voice with me. I'm merely the messenger. The insurance company decides on the rules that govern its policies. I have specific instructions to convey: you must travel to Toronto to collect your cheque in person. You may refuse, but in that event, you forfeit the policy."

"I get it now," Mulino snarled. "You count on people like me to give up, and then you keep your precious insurance money. I have news for you and your vaunted company—I'll make the long trip. Just tell me when and where I need to be."

"Splendid. The location is known to you. The cheques will be delivered to the home of Lilian Caulfield. Mason's widow has agreed. I'll be presenting them."

"For the fat cheque you're giving her, I'm sure that her motives are not magnanimous. Who else will be there?"

"Brian, Lilian's son, the two stepdaughters of the widow and a woman named Pharo Simmons."

"Who is she?"

"A friend from Buffalo. Lilian had moved to that city with her first husband, because he managed a bank there."

"Oh yes, I recall meeting a Pharo at the Caulfield home—in the company of a colored boy. I recall her being mentioned by Lilian as having a cottage on Smoke Lake."

"I can only report to you what Lilian disclosed to me. Pharo is her close friend."

"My only interest is to obtain my share and depart swiftly. Tell me, what *is* my share of Mason's will?"

"That, sir, is strictly confidential information until the meeting in Toronto—another company policy. We don't want the family and friends squabbling about their respective shares before we distribute them. You'll get your money soon enough, Mr. Mulino."

Mulino moved forward and stood inches from his guest. "I don't like you, Whitaker," he said with contempt. "You led me to believe I'd get a cheque today. But you can mark down that I'll be there. I'll purchase my train tickets in the morning. I have my film script to study to keep me busy."

His mission accomplished, Whitaker Chambers turned and left the room, hiding his broad smile and bitten lip from view.

*

Pharo Simmons rushed to the kitchen table carrying the cable from Sir Arthur. She had given up hope of receiving another word from the author of the famed Sherlock Holmes novels. And yet here it was in her tingling fingers: the words from the master author himself. She laid it on the table and began to read:

Dear Pharo,

I apologize for not writing sooner. You'll realize from following the news that Europe is descending closer to war. Germany has declared war on France, and Russia is standing by, ready to assist the French. As Russia begins to organize for war, can Great Britain, the third partner in the Triple Entente, be far behind? I walked to my pub in London today and passed cheering crowds. These fools are pushing my spineless government to war. Our young people are rushing to sign up to join the military like it's a grand spectacle that might pass them by.

Our dear son has enlisted and will be among the first to be shipped to the front. I fear modern warfare will be ghastlier and more devastating than anything the world has experienced. Of course, I'm forbidden to say these things to my dear wife. Like a mourner anticipating the certain death of a beloved, Lady Doyle is consumed by the prospect of our child serving on the battlefield. I hugged my son more tightly than ever, when I bid him farewell.

I am comforted to know that you are carrying on with the investigation of Mason Caulfield's murder, and eternally grateful for your reports of progress in your work. I do have one snippet of news to pass on: at my prodding, my former colleague in Rimini, Willie Hornsby, met with the police in Bologna to check at the apartment of Mulino's twin brother. He introduced my name and promised the officer a signed copy of my book. A family had moved into the apartment and politely agreed for the police to survey the apartment.

When a sofa was moved, a patch of dry blood was revealed on the carpet. Blood had soaked through to the floor.

Willie sought my advice upon his return. I sent him a photograph I obtained of Rudolph Mulino and gave him a list of questions for the officer:

— Was the sofa in the same location when the family moved in?

— Did the police interview the residents of the apartment above and below Mulino's apartment? Did they overhear an argument and struggle?

— Did any of the neighbors observe the Mulino twins in the area of the building?

Willie updated me on his progress. The family

confirmed that the sofa and other furniture had been left by the former renter and hadn't been moved. The police went from apartment to apartment in the building with the photograph of Rudolph Mulino. A musician on the first floor, shown the picture, remembered seeing the twin brothers enter the building through Mulino's window and being struck by their close resemblance.

Clever Willie checked the timing of that sighting, and it coincided with the end of the filming of Roman Holiday for Two.

The police in Bologna agreed to open an investigative file, but no murder investigation has yet commenced. That will await the fruits of your assiduous efforts in the investigation of Mason's death. I agree with your plan of attack. You have my full support. I do hope that it is successful.

I don't know if you engage in prayer. I cannot say that I am a particularly religious person. But it is fitting to resort to prayer for peace in the world, peace for mankind.

Your confederate,
Arthur

I agree with your plan of attack. Pharo imagined reading Sir Arthur's words aloud at the next Sherlock Holmes Club meeting. An endorsement akin to the Pope's approval of an ecclesiastical service, she thought.

What to make of Sir Arthur's revelation that Luigi Mulino possibly murdered his twin at his apartment? How had Luigi disposed of the corpse? Why was Rudolph at his brother's apartment? Perhaps Luigi lured him to Bologna to return his initialed ring. Might there be a record of a train ticket in Rudolph Mulino's name from Bologna to Rome?

As Pharo pondered these questions, the telephone rang, and she rushed to pick up the receiver.

"Pharo, it's Graham here. I just received a telegram from Mulino. His train is set to arrive in Toronto on August 10th."

"Congratulations, my friend. A peerless performance on your part. I'll be back to you shortly with the date of the meeting at the Caulfield home."

*

Pharo set the final part of her plan in place after being briefed that Mulino's train travel would bring him to Toronto. A meeting was set for August 11th at Lilian Caulfield's home in the morning. Burford had insisted that Booker attend with Pharo for the meeting. Lilian had been eager to set up the meeting at her home after Pharo reviewed her findings. The involvement of the Canadian police would be most welcome, but time did not permit Pharo to travel again to Huntsville. Booker was to arrive with the cab to pick her up at 8:00 that evening, and they would take a night train to Toronto. She only had sufficient time after receiving Sir Arthur's cable to pack and have dinner with Burford in their dining room.

There was a possible hitch in her plan, Burford impressed upon her. "You will present the findings of Sir Arthur in Italy and the conclusions of your knot expert. But what assurance do you have that the crafty Mulino will succumb and be prompted to confess?"

Pharo said nothing.

"And if he protests, what next step do you propose?"

Pharo had no answers. "But I am prepared to assume the risk. Mulino has murdered thrice, including his own flesh and blood. My best efforts to ensnare Mulino may absolve me of the blame for permitting a devious killer to remain free."

Burford reluctantly agreed, on one condition. Detective Jacob would also be present, inside the home of Lilian Caulfield, armed and prepared to intercede if Mulino became violent.

"His propensity is to kill whoever impedes his goals and desires," Burford insisted, "and he'll do it again without hesitation."

"I will be his foil, my dear husband. And if the French detective's presence allays your fears, I will be content with his presence. But this scoundrel will be brought to justice!"

Chapter Thirty-Nine

In Toronto, Pharo and Booker took a cab straight to Lilian Caulfield's house. They arrived half an hour early and decided to walk around the neighborhood until the meeting began.

"Pharo!" The voice came from the front yard of Lilian's home.

Pharo turned to see Brian running toward her, a baseball bat in one hand and bottle caps in the other.

"Hi, Booker," he said as he reached them. "Wanna play with me? You can stand on the other side of the yard and try to catch the caps."

"We have to meet some people at your mom's house, Brian. We'll be happy to play with you after."

"My stepsisters are there. They don't speak to me. They aren't very nice to my mother."

Pharo was indignant. "Well then, they deserve to be shunned. You're adorable, Brian. Who couldn't be friendly to you?"

Brian beamed. "Do you promise you'll play with me?"

"We promise," Booker said. "I played outfield on my high school baseball team. I'll catch a few of your bottle caps."

Just then, a cab pulled up at the Caulfield home, and Pharo recognized the passenger instantly. "Rudolph Mulino," she whispered.

Brian turned away at the mention of the name.

"You told us that Rudolph wasn't genuinely nice to you, Brian. Was there a reason that he gave you?"

"I saw him come out of my parents' bedroom. He grabbed me by my collar and lifted me off the ground. He said that if I told my mom and dad, he'd strangle me. He made me swear not to tell." Brian looked up at Pharo, pleading. "Please don't tell Rudolph I told you."

"Your secret is safe with us. One more thing. You said your mom and dad. Did you catch Rudolph in the bedroom before your dad died?"

"Yes, it was a day or two before he left for the canoe trip."

"Rudolph is in the house. He didn't see us chatting, Brian. Don't be frightened. Come, Booker," Pharo declared, "it's time to make our entrance."

Lilian greeted Pharo and Booker with a hug and led them into the living room, where Rudolph Mulino was occupied in idle chat with Mr. Chambers from the insurance company. A couple of scowling faces exchanged looks with her from across the room—the stepdaughters. Both were in their twenties, she surmised, and were dressed smartly for the occasion of acquiring their desired prize. Pharo overheard their shared whisper. "Who is *she*?" The pair resembled a pair of ravenous dogs sensing a rival about to pounce on their plate of meat. Pharo held back from uttering that Brian had described their pouting cheeks perfectly. She only hesitated because revenge against their brother might follow after she left.

"Greetings, everyone," Chambers said stiffly.

Pharo pressed on her lip to keep from laughing. She'd regale the members of the Sherlock Holmes Club with the vintage performance she was witnessing.

Chambers continued. "I have the distinct honor of delivering the cheques this morning to the beneficiaries gathered in Mason Caulfield's former home. But before I do, Pharo Simmons has asked to say a few words."

"Who cares if some friend from Buffalo wants to blabber a few platitudes? Let's proceed with the reason we're here. No more dallying. Let's get to Mason's will." Rudolph's upper lip curled as he spoke.

"I can vouch for Pharo," Lilian declared. "She's a dear friend and I'm honoring her request to speak."

Pharo stood and nodded her head in the direction of Lilian Caulfield.

"I shall be brief," she announced. "When I discovered that the insurance company of Mr. Chambers was prepared to deny the claim because suicide was the suspected cause of death of Mason Caulfield, I embarked on a mission to refute that absurd conclusion. With the capable assistance of Sir Arthur Conan Doyle, I can relate to you that foul play was responsible for Mason Caulfield's death. Yes, it was murder," Pharo continued, letting her eyes settle on Rudolph Mulino. "And the man responsible is seated to my left."

"What preposterous nonsense this is!" Mulino shouted, and stood abruptly. "I'm leaving."

A man holding a revolver pointed at Mulino emerged

from the shadow of the kitchen, and said, "Stay where you are, *Monsieur*."

"Allow me to introduce you to, Detective Jacob," Pharo said calmly.

"A most interesting story. We are your rapt audience. Please continue, *Madame*."

"Rudolph Mulino, *not* his identity, has murdered three times." She counted them on her fingers. "Once a twin brother in Bologna, one time in Smoke Lake, and once in Huntsville. I shall focus my attention on the murder at Smoke Lake. Mason Caulfield was hit on the back of his head with a large rock—by Rudolph as they walked along the lake's edge. Rudolph then dragged Mason's body to the shore and placed it in a canoe. Rudolph paddled to the middle of the lake and used a rock tied to Mason's body to sink his body to the bottom of the lake. He left the canoe and paddle to float away, and he swam back to shore."

"Lies, all lies!" Rudolph protested. "Why wasn't the canoe found? Lilian," he said with a triumphant smile, "this accusation against me is preposterous. You mustn't believe a word of it."

"I was confident that you would say that, of course," Pharo replied. "Only in the cinema does the murderer confess. The missing canoe bolsters your case for innocence, but only an amateurish police investigation has saved you from its discovery. Somewhere in the brushes surrounding Smoke Lake, the canoe is hidden."

"Did you hear that? My false accuser now professes to know more than the police!"

"Shush, Rudolph," Pharo said with a dismissive wave of her hand. "I was left with one baffling mystery to solve. Why? Why was Mason killed in the wilds of Algonquin

Park? I struggled with this puzzle for weeks—but now, alas, it is solved. It starts with the break-in discovered in Lilian Caulfield's home on the day of her husband's funeral. A window was shattered at the rear of the house to gain entry. Except that there was no break-in. Before leaving for the commemorative service, Rudolph ran back for a few seconds to break the window. It was a ruse, of course. The jewelry the robber was supposed to have pilfered from the bedroom of the Caulfields was actually taken days earlier, *before* the canoe trip to Smoke Lake."

Lilian Caulfield gasped.

"Rudolph might have succeeded with his devious plan, except for one thing: Brian Caulfield caught him leaving the bedroom. He threatened Brian to make him keep silent, and the ploy succeeded. But Rudolph had a dilemma when he left for the trip to Smoke Lake. What to do with the precious gems he'd pilfered? He could hide them—but he chose instead to bring them on the trip. During the fishing trip, he had laid the jewels on his bed to admire his plunder when Mason barged into his cabin to chat. Mason recognized his wife's jewelry and reproached Rudolph for his betrayal of their kindness. Rudolph's treachery having been exposed, there was only one option for him to engineer a tidy escape. He brought out a pistol, and, pointing it at Mason, ordered him to the path. Following behind, Rudolph grabbed the rock and struck Mason with it."

Rudolph sneered. "What proof of this imaginary tale do you have, I ask?"

"I have the proof in my closed fist," Pharo answered. "You see, I returned to Smoke Lake with my associate, Booker. And in your cabin, Rudolph, I found a single ruby of an unusual shape that Lilian Caulfield has identified as

her property. You slipped up, Rudolph. The evidence linking you to Mason's murder lies in my clenched hand."

Pharo opened her fist to reveal a sparkling ruby jewel.

"Why you clever lady," Rudolph said. He reached into
his jacket pocket and pulled out a pistol, brandishing it
at Pharo's head as he approached and held her tightly.
"Detective, put down your gun, or I shall have to shoot
Pharo. You seem to be acquainted. You won't want her
blood on your hands."

At that moment, a bat swung, and the gun flew out of
Rudolph's hand.

"Let go of her," Brian shouted, crying. "She's my friend."

Rudolph Mulino lay writhing on the floor, holding his
arm. "You've broken my arm, you fool," he said.

Jacob crouched over him to examine the break. "That
was the exact point of the exercise, *Monsieur* Mulino.
Brian Caulfield performed the task admirably. *Magnifique!*
His stepfather would be proud of him."

*

Pharo stood watching as Brian hit the caps in the air, and
Booker valiantly tried to catch them in mid-air. Police cars
arrived at the Caulfield home in procession, and eventually the game paused as Rudolph Mulino was ushered out
of the house to a waiting ambulance.

Booker and Pharo stood side by side as Mulino was
marched along by two armed constables.

"You never told me that you recovered a ruby at Smoke
Lake," Booker said. "You could have trusted me."

"Indeed, I should have, Booker. I waited for confirma-
tion from Lilian Caulfield after my discovery. We made a

pact to tell no one until Rudolph—or I should say Luigi—had been apprehended."

"I forgive you, Pharo. I've been keeping a surprise from you as well."

"What is it?"

"Mitchell and Neeru are engaged to be married."

"Wonderful news. I had no idea that they were involved in a relationship."

"Mitchell told me that if they have a son, they will name him Leo, after Leo Frank."

Just then, a shout from Brian could be heard from across the yard. "Hey, let's play, Booker!"

"In a minute," Booker called back. He stared at Pharo admiringly. "Sherlock Holmes is real," he said.

"Oh, Booker... that's the sweetest thing anyone ever said to me." She hugged him tightly and kissed his forehead.

Chapter Forty

Detective Eli Jacob stood and raised his glass of champagne to propose a toast. "*A la Victoire!*" he said with the rapture of winning a fierce armed battle. He peered down at one of the guests at his table, her glass held high. "And to you, *Madame* Simmons, I salute you for the great courage you showed in pursuing this rogue imposter, Mulino. He is safely behind the bars of a prison cell. He will not have the opportunity to harm anyone else."

"Did he confess to killing Mason Caulfield?" Burford asked as Jacob sat to his dinner.

"*Mais non*, not that I expected him to. He was shrewd in his dealings with the Canadian police. He admitted to stealing a few jewels from Madame Caulfield's dresser. This explains his reaction to Madame Simmons' accusations. But a killer? *Jamais*! Never! I credit your clever wife for unraveling Mulino's crime. At my urging to Detective Sperling, a senior detective in Toronto, the police combed the shore of Smoke Lake in the area of the camp. They made a startling discovery. Hidden in the bushes, they found a canoe and underneath it, the body of Mason Caulfield. The overturned canoe had shielded the body from the moose and bears in the woods. There was a deep gash to the back of the dead man's head, caked with dried blood."

"I must share this information with Sir Arthur," Pharo said. "He was right from the start."

"Permit me to finish my story, *Madame*. The corpse of Mason Caulfield was not the only important finding made by the police. It took a man with resolute strength to drag the canoe and body deep enough into the bushes to be missed by the police in their first search of the area. On the path from the lake, the police found a ring on the ground. It will be familiar to you, Madame Simmons. It contained the letters 'BFC'."

"Rudolph Mulino's ring from his soccer club!"

"Oui, *Madame*. It must have slipped from the killer's hand as he covered up his crime. And *tres important*, last seen in the possession of his twin brother. Because of your astute investigation that you shared with me, the police have conclusive evidence against the killer in their possession."

"I'm happy for Lilian and Brian," Pharo said. "They can have a proper funeral for Mason now."

"And I'm pleased that you'll be safe from this killer," Burford added.

"I am assured that he will be sent to the most secure penitentiary in the country. And he will find a most suitable neighbor beside his cell."

"Mortimer Hanus?" Pharo asked.

"Oui, *Madame*."

"I shall join you in your toast now," Burford said. "To my dear wife whose plucky spirit saw two scoundrels meet their deserved fate. And to the industrious French detective who has rescued my family yet again from harm."

Three glasses of bubbly champagne clanged together in unison.

Acknowledgments

The cover design is a photograph of a painting by the Canadian artist, Jennifer Ross.

The following books and articles were relied upon in research for the novel: John Dickson Carr, *The Life of Sir Arthur Conan Doyle*, Da Capo Press, 2003; Arthur Conan Doyle, *The Complete Novels of Sherlock Holmes*, Fingerprint! Publishing, 2017; Leonard Dinnerstein, *The Leo Frank Case*, The Notable Trials Library, 1991; Gordon Martel, *The Month That Changed The World July 1914*, Oxford University Press, 2014; Rupert Colley, *1914 History in an Hour*, Harper Collins, 2013; Simon Burnton, *How suffragette pavilion fire outraged Tunbridge Wells... and Conan Doyle*, the Guardian, November 10, 2020; *'An Innocent Man Was Lynched': Reporting exonerated Leo Frank in the murder of Mary Phagan*, Tennessean, February 20, 2020. I also utilized the archives of the Globe and Mail and the Atlanta Journal-Constitution.

I thank Bill Gallagher, a criminal defense attorney in Cincinnati, Ohio, Robert Chisnall, a forensic knot consultant in Kingston, Ontario, Neha Chugh, Ian Colford and Denise Smith for their valued assistance.

About Atmosphere Press

Founded in 2015, Atmosphere Press was built on the principles of Honesty, Transparency, Professionalism, Kindness, and Making Your Book Awesome. As an ethical and author-friendly hybrid press, we stay true to that founding mission today.

If you're a reader, enter our giveaway for a free book here:

SCAN TO ENTER
BOOK GIVEAWAY

If you're a writer, submit your manuscript for consideration here:

SCAN TO SUBMIT
MANUSCRIPT

And always feel free to visit Atmosphere Press and our authors online at atmospherepress.com. See you there soon!

About the Author

STEVE SKURKA is a highly respected criminal defense lawyer in Toronto. He has defended a number of landmark cases in Canada including the racial profiling case of R. v. Brown involving a former player on the Toronto Raptors basketball team. In other precedent-setting cases, he led evidence of marijuana-induced psychosis to significantly mitigate his client's sentence and relied on the battered child syndrome in a homicide case. Steve taught criminal procedure at Osgoode Hall Law School, acted as the legal analyst for the CTV television network, and wrote a book about the sensational case of media baron Conrad Black. *Pharo and the Clever Assassin*, published in 2021, is Steve's first novel in the Pharo series.

Printed in the USA
CPSIA information can be obtained
at www.ICGtesting.com
JSHW020208110224
56982JS00003B/12